Arc-Less

Beau Bruin

MAULED MEDIA

To My Mother, Ursula
I taught myself to read. You taught me everything else.

To Rhy
We share a love of story... and each other. It's really hard to not be sarcastic here.

For Penelope
I wrote most of this with you warming my feet in an already hot apartment. You were a
spiritual co-writer, there for almost every word. Most of our time together culminated
in this project. It's sad to not have you here at this stage still. You reminded me to take
breaks, for your walks, and for a very long time that was the only self care I did. You were
a great pup, in my eyes the greatest. Sleep well little one.
Can't Stop. Won't Stop. Pitstop.

Chapter 1

A fistful of braids. That's all it takes to start a fight. Greasy, boxy little tendrils slip between my fingers as I snatch Alani by the back of her head. I try to rip the braids out at the root, but I can barely drag her across the dusty linoleum. She fights to get her feet under her. Each time I yank her onto her butt.

Alani whines and cries out, trying to untangle my fingers from her hair. "Let me go bit—"

My fist crashes into her face, leaving a big red mark. The thud makes all the other students whip out cell phones and "OOH" collectively.

Beating your middle-school bully's ass in the foyer is a hell of a way to kick off freshman year. I almost made it through a day of school without getting eyeballs-deep into trouble. The day was going pretty damn good too. I got here early for once. My uniform was clean, I only fell asleep in two classes, we had pizza for lunch, and this dude in sixth period agreed to do my homework since I covered for his more-than-fashionably-late entrance on the first day.

Then she opened her mouth, and next thing I know I'm dragging her through the school. At least I'm winning. Well, I'm pretty sure I'm winning.

Alani gets her feet under her and uncoils. Her height pushing nearly six feet makes it hard for me to keep a grip on her weave. From my view, her head nearly touches the "Welcome Students" banner stretched across the hall.

A guttural scream erupts from Alani as she slams me against the lockers with a loud clang. The steel feels cool on my back. My pleated uniform skirt rides up a little, revealing the biker shorts beneath.

Someone in the crowd yells, "World Star!"

This is definitely ending up online. Also, who still yells that? What decade are you in?

"Callisto! I'ma beat your ugly little four-eyed ass!" Alani yells.

It's mean but accurate. I do wear glasses, and nobody is calling me cute. They would have to talk to me to do that. Short, a little pudgy, and hair that's almost always in puffs.

Pinning me against the locker, her long fingers worm around my throat. Well, I'm tapped. I don't spend every minute of every day working out. I actually spend every minute of every gym class trying not to work out.

As she squeezes the life out of me, an Insta-story from middle school pops into my head. This is the bitch who made a hidden camera documentary about me wearing the same pants, tallying each passing day with stains. She made my life hell and put me on blast to the universe for clout so she could say, "Look at Callisto; she has no money for clothes!"

Anger pumps through my veins, and suddenly I forget to be tired. Uppercuts put people to sleep or make them let go. My knuckles kiss her chin. Stunned, she backs up.

This is all her fault.

Do I want to look like the hood girl who beats up varsity athletes for calling them "Ca-lez-toe?"

No.

Do I constantly want to defend my best and only friend, Yesenia, from all the dead mom jokes this bitch makes?

Not really.

Am I going to take this shit for four more years on top of the three I just dealt with?

Hell no!

WHAM! A leg hits my side. I double over as a deep throb shoots through me. Damn, that hurt. Her legs are so long she could probably kick me from the other side of the hall.

I can't see through all the tears. They're not pain tears. They're anger tears.

Using her hair, I whip her headfirst into the lockers. These "OOHS" are encouraging, like I'm doing something right. I even hear a few snickers. But this trick might as well be the Terminator.

Giving credit where credit is due, her recovery is amazing. I'm wheezing, and she's already on her feet again. She runs like a goose, gangly limbs going everywhere, but she tackles me like a football player. I know enough to tuck my chin so my head doesn't smack the school logo on the floor beneath us: a silver-and-black space shuttle in a circle of its exhaust. *Blackburn High Launchpad of the Shuttle.*

Alani mounts me, but I hold her in some MMA move I saw online to stop her from just pounding my face in. Still, she tries, flailing wildly, saying crazy crap like, "You've messed up," and "Imma beat you till your momma don't love you no mo. You know who I am. You shouldn't have stepped to me!"

Listening to her, you'd think I'd started this. The nerve of this girl! I mean, I did start this fight, but ya know I didn't want to.

She keeps swinging. Her slaps sting my forearms. All I do is wait—wait for an opening to shove my fist in. She keeps going and I keep waiting, doing my best to put my current situation out of my mind.

I focus on how her face twists as she screams, the fury of her snarl, the smell of her perfume fading midway through the school day and how it mixes with the cleaners used to mop this floor.

Next thing to strike me with stunning detail: the specks of blood on our white blouses.

Mom is going to kill me.

Sneakers squeaking, keys and coins bouncing along with every footstep racing toward us.

Her blows are a distant memory.

I'm numb and don't feel so good, like I have a sudden fever. Sweat coats my forehead. My mouth is muggy like a humid day—barely any spit. My pulse spikes. My heart thunders in my chest loudly. I can't hear anything else. Oh God, am I having a heart attack?! Can fourteen-year-olds have heart attacks?

It's like feeling someone else's heartbeat pulse through me.

THRUM! THRUM! THRUM!

What is that?

A bassy tornado of pressure and pain forces my hands to my ears. It stops the fight faster than any teacher could. They, like everyone else, stare at the unspectacular gray box blaring above the school's main entrance: the geiger.

This makes sense. Usually, the drills are scheduled way in advance. We've heard about them going off at other places—airports, bus stations, DMVS, the mall, other schools—but never this school.

Personally, I find it more fascinating that no one knows what the hell these things do. We're told they scan for Arcs, super-powered peacekeepers working for the UN. So I don't get why the government treats them like guns.

Anytime I ask this question, though, I get "Mind your business, Callisto." Or shoved into doing a drill though no one can tell us what it's really for.

Teachers suddenly remember they have a job to do.

"Get to class!" one yells, spurring the hallway into motion.

"Out of the halls! Out of the halls!" an administrator tacks on, their voice drowning against the siren.

Neither I nor Alani can focus on that. We're trying to kill each other, after all.

Two burly security guards wearing black polos with the school logo scoop both of us up, tossing us in the principal's waiting room along with, like, a dozen other students.

"You two sit," one of them says in the thiiickest Alabama accent I've ever heard. Like damn, dude.

No lie, I'm really tired. That's the sole reason I listen, crumbling into the seat on the opposite side of the room from Alani. Sitting in front of the vice principal's office is like having box seats to a game. Only it's chaos on the other side of the window. Blackburn's halls become a ghost town in seconds.

Active shooter drills have ingrained in us the need to clear out quickly along with a deep paranoia.

Alani stares daggers at me. "Ol' weak-ass punches," she mutters.

The red welts on her light-skinned face say otherwise I marvel at my work, and a sudden pang of guilt hits me. It shouldn't have gotten to this point. Sigh, but I'd do it again.

My ratty book bag plops on my lap as Yesenia wades through the crowd of kids all cramped in this office. She's taller than me by a couple of inches; curtains of straight dark hair perfectly outline her enviable, heart-shaped face. Yesenia should be a model, but she insists she's "small town cute at best."

I'm the shorter, browner, bustier of us. Even with my dad's complexion, I without a doubt wear like seventy percent of my mom's Iranian heritage.

"You almost made it the entire day," Yesenia says.

"I would've made it if someone could keep their mouth shut," I say just loud enough to invite the fight to start up again.

Yesenia and I glare at Alani, who's intentionally not looking at us. Yesenia is useless in a fight but a great hype man.

"You're probably going to be suspended, but I appreciate it, Cal," Yesenia says.

First days are the hardest for her. This one especially so. We've been friends since kindergarten. Back then, all it took was a Bratz doll and a then-mutual hatred of school. Somehow even back then I knew I would hate places like this, but she didn't want to be away from her mom. Yesennia was scared her mom wasn't going to be there to pick her up. When she got sick, that fear became a little bit more real. Still, Mrs. Barros made sure to always be there to pick Yesenia up from the first day of school. Even when she couldn't drive and should've been bedridden, she would ride shotgun. This is the first year she won't make the trip at all. So Bimbo Slice picking today of all days to mess with her isn't cool.

"You and I both know she had it coming," I say coyly.

"Yeah, but we're supposed to be new and different people."

"There's no way to reinvent yourself when you've been going to school with the same people since elementary. People know who we are," I say, to her disappointment.

Her thick brows furrow like caterpillars about to butt heads, the telltale sign she's upset.

"Maybe you're right. I just didn't want to be the girl with the dead mom for the next four years, ya know? But I guess that's who I am forever."

Yesenia's sad revelation hits her in waves. What can I do about that? I can punch other people when they pick on her. I can't do that when she does it to herself, or can I? Playfully, I punch Yesenia in the arm.

"OW!! Cochina, that's going to bruise." She rubs the spot gingerly.

"I beat up people who mess with my friends. No exception," I say.

"Even if it is your friend?"

"I said no exceptions," I say with a very forced, fake menace.

Yesenia laughs, and after a second she says, "Thanks, just promise me you won't drop out."

"I mean, that's always a possibility." I laugh as Yesenia playfully punches me this time.

Don't get me wrong, I've thought about it. School has never felt like the place for me, but this is what kids do. Camp here for seven hours a day, "learning." Besides, my mom would never go for it. I can hear her scolding me already: "I didn't move to this country and work four jobs so you can be a failure."

Ironically, it's part of the reason I know school doesn't work. My mom is the smartest person I know, speaks like eight languages or something, got great grades, and has never earned more than minimum wage. Places like this don't prepare you to live a life; they prepare you to do what you're told. But what else am I going to do?

"You know I can't," I say.

"Yeah, your mom would literally kill you," Yesenia says offhandedly like she's stating the sky is blue.

"To be fair, getting suspended on the first day of school, she might just kill me anyway."

"I'll tell her how much I need you around. I don't think I'ma make it the next four years without you around, Cal. I'm serious."

Alani mockingly makes kissy faces behind Yesenia's back.

"You won't have to," I say.

The alarm stops.

Our security guards poke their heads in again.

"All clear," Bama says as Mrs. Stephens, our principal, steps out of her office, still on the phone.

After the vice principal got sick and left for the day, she spent like forty minutes at this morning's orientation talking about discipline and order. So between the alarm and our fight, I imagine she's not happy. Her scowl is a dead giveaway.

The professional, stern-looking woman holds her hand over the phone's receiver.

"Who are our problem kids?" she says.

"The one with the welt," Bama says, pointing to Alani. "And the one with the puffs." He points to me.

Ugh.

"You two sit. Everyone else to class," Mrs. Stephens says, and ducks back into her office.

"I'll hit you up later," Yesenia says as she files out with everyone else, leaving just me and the bully.

Suddenly, this cozy little waiting room, with its comfy chairs, thank-you notes from alumni, and shining view into Blackburn's majesty, is cold. There's an ocean of distance between me and the lanky asshole as we sit on opposite sides of the room.

It's not far enough.

The door to the principal's office sits closest to her. Next to me, the vice principal's door: closed and dark.

Alani mutters, "You lucky that alarm went off. I was going to—"

"Do absolutely nothing," I say, cutting her off. "You only talk so much cuz you can't fight. Ain't you supposed to be in varsity? Don't that mean you tough?"

I may not have any school spirit, but I've had to wait around after hours for Mom to pick me up. Occasionally that means going to volleyball games to kill time and overhearing coaches question this girl's toughness. It's a sore spot for her, one that I fully intend to jab as hard and as often as I like.

"Oh, High School Callisto bold. But she can still get her ass whipped!"

"Wrong!" I say with all the harshness of a game show buzzer.

Alani shoots to her feet, fuming, just as Mrs. Stephens's door swings open again. The woman's eyes dart to me, then the varsity athlete towering over her.

"In," she commands with a wave of her arm, ushering Alani to follow her.

They duck into the room and the door closes, but not before our principal glares at me again.

Yeah, I'm definitely getting suspended.

As the door latches, the light in the office closest to me suddenly pops on, spilling under the door and through the small tinted partition. Mr. Bernerd's office was empty earlier. I'm sure of it. He definitely went home.

... Something isn't right.

The entire time I've been in this office, I could sense the emptiness, but now I have that feeling like the call is coming from inside the house and I'm not alone.

All the doors come through this waiting room. No chance someone entered from the other side.

Maybe I'm just trippin'. I mean, I'm already in trouble. That's what this is. Maybe Mr. Bernerd has nothing to do when the alarm goes off, like Mrs. Stephens. Maybe he slept through it all. Maybe he didn't leave, just went to his office and laid down.

That's got to be it, right?

Goosebumps raise on my forearms, and my palms sweat. I muster what little spit I can to gulp down.

An inescapable feeling of being trapped swallows me up. It's somewhat claustrophobic, no doubt due to how tiny this place is now.

No, this is all wrong.

Before I can grab my crap and flee, the door springs open, just a bit at first, before it's pushed all the way by a well-dressed man. He stands in the entry, one hand firmly in his pocket. There's no way he could afford clothes that nice with what they pay teachers around here. A perfectly tailored ash-blue suit, golden tie clip, and cufflinks, his tie the color of fresh-cut wood.

Nothing about him says he's very big, but somehow I know that's a lie. My instincts scream that what I'm seeing isn't real. The man's dark skin seems to give life to shadow, like a nightmarish astigmatism. All I can focus on is him and even then he's just a blur, but his every sway and shift in posture causes the shadows to dance. Is it because he's back-lit, or does my prescription just suck that much? No matter what I try, I can't focus on his face. My eyes and knees sway to different rhythm. The room spins. My stomach churns threatening to ressurect undigested lunch. What the hell am I looking at?

An unnerving bass shakes me to my core, invoking all the fears I so desperately try to ignore. My heart pounds in my head. It takes a minute before I recognize it as a man's voice: sinister, wielding some sort of ungodly power in a simple phrase that sends shivers down my spine.

"Come in, Callisto," he says, and suddenly I know I don't want to be here.

CHAPTER 2

Crossing the threshold into this unfamiliar room, I brace myself like I'm about to skydive.

The Well-Dressed Man ushers me to a waiting office chair. Up close, the veil of blackness peels back just enough to reveal a hard face that hasn't seen the business end of clippers in a while. His overgrown facial hair clashes with his expensive suit. He looks like someone who loses sleep often enough that he doesn't mind. How come I can see him now, but I couldn't before?

Behind me, the door slams shut, locking me inside with my fears, bad feelings, and The Well-Dressed Man.

My seat across from the heavy wooden desk puts me directly in front of him as he leans against it. I look anywhere but at dude.

This office doesn't match the waiting room, but it matches the man perfectly. Everything seems too expensive to be in a school: the leather desk chair, the migraine-inducing sweet potpourri, he even has those auto roller blackout window shutters.

Wait. Why? Classes and hallways surround this office.

The Well-Dressed Man clears his throat.

"Sit." He guides me to the luxury chair.

He's careful to stay on one side of me, never crossing the big-ass piece of old technology sitting on the desk that's now pointed at my face. It's a mess of ribbon cables, coiled wires, and a fixed directional mic-looking thing—definitely a product of some long-forgotten decade like the 80s.

"You've been busy, Callisto," the man says, no longer sounding like a demon, just a vaguely British dude, every word as crisp as a new dollar bill.

From his jacket pocket, he pulls a mini tape player, scribbles something on it, and clicks record.

"State your name, age, and how you identify... for the record."

"Uh, Callisto Kader, fourteen years old, female," I stammer.

"Do you know why you are here in my... office?" the man asks, as if it isn't his office. And I know it isn't. I've seen Mr. Bernerd, and he ain't who I'm looking at. So who is this guy and why am I here?

I remain quiet. Stating things on the record has never worked out for me. Still, my eyes dart to the recorder just enough to give away the game.

"Right, you don't want to be heard admitting fault. What if I assure you this is just for me?" the man says.

I remain silent.

"Well, I don't really need your admission. I have evidence." The man delicately places a photo in front of me. He stands back to watch my reaction.

Cautiously, I lean forward to peek.

...GTFOH!

Public schools have cameras, that's a given. But this is something else entirely. It's me, mid-uppercut, doing something strange with my face as Alani's head snaps back, but it's so vivid, almost like looking in a mirror. No, it's more than that. There are scrapes on my chin I hadn't yet noticed. I'm convinced if someone were to touch the pic, I'd feel it.

And if that weren't weird enough, it's holographic sort of changes as the light hits it. I kinda wanna post it on IG. As cool as it is, I can't let him know I think so or admit it's me.

"Photoshop," I say flatly.

The man laughs.

"And the alarm going off at the same time is just a coincidence?"

"Alarm?" What the hell does that geiger thing have to do with the fight or why I'm here?

"The geigers are a hold-over from our earlier, more contentious days. Some of the older families left before they were commonplace. Every now and then, though, geigers make themselves useful. Like now. You're looking at a recorded event horizon. The box exposes the film inside to the light and whatever radiation is around. The result is..." He gestures to the picture.

He totally made that up.

The Well-Dressed Man looks at the tech on his desk and then back at me.

"I'm curious. What did the alarm sound like to you?"

That's a weird-ass question. I'm not answering that. All of this feels like a trap.

The man grows tired of listening to me say nothing. Finally, he sighs, exasperated. "We'll play it that way. Tell me about your family. You live with your mother, but what do you know about your father?"

... Why the fuck is he asking about my family?!

Why hasn't he just suspended me for the fight and sent me on my way with some ill-advised attempt to motivate me like, "I'll be watching you making sure you fly straight?" I guess he'd have to be a school official to do that? Maybe he's a superintendent? But why does he want to talk about my family?

Again, I find myself staring at him in silence. He waits on my answer coldly until something clicks and his intense gaze lightens up.

"You really don't know?" the man says.

"Is my mom alright?" I ask immediately, expecting this to be the part where he tells me I'm suddenly an orphan.

"Yes, she's fine, as far as I know. I will need to speak to her," he says.

Okay, officially this is bad. My mom says it every morning: "Keep your head down, Callisto." But I don't listen. Now some stranger is here droning on in riddles. Asking about her and the guy who donated DNA to me.

Why?!

Is this Child Protective Services?!

The way he's dressed screams government enough to freak me out. Definitely, CPS. My mom is going to kill me.

Oh god, he's still talking!

"—there is no need to worry. It falls under my charter to bring you with me and keep you safe. The others will see that you're acclimated."

What the hell is he even talking about it? Damn it, I wasn't listening again. He's taking me away from my mom, isn't he? I need to call her, but my phone is dead. I can't believe that I actually regret playing games in class.

Ugh. Fine, fine. I just need to get out of here.

"You don't look like you're following," the man says, staring at me.

I smile nervously. In our race to both say what's on our mind, we speak over one another.

"You're an Arc," he says as I ask, "Can I go to the bathroom?"

Wait, what?

"Out the door. On your left," he says.

Slowly, I get up and throw my bag over my shoulder, making my way to the door.

What was that he said? I'm an Arc? How? Don't they all have cool abilities like helium hair and magma eyes? My only skill is getting in trouble or running away from it, like I'm doing right now.

Outside his office, I'm greeted by an orchestra of ringing phones and busy business people.

WHERE THE HELL IS THE SCHOOL WAITING ROOM?!

How did I get here? Where is here? And who are these people? My chest heaves like I have asthma. I'm causing a scene.

Cal, don't cause a scene.

Okay, there are four walls. Four walls made of windows in a high-rise overlooking downtown.

What?!

"Can I help you?" someone asks.

Apparently, my bugged-out eyes and near-manic expression let people know I'm not doing so well. Interesting reason for that.

I'm not doing so well!

The door I just exited isn't even the same one I entered. What the hell?!

Don't get distracted, Cal. You're escaping.

Pushing past the adult who knelt to help, I head towards what I hope is an exit.

All the unimportant details that do make sense start to calm me. Like that plant. It's green. It's in an office. Offices are supposed to have plants and cute desks with little brass legs, bland overhead lighting, paneled ceilings. This is just one of those business spaces people rent offices out of. Right, all of this makes sense.

What doesn't make sense is sudden Callisto in an office, but I can make sense of how I got here later.

Finally, I make it to the elevator, and down it goes, opening to the lobby someone spared no expense for. There's an indoor fountain, glass ceiling, and fancy waters at the receptionist station.

Cool. Cool. Cool.

A doorman does his job, swinging open a hefty wooden door into the mall, inviting in its noise. This transport is less mystifying. There is a business center in the middle of the mall downtown.

Okay, focus, Callisto. You need to get the hell out of here.

I don't blend as much as I should. If this were any other time of day or a weekend, no one would think twice about a teenager loitering here, but it's still too early for school to be out and I'm in my freaking skirt and blazer school uniform combo. With blood speckled on my shirt still and my hair firmly looking like a bird's nest, someone is going to stop me. I can feel it. None of this would be happening if I weren't SUDDENLY DOWNTOWN!

Walking faster and faster, I race The Well-Dressed Man's realization that I'm not coming back and phantom truant officers.

"Hey!" someone calls.

I imagine a bounty hunter armed with pepper spray and those zip-tie cuffs behind me, trying to wrangle me back into the office or back to school and charge me a hefty fine for skipping.

Fighting every instinct to look back and confirm the weird image that popped in my head, I walk faster and faster until my legs do that bendy thing where they want to run.

Can't run. I'm a teenage black-ish girl, the key mixture of demographics where people assume I steal shit. I don't have time to prove them wrong and somehow not get taken away from my mom by the CPS guy upstairs.

My heart races as I near the exit. Two pairs of auto sliding doors. Perfect.

Outside, southern autumn waits. A slightly cooler summer that occasionally gets stupid hot or stupid cold depending on whether I took a heavy jacket to school that day, so it can do the opposite of what I'm dressed for. Climate change is very real.

The sweetness of freshly baking mall cookies and offensive odor of poured asphalt from nearby construction confuses the senses as a serious wind rips through the mall as the doors open.

Stepping inside, I look over to the small booth between the inside and outside doors. A security guard station. Nothing to worry about...

THRUM! THRUM! THRUM!

Godammnit! Not this again. The alarm rings both like a fire alarm and the same sub-woofer, car window open tornado. I nearly crumble.

Locking eyes with the security guard, there's this near-perfect moment where I can tell what's about to happen. He's going to lock me in here and wait for the authorities. There's some emergency button, but before he can slam his hand down, I dive out of the little door prison. It's enough to topple the woman in front of me.

"Sorry!" I yell, already sprinting.

The security door opens.

"Code Curie," the guard yells into his walkie-talkie while giving chase, but I'm nearly down the block when the mall doors finally slam shut. The security guard had less than a chance in hell of catching me.

At this rate, I'll be long gone before anyone can do anything. The real goal here is figuring out how to get home. I live twenty or so minutes from my school by bus, and this is twenty miles farther inland, so it's going to take me forever when you factor in waiting. I just have to find the right busssss... shit.

Whirring sirens interrupt my thoughts. From every direction, police cars and unmarked vehicles race towards me. Some even jump the curb.

"What's happening?" I say, stopping for the first time at the intersection. Down every street, there is some sort of law enforcement vehicle racing towards the mall. Some even go against traffic.

<They will take you. Run!> a girl's voice, like a whisper, speaks in my head.

That was weird. Really weird. With her voice comes a genuine fear. My heart nearly leaps from my chest, and my limbs tremble.

Why are they coming for me?

The chaos of sirens and the mall alarm harmonize into a song of terror that follows me as I escape and reflect on my bad luck. All this because I had to punch one girl in the face. If the CPS dude wasn't going to take me from my mom, these people definitely are.

A lifetime of avoiding the authorities doesn't make you a pro at evading them.

"Stop running!" my security-guard pursuer says.

Taking a better look at his uniform, I can tell he's an actual cop. That explains why he never gave up the chase. Even now, he points at me, trying to signal other officers. Well shit, I guess more than a chance in hell at catching me. A nearby crowd surges sweeping me into a nearby building.

THRUM! THRUM! THRUM! Again, an alarm rings!

The panicked crowd pushes. I push back while trying to get to a pillar, peel off this damn blazer, and rummage through my backpack for a light-blue butterfly hoody. I drop all of it. Damn it. I scoop my crap into my arms. Trying to remain hidden. Terror in a woman's face tells me about all the chaos I unleashed. No one here has any clue what's happening.

Neither do I.

My palms sweat, and my chest is still heaving. My lungs burn. With jittery hands that seem to move slower than everything else, I finally manage to stuff the stupid blazer in my backpack and pull the hoody up enough to try to hide my hair. That's the thing I'm sure someone noticed fleeing the crime scene.

Was there a crime?

Breathe, Cal.

I can't.

Through the glass, I watch cops flood in from the street, pushing against the tide of outgoing traffic. Their hard boots thud dully against the floor. I pull as much of myself as I can behind a big pillar. Hoping that no one turns around.

"Pssst."

An older Iranian man, subtely beckons me. His balding head and pleasant face make him seem like the unassuming sort of person you'd want greeting all your workers from his security kiosk. His eyes dart from me to the cops straight ahead of him, and he subtly tilts his head behind him. Crawling along the floor, I make my way behind his desk. A door leads, well I'm not sure where it leads. Nor do I care as long as it's not here. As I'm about to scoot, he gestures for me to stop.

I hold my breath and my blood runs cold as a cop's voice sinks my soul.

"Iman?" he says. "We're looking for a little girl. She came out of the mall, probably with the crowds as the alarm went off."

Forever seems to pass before my buddy Iman shakes his head.

"No... I don't see anyone come in. Just people going out. What did she do?" he asks.

"She's wanted for questioning. If you see her, do your job," the cop says harshly. "Come on."

Questioning my ass.

Iman mutters something in Farsi. I don't know what it means exactly, but given how much my mom says it to me, I'm pretty sure it means "asshole." Iman clicks his teeth twice.

I say "thank you" as best I can remember from my grandmother's WhatsApp Farsi lessons.

The security office door leads to a maze of narrow service hallways used for deliveries. Huge arrows on the floor make it easy to find your way. Finally, I reach a small security booth. Two guys on their lunch break hang out inside. Across from them, the loading dock. Freedom waits on the other side of that door.

Spilling out onto the back streets, I'm greeted by all manner of sirens still ringing in the distance. Not distant enough. With no real goal in mind, I walk in the opposite direction. That's all I know to do.

I'm thirsty, no spit in my mouth, my forehead slick with sweat, and I'm tired, really tired.

Cars whooshing on the highway get my attention. I sort of know where I am. When my mom used to commute to the city, I'd always see this footbridge arching over the highway. That's exactly where I head. As I climb, a gust of wind carrying the smell of piss threatens to pin me against the chain-link fences. It's the only thing stopping me from falling to my doom thirty feet below. Back where I just came from, the sheer amount of sirens from fire trucks and ambulances and cop cars is sort of ridiculous. All that for me, and I'm not out of the woods yet.

Reaching the other side, I stop in my tracks as a police cruiser rolls by slowly. An officer with her window rolled down, clearly looking for me, but her gaze rolls past me as if I weren't even there. The cops pull off to circle the block. As they leave and my soul returns to my body, a girl silhouetted by the sun stands on top of the footbridge, and as I blink, she's gone.

A siren too close for comfort reminds me that I'm kind of a fugitive right now.

It's not much different from how I already live my life. Make yourself small don't draw attention to yourself. Which is hard in this part of the city. On the bus, I count the tagged walls as they become more and more, and high-tops replace flip-flops. The bus crowd shifts from people who opt to ride it to people who have to. With each block that passes, I get smaller and smaller, shrinking into a sea of faces that look like mine until I'm just a girl with afro puffs instead of THE girls with afro puffs. No matter how comfortable I am in my own habitat around people who look like me, the dread never goes away.

It feels like they are watching, plotting or laying a trap. I wait for a roadblock to pull everyone off the bus, but it never comes. Cop cars racing past us make my blood pressure spike, but no one other than me and looky-loos seem to notice.

My stop feels too good to be true. There's irony that I feel safest in this unsafe neighborhood. Its familiarity swaddles me in my favorite blanket the way Mom used to when I was little, before we lost the house... and the blanket.

Our street is characteristically dark. The light has been out for months and no one has bothered to fix it. Dogs bark, and somewhere glass shatters.

I imagine footsteps behind me. I'm alone. I know I am, but that doesn't stop me from looking, nor has it made the hair on the back of neck lie down.

The ragged chain-link fence hiding in hedges I usually loathe is such a godsend. On the other side sits our place, a dingy little detached mother-in-law suite tucked behind a McMansion.

It was the cheapest thing Mom could find, and we're getting what we pay for. Our living room is on sub-floors, and we deal with shoddy plumbing, a leaky roof, and the ever-present stench of rot. Stillness and funk greet me as I unlock the front door. There's no sneaking in when you live in two hundred square feet of unrenovated sadness. Mom watches reruns of 90s sitcoms on our little twenty-inch television, laughing her head off.

"You're late, Cal," Mom says coldly.

"Sorry, Mom."

"You're fourteen. Girls go missing too often for you to pull this kinda crap."

"I understand."

Mom's eyes dart to a bloodstain on my uniform. She saved and called in favors to get this one made for me. The look tells me everything. She's disappointed.

"I'll wash it, Mom."

"I guess you'll have time, since you're suspended."

"You, ah, you know about that?"

"Yes, Cal. I know about that. A week for fighting. I can't even talk to y—. You know what, I've been on my feet all day. Can I chastise you tomorrow?" She turns around before I can answer.

Ohhh, that's not good. She lives to scold me. She must be super tired if she can't do it, or there's something else going on.

Mom is a beautiful woman. Her skin, which usually seems to glow, is dull in the blue light of the TV screen. Her smile and bouncy, infectious charm are gone. My mom's a husk of herself. I suppose I should count my blessings that I'm not getting whipped or cursed out because of school. But the dread of imagined footsteps following me worries me more than my mom's eerie calm.

I look around our little box, trying to picture which direction they will come from. Four plain, dirty-ass walls; the wood paneling splits where it can. There isn't a kitchen, just a sink that's used for both the bathroom and washing dishes. I guess you could call it a kitchenette. It's little more than you would find in a hotel room. The bathroom is a closet with a toilet and standing shower, both of which work far less than they should. Only two small windows and a front door. The back room this place technically has is full to the brim with out-of-season furniture. Yes, we're paying to squat in someone's storage locker.

Why do we live like this? Part of me wants to moan and cry about it, but I never do. I can't. For one, we have enough trouble as it is, clearly, and she already spared me. But I get the feeling it's not over yet. My eyes settle on the front door. Without a doubt, that's the only way in and out of this place. Unintentionally, I stare, waiting with bated breath.

"Cal, you make a better door than a window." Mom gestures for me to move from in front of the TV.

"Oh, right. Love you," I say, scooting out of the way.

"Mmm. If you love me, you wouldn't make me worry," Mom mutters offhandedly.

My sad cot sits in the corner of our only room with not even a privacy curtain. There's nowhere to hide from Mom or her sitcoms. With no other rooms available, I peel off my uniform just five feet from my mom and get into my pajamas. I'm too tired to wash downtown chaos out of my hair. I'm sticky from all the running and the panic.

But as I lie down to sleep, I don't. I can't. I just stare at the door.
And wait.

Chapter 3

—·—

"Grab your things, we're leaving," Mom says in a harsh whisper.

My eyes open to the sort of darkness twilight brings. It's either too early or too late. I don't remember falling asleep, which makes waking suck just that much more.

Mom doesn't wait for me to get up. She's already hustling things out of the house, only pausing in the doorway to snipe at me. "Come on, girl."

Her clothes, more than her words, make everything click. Any other day she'd be in her uniform, ready to drop off mail for her first shift before heading to her second job. Right now, she carries boxes of our little dishes in jeans and a T-shirt.

Yeah, without question, it's this again. Of course, after everything that happened yesterday, this is when my mom decides to skip out on rent.

The propped-open door lets in the cool morning air.

My life is trash and this is straight up bullshit. I want to scream, but that doesn't help anything. Instead, I roll off my cot, yawn with breath as hot as the coming day, and grumble, "I'm up. I'm up."

Mom never explains why we're doing this, but I know. I know we're already a month behind on rent that she doesn't have, and the first is coming up. It's not one of those things I imagine parents want to talk about. I think it makes her feel like a failure or something, but I get it. We're doing the renter's equivalent of dine-and-dash.

Honestly, I won't be sad to see this place go, but I hate moving, if you can even call this that.

Unzipping the suitcase I live out of, I grab my checklist from the inside pocket.

We learned our lesson the hard way. So many things got left behind the first time we got evicted: clothes, shoes, whatever wasn't necessary. Now, we keep it simple: clean laundry, dirty laundry, TV, house essentials, suitcase. A spot check and we are gone.

"Your uniform, girl," Mom says, reminding me to grab the crumpled heap I left on the ground. "It's going to be all right. I promise."

Her sometimes-non-existent accent is now at its thickest. It happens whenever she's really stressed. It's like her brain short circuits to Persian. Maybe the last time she was truly happy was when her accent was more pronounced, before I was in the picture.

Doesn't matter now, though; I'm here and I know it's not okay. Mom's words used to be such a comfort to me, casting an illusion that would allow me to sleep at night, but I've seen through it too many times for it to keep working. We've been here one too many times, and believing it at this point would just be wishful thinking, or I would be stupid. It takes everything in me not to say something to make all of this worse, a skill I haven't always been great at.

Under the broken streetlight on the other side of the hedge, our car waits with open doors. The few things we own get stuffed in the trunk or backseat. Mom and I work fluidly in mostly darkness—only a few trips as to not draw attention to ourselves. If you saw us and didn't know any better, you'd swear we were robbing the place.

All packed up, we hop into the car. Shifting into neutral, we roll silently downhill like a Volvo-sponsored roller coaster. Near the bottom, Mom starts it. The car sputters for a second before turning over. Mom looks at the dashboard. "Damn it."

"Everything al—"

"Everything's fine, Callisto!" Mom snaps. "Put on your seatbelt."

And just like that, the place I knew as "home" for the past three months has been left behind again.

A short time later, we sit in a McDonald's, eating silently. The other morning homeless and party girls sobering up from the night before hang out in the lobby, filling it with loud laughter and coughing fits.

Mom tries to think of something to say to make this okay, grasping for anything but settling on nothing. Her shame, like warmth, I can feel across the table. When she's not staring at me, she's doing her best to hold back tears.

All of it makes me feel small.

"It's fine, Mom." I eat the hotcakes we bought with money we don't have.

"No, Cal. It really isn't." Her tears break free just enough for her to delicately wipe them away. Being sad doesn't mean you have to smear your makeup.

"So, I'm off the hook for being suspended?" I ask jokingly.

Mom stares daggers at me that trigger the PTSD of past whoppings. Got it, too soon.

"Why you fighting?" Mom asks.

"Some people deserve to be punched in the mouth," I say under my breath.

Mom's unexpected chuckle makes her choke on her coffee, but it's not enough to lighten her mood. If anything, she doubles down.

"Not every fight is your fight, Cal. All I need is for you to go to school and get good grades. To be less of my lazy child and more of my brilliant one."

"Yes, Mom."

"But if you ever come home that late without calling me, I'll have to give this talk to my replacement kid."

"My phone died," I say sheepishly.

"If you weren't playing games on it in class, maybe it wouldn't have."

How did she know? How does she always know?

"Where were you?" Mom asks finally.

"Fell asleep on the bus home, rode it to end of line, then had to come back," I say too easily.

Thinking of lies in my spare time has become a hobby of mine. At the rate I get in trouble, I'm always going to need 'em.

I learned from the best. Mom's told dozens of little lies to keep me safe or to control me. Her favorite one, and the one I find to be the most untrue: "You're a spitting image of me when I was your age."

Usually, I call bullshit, but as she gazes out the window, distracting herself with the world as I sometimes do, exhaustion and stress tugging at her beauty, graying her dark, silky hair and dulling the hazel-green eyes we share, I can see it like a peek into my future. I see myself in her and the life she's lived.

And it's sad.

"Go brush your teeth. You got yourself suspended, so I'ma have to drop you at Angie's and you can take care of your uniform. Don't make trouble for her," Mom threatens.

There's no greater discomfort than an early-morning sink bath in a gross McDonald's bathroom, unless of course the familiar ache in your lower back tells you that your period is coming.

Just greeaat. Fan-freaking-tastic.

A fresh shirt and jean shorts do almost nothing against the funk still permeating from my pits. Ugh.

The morning started so fast, but watching myself in the mirror as toothpaste foams in my mouth and dribbles down the my chin, past the scrape from the fight, it's the first time I've had to think. Well, not so much think but have the fear, panic, and confusion from yesterday flood in. The dude in the suit, the things he said, the cops chasing me, and that voice at the bridge.

Everything was so loud yesterday, but now it's eerily quiet.

No, I can't let myself think about it; that's just inviting trouble.

I try, but it's all a little too invasive. The smallest details about that meeting come back to me in stunning clarity. I don't want them too.

Cupping my hands over my ears, I try to think about anything else. The bathroom door opens and a disgruntled worker waits to mop. I've never been so happy to be embarrassed, because now, everything is moving again. No time to stop.

"Sorry," I mumble, gathering the rest of my things and fleeing to our table.

Mom and I go back to pretending to eat so we can loiter in peace. We sit in silence as time ticks closer and closer to the day starting. Mom would typically be gone by now. I'd usually awake to a text that would tell me she loves me, but today she hovers. Mom doesn't enjoy upending my life, and abandoning me is just a little too much in her book. Might be something to do with how she and I are all each other have now.

For the moment, her sadness hides behind fatigue as her eyes droop, tired. I can see Mom actively putting it out of her mind to focus on the now and be happy. Other than car camping and, ya know, being suspended, this is exactly what she wanted: me going to a good school so she doesn't have to worry. Even though I make her worry.

Somehow, I know she's not focusing on surviving for the moment, just her victories to lift her up.

Our busy days nip at our heels, but we take our time "eating."

"Eat your eggs," Mom says, referring to the poisonous yellow fluff. She doesn't believe in allergies, which is weird, but immigrant moms, what are you going to do?

I forcibly scooch them to the side with the plastic knife, accidentally sending a bit flying across the lobby, and glare at her as if intentional. Mom laughs, and just like that, the morning is salvaged.

"Come on, I have to go to work," Mom says, packing up our stuff, and then we're off to the next stop.

BANG! BANG! BANG! The metal gate rattles as I knock.

A one-woman operation in the middle of the hood is an easy target, which is the reason for all the security gates.

Several locks click and turn before the door opens, and then several more before the security gate. A mop of brunette hair with a silver streak suspiciously peeks through the gap. Angie Arnaud, the fortyish French white lady, lights up when she sees me. She's my mom's oldest friend. They met on the plane when they immigrated and have been inseparable ever since. Her shop is in a rundown strip mall. The washateria in the complex is convenient, to say the least.

"Good morning, baby!!" she says, her accent thick as if she left Martinique yesterday. She waves to my mother, who hangs out the window while reversing.

"I'll be back after work," Mom yells as the car zooms off.

Ms. Arnaud leads me in. The wheels of our laundry hamper catch every crack in the pavement as I enter Ms. Arnaud's tiny shop, making an uncomfortable dragging noise in between.

There's little more than a display area and cash register behind the security gate. Her mannequins wear these very involved quinceañera dresses: giant skirt parts, tight corset parts, and the brightest colors. She focuses on birthday dresses because proms come and go, but birthdays are eternal, and at $2500 a pop, she's making bank. You can say what you want about the lady, but she's not an idiot. When she's in the back singing pop songs off-key to the radio and sewing out of her mind, she's probably counting her money too.

"Some girl sex your boyfriend and you beat her up, eh?" Ms. Arnaud jokes.

Ms. No Filter strikes again.

There isn't a single thing she won't comment on. Ninety percent of the time it's inappropriate, and a hundred percent of the time it's also inaccurate.

I could correct her, but for what? She's a nice enough lady, and it's not like she'll ever learn. Plus, Mom would be pissed if I went off on her and she had to come back and pick me up.

I force a smile. "Morning. I'm going to go start laundry."

Turning around, I pull the security gate shut.

Outside, a cool breeze carries the smoky aroma of barbecue from a nearby restaurant. Goosebumps trail down my legs and arms. I zip my hoody closed.

Places like this strip mall just seem to exist, forgotten about from the time they were built. Dingy and out-of-date marquees missing letters. Some walls are tagged, others hastily painted over with mismatched paint. Four businesses are the only thing keeping the entire complex open. Inside boarded-up storefronts are no doubt homeless, taking shelter as summer turns to fall.

A car is the only difference between us and them.

Dope boys on the corner blend like chameleons, clocking everything that moves. Unsurprisingly, their leers forget that I'm fourteen and they're easily in their mid-twenties. Four of them sit there about to punch the clock on an all-night shift. Not a word is said, but they're not necessary to make me feel unsafe; their eyes and clouds of sweet-smelling tobacco blown my direction are enough. Probably the best I can hope for. Outright rejection leads to a confrontation that you can't always walk away from. Counting the times my hamper wheels catch cracks makes a pleasant distraction from depressing surroundings. Focus on the wheels and nothing else.

Drag, click. Drag click. Drag click. And in no time, I'm standing in front of the yellowed, scuffed plexiglass doors, greeted by the loud tumbling of shoes in a dryer.

Inside, three women wash enough laundry for a dozen households. Thank god there are a few untouched machines. Nothing is worse than having to wait at a laundromat. Rows and rows of washers and dryers. On the far back wall, the supply closest and vending machines.

Warm linen, detergent, and the overwhelming scent of softener only slightly hide the stench of mold.

After separating and loading laundry, I get to work soaking my uniform. According to Ms. Arnaud, "Everything I make is delicate and must be washed by hand."

Do I have everything? Pleated tartan skirt, white blouse, sweater, knee-high socks, blazer, and cardigan. It's all here, and somehow, it's all stained. I understand how blood got on my shirt, but the cardigan was in my backpack. Not only are they useless, but they're blood magnets as well, apparently.

Filling a bucket with detergent and water, I dunk what looks like anime school girl cosplay in and listen to the machines churn. I'm in no rush to be anywhere, and for me that often means gazing through hazy scratched-up windows thinking about everything and nothing, taking in the weird, taboo malaise that comes when you're not in school during the early hours of the day. Everything is sort of a boring secret they don't want to let kids in on, and that's why they tuck us away for school. We're trapped, and everyone else is just out here... being boring AF.

While my uniform soaks and phone charges up, I watch the little flatscreen in the corner.

On the news, a pair of anchors, who may be the most gorgeous people I've ever seen in my life, make small talk and chat about local crap. No mention of anything that happened downtown yesterday.

Okay, I know I'm trying to not think about it, but that's odd, right?

One of the women folding a mountain of basketball shorts gets sick of that and switches it to a telenovela.

As much as I love them, it's hard to focus when there are questions floating through your head. Everything about yesterday bugs. What even is an Arc, really? I mean, it's not really my fault I don't know. Nobody seems to know. We're not really taught anything but how to pass tests. All we got on Arcs was that they're supposed to have special abilities, whatever the hell that means.

A short Google search gives me absolutely nothing. The more I dig, the more it seems like the internet is fighting me. This rabbit hole eventually lands me on the wiki for the US military. A single blurb reads: "Arcs took over as the UN's military arm shortly after its founding. Their society, traditions, and members are a closely guarded secret. They are thought to be the most secretive combat force in the history of mankind."

"That's it? Cabron!" I say to myself.

"I had no idea you spoke Spanish," the Well-Dressed Man says, sitting next to me.

"Jesus!" I say as my heart races, threatening to burst from my chest.

Dude sits next to me still wearing a suit, but this one is less pricey. I think he's trying not to stand out.

"Hablo un poco," I say.

Which is a lie. I'm fluent. My best friend is Mexican, and telenovelas are always on.

"How'd you find me?" I ask.

"You didn't make it easy. First, I went to the location on your records and found a vacant lot with mail forwarded to a P.O. box. So, I considered that a dead end. Then I made my way to the mother-in-law suite. You guys weren't there either. Your landlady, Ms."—the Well-Dressed Man pulls a piece of paper out of his pocket and reads—"Elza really wants to talk to your mother, by the way." He shoots the crumbled little bit of paper into a nearby wastebasket.

"Considering you ran yesterday and your place was cleared out, I thought you really didn't want to see me again."

"I didn't. Still don't," I say, looking around, really wondering the answer to the question he's apparently not going to answer.

"You wound me, Callisto."

"Look, CPS dude, I'm not going anywhere with you. I'm staying with my mom, and if you don't want me to scream, I suggest you leave."

"I'm not CPS, Callisto, and don't call me 'dude.'"

"Fine. Mr. Rhys, why are you looking for me?" I ask.

"And?" he asks, sipping coffee from a paper cup he brought with him.

And? And?... The answer to both our questions seeps into my brain. The last thing he said to me as I left his office yesterday. The reason for my Google search.

"And what did you mean when you said that I'm an Arc?" I say, dropping my voice so as to not be overheard.

"That's the logical conclusion, isn't it? You set off a geiger; you're an Arc," Mr. Rhys says with a smile.

Mr. Rhys... oh ha, like mysteries, I get it.

Wait, he never said his name. So how did I know it's Mr. Rhys?

<And you're not the only one.> His voice pings in my head, making my teeth rattle and my mouth suddenly taste like almond creamer. Yuck, I hate almonds.

"That's freaky. I don't think I like that. Don't do that," I say.

"Just making a point, Callisto."

"What are they? You. Us?"

"A secret state of soldiers. Each with a gift. We govern ourself and operate in accordance with the UN."

"Why?" I ask.

"So I take it you weren't listening yesterday."

"Nope."

"I guess I have to repeat myself."

"Pretty much."

"Okay, so let's start with the basics. One, again for clarity, I'm not from CPS. Two, I'm not here about the girl you punched in the face, but from everything I've heard, I'd say she deserved it."

I'm liking him a little more now.

"I represent The Faction, the governing organization of Arcs. We are the largest collection of Arc families. The 1952 S.O.S. Treaty charged us with public defense as well as the recruitment, enforcement, and protection of our kind. In trade for our autonomy, we agreed to become the military arm of the world."

All it took was three sentences, and he's told me more about Arcs than any social studies teacher or twenty-minute internet search.

"Yo, should you be saying this in front of everyone?" I ask, now sloshing away at the stains on my blouse.

"Do you think they even know I'm here?" Mr. Rhys says.

"Wait, you can do that? Like, make people not see you?" I ask.

"What do you think?" Mr. Rhys asks, gesturing to the people who are going about their day oblivious to us sitting in stiff plastic blue chairs and talking about whatever we're talking about.

"Truth is, people ignore ninety percent of the things they see, anyway. I just added us to that. We're still here; they'll just never notice or hear us."

"Okay, that... that's kinda cool," I admit.

"Thanks. I can be impressive when I try."

"With the way you dress, I say you try often."

"Nothing wrong with trying," Mr. Rhys says. "So, do you remember the big-ass piece of old tech sitting on my desk yesterday?"

"So you heard that too?" I say.

Mr. Rhys nods. "I hear most things."

Creepy. Oh, I guess he heard that too. "Um, yeah, I remember it."

"That was a Mark 1 geiger, the Eisenhower. It's more accurate and sensitive than the ones in doorways. It was pointed right at you and didn't go off. What the world doesn't know is that all Arcs are lightly irradiated. We can't hide it, dampen it, or stop it. That device was designed for the specific purpose of finding people like us, but I had it pointed at you and nothing. Now, how does that happen?"

"Easy, I'm not an Arc."

"I thought so too. I was about to untell you everything and send you on your way, but then..." Mr. Rhys responds.

"I set off another one," I say.

"Two of them," he corrects.

Shit shit shitty shit shit. I could've been free of all of this if I had sat still.

"You could've been. Yes," Mr. Rhys says.

"What does 'untell' mean? And why didn't the big thing go off?"

"Untell? I think that's fairly self-explanatory right?" Mr. Rhys says, gesturing to his head with one finger and sort of flicking away from him.

Ohh, he means make me forget. He can do that?

"I can. As far as the Eisenhower goes, the answer is the most important one anyone can ever give."

"What's that?"

A concerned and curious look stretches across his face as he says, "I don't know."

I've never met anyone like him before. There's intention behind everything he does, including the way he dresses and the way he sits. His long legs planted firmly on the ground. The ankles of his pants ride up just enough to reveal checkered red, white, and black dress socks. As relaxed as he seems, he's still ready to move if an occasion calls for it. All of this should be off-putting, but it's not. And that terrifies me. I don't like people, especially new people, but here I'm fine. It's probably because I have questions, and I like when people answer my questions.

"Kay, why were the police chasing me?" I ask.

"Legally? Our movements are heavily monitored, because they view each one of us as a potential weapon; intermingling with civies requires special permissions. Truthfully, however, since there have been Arcs, there have been people trying to recruit and extort us for our abilities. And though we have a signed treaty with the United Nations, individuals will ignore and exploit people like us for their own agenda. No government excluded. So, when they find a rogue Arc, not from one of the major families who slipped up and made their way into polite society, they approach you with a choice. Die for their cause." He stops in an uncomfortable pause.

"Or...?" I say.

"Or you don't walk away from that meeting. Neither will your parents. Your friends. Or anyone you've ever loved."

That's... That's not good.

"And behind door number three?"

"Let's just say it's a good thing you ran. I'm offering you survival. That's what you do, isn't it?" Mr. Rhys takes a long sip of his drink.

"Kinda hard to survive in an army. Besides, I'm not much of a joiner."

"It's too late for that. You're joining one side or the other. You're one of us or you're one of them. Easy peasy."

"Last I checked, I'm an American. Like, free will is our schtick," I say.

"Technically, the moment you set off that geiger, your nationality changed whether you knew it or not," Mr. Rhys says.

"I didn't sign up for that."

"We're in uncharted waters here. No one who's ever set off a geiger once has not set off one consistently. It just doesn't happen." Mr. Rhys loses himself in thought.

"So, what do we do?"

"Something radical, I guess. How do we keep you away from the bad actors, is the question."

"Bad actors? Like those horrible insurance commercials or...?"

"No, bad guys. Nefarious intentions. People who move in the shadows."

A specific detail from yesterday comes to me randomly. The police cars were on the scene instantly, and so were unmarked SUVs.

"Do these bad actors drive SUVs with tinted-out windows and no plates?"

"Sometimes. Why?"

Before I can say anything else, Mr. Rhys interrupts. "Oh."

He stares off into space like I did. I recognize being lost in your own thoughts, but I guess in his case he could be lost in others' thoughts as well.

One of the abuelitas doing laundry jumps in fright when she notices him sitting next to me.

"Mr. Rhys," I whisper, snapping his attention to me.

My eyes lean in her direction the way Iman's did yesterday. Just like that she's oblivious again. It's so odd.

"Right. That changes things a little." Mr. Rhys' posture shifts, and I guess so does his strategy. He softens a bit from being a sort of rigid adult figure to the kind of adult on public access television that actually listens to kids.

"School doesn't prepare you for life. That's sort of your mantra, isn't it?" Mr. Rhys says.

My clothes slosh in the bucket. It's official. I hate having conversations with a telepath.

"My school does," he continues.

"So you run a school now?" I say, focusing harder on the television as the very obvious evil twin plotline takes hold.

"No, Callisto. I recruit and train Arcs to fight in wars all across the world against enemies both foreign and domestic."

"Like the ones coming for me?" I ask.

"Especially the ones coming for you."

"So if they were there that quick, they'd have to know about me, right?" I ask.

"Not necessarily, but it's more than probable that they knew about you."

"Why are they coming after me, specifically?" I ask.

Mr. Rhys thinks for a second, smiles a bit, and answers, "I don't know, but I'd like to find out."

"And you can do that if I join your school?" I ask.

"Yes. You'd be a guest in my organization. We'd keep you and your mom safe," Mr. Rhys says.

That's the second time he's alluded to her being in danger because of me, and given everything my mother has sacrificed to get me to this point, I can't really risk her life because I said no to something as batshit as joining super-soldier military academy.

This is all very overwhelming. I just want to do the laundry I didn't want to do and not answer questions about my future. That would be nice.

"Maybe," I say.

Mr. Rhys looks frustrated—the way most adults look while talking to me, but unlike everyone else, he takes a deep breath, calms himself, and tries again.

"Callisto, I have to say, for a fourteen-year-old, you sound and think older than you are. My guess would be that you've been forced to live a lot of life in a very short amount of time. You've seen things some people won't see in their lifetime."

"You don't know me."

"True. But I know you're capable of thinking this through, and you have no problem saying what's on your mind. So, what's holding you back?"

I kinda appreciate him not rushing through this, even though he says I'm stuck like this stain on my blouse. Blood is notoriously hard to get out of clothes. I can't even remember Alani bleeding. For a moment I distract myself by churning away at the clothes in my bucket before I can feel Mr. Rhys' gaze prying a response out of me.

He won't leave me alone unless I say something.

Part of me really wants to tell him what he wants to hear so he can go away and I can be done with this, but the other part of me just starts talking. "I know what to expect from this washateria, I know what to expect from the dope boys outside, from Ms. Arnaud, from my mom, from teachers, and from future coworkers when I'm working some busted-ass retail job. I know this neighborhood and the kind of people in it. I know what everyone around here grows up to do. I like knowing."

"Do you like knowing, Callisto? Or do you just hate not knowing?" Mr. Rhys asks earnestly.

"That's not my point," I say. "My point is that I don't want my life to change. Even though it's not great, I don't."

My life is a bubble of my own experiences. I can handle that bubble.

"Bubbles are fragile and, by their very nature, they are meant to pop," Mr. Rhys says.

That's not what I wanted to hear. He knows that. I get up to move clothes from the washer to the dryer. Mr. Rhys follows, somehow still invisible to everyone else. No one even thinks twice about me talking to myself. I head to the back supply closet where they keep the extra dryer sheets. You have to pay for them, but given the amount of business Ms. Arnaud generates here, they let me get away with a few freebies now and then.

"Someone knows who you are, and they're probably watching you." Mr. Rhys's words act as a gentle reminder of the deep crap I'm in and implore me to answer him. My options right now are to not believe this Arc who has come down to a dingy washateria in order to recruit me and possibly save my life. Or risk my mom's and my safety because I'm letting a bad feeling outweigh what I know is real. I know people were chasing me. I know he's here answering questions and offering a way forward.

"So I join your school then," I say, cranking the knob to adjust the heat.

"We'll keep you at Blackburn, and from the outside, everything will look the same. But it will be easier for my people to watch you and keep you safe on our grounds."

"So I'll be going to two schools?" I ask, instantly regretting my decision to say yes.

"To put it simply, yes. It'll be like a secret school within your regular one."

"What happens when your team takes care of these bad guys and figures out I'm not one of you?" I ask.

"Like I said, you'd be a guest. If that happens, then you will forget we had any of these conversations and your life will pick up as it was, uninterrupted. Does that work for you?"

"It does." I return to my bucket, now satisfied the stain on my uniform is gone. Then words from yesterday ring in my head. My mom's offhanded mutterings. If I love her, I wouldn't make her worry.

"But I don't want to tell my mom," I blurt quickly. "All of this is just going to make my life hell in the meantime. She shouldn't have to worry about it if it's all going to go away, anyway."

"You sure that's why you don't want to tell her?" Mr. Rhys asks in another bout of honesty.

For a second, I'm genuinely lost for words.

Why is he asking that? Am I missing something? Does he know what I'm thinking more than I do? Conversations with a telepath are ibuprofen-inducing.

"I am," I say shakily.

Mr. Rhys plays the silence before finally saying, "Then I'll see you at school tomorrow."

Standing up, he carries his empty paper cup with him as heads towards the supply closet. Does he need dryer sheets? As he opens the door, on the other side sits a field of swaying grass. It's authentic enough to smell the dirt and stink of manicured grounds. Where the hell are the shelves? It's just like the waiting room all over again. Before the door closes, something else strikes me that suddenly.

"But I'm supposed to be suspended!" I blurt as everyone who paid no attention to The Well-Dressed Man now suddenly eyes me. Great.

Chapter 4

"Gui Lugo," says Mr. Brown.

My homeroom teacher literally gatekeeps. The line snaking outside his classroom adds to that first week confusion of kids unsure where the hell they are supposed to be, just so this guy can guess people's names. When your basketball career flames out and you're forced to be a teacher, you take pride in what you can.

I can't believe I got up at six am and took two buses for this.

Leaning against the brick wall, edging closer and closer to a desk I can sleep on. A couple students looking at me make me a little paranoid. People not being able to take their eyes off me is new and I'm not sure I like it. Maybe I'm being a little self-important. Maybe it's my period. Maybe one sink bath isn't enough to wash away two days of bullshit.

I don't have enough bandwidth for them, or this day, for that matter. I'm starting secret super-soldier school, I think. I wasn't given a lot of instruction, just "show up." I'm here because, like most things I do in my life, this option is least likely to lead me somewhere worse. In this case, it's an early grave. Mr. Rhys made that very clear yesterday. For once, I'd like good options.

"I thought they suspended you for a week," Yesenia says.

Speaking of eating up bandwidth: she's my best friend. I love her and would never hurt her, but god, her chipper-ass voice is going to get her decapitated this morning. She reels back when I look at her.

"Don't make it a thing," I say, trying not to yawn in her face. First night in the car is always the worst. At best, I got thirty minutes of rest. No matter how many times we do it, I can't sleep in the car. New places in general are hard for me, but that doesn't stop Mom from shuffling us from place to place. Like, I get it, we can't afford rent, but how hard would it've been to ditch a month earlier, instead of the first day of school? I wish I were still suspended. I could be curled up on petticoats in Ms. Arnaud's storeroom right now.

"Don't tell me. Don't tell me, uh, Har, Harvey Townsend." Mr. Brown daps up the teenager with the giant fro.

It's Yesenia's turn.

"Yesenia Barros with the good hair," he says to my cringe.

Then it's me.

I wait outside his classroom as he tries to conjure my name. His face twists and contorts in confusion before falling blank.

Well, that failed. He flips through his little book.

"You sure you're in my homeroom?" he asks.

"Yeah."

As he flips some more through his book, the couple of kids behind me groan. If they think they're annoyed, I'm not even sure I'm supposed to be here today.

"Name?"

"Callisto Kader."

"You're Callisto Kader?"

"Yeah?"

Yesenia's face tries to tell me something, but she's not good at giving subtle or even overt signals. Every time it just looks like she's trying to levitate me with her eyebrows. I guess if she were an Arc, she could.

"You sure you're Callisto Kader?"

"Yes!"

Mr. Brown's eyes dart to his left as Mrs. Stephens marches out of his classroom.

"Good. Come with me," she says. Her long, slender fingers beckon me towards her office.

The class "ooohs."

Blackburn is the newest school in the district. So like twenty years or something. Technically they built it from the bones of a previous high school and apparently just had money to throw at things, because everything is very... trendy. There are concrete floors and faux brick everywhere. It's a shining example of bastardizing something classic. I always feel like a stain here. The one soiled thing in these refurbished halls.

At the heart of the school sits a courtyard where the botany club does botany things. Huge windows lead out to what may be the greenest garden I've ever seen. The lockers hugging the walls are new and mostly uniform, except where I drove Alani's head into one. The occasional classroom door interrupts the rows and rows of book closets. I peek into one of the classrooms through the glass panel in the door. Every student just looks like they are being programmed. Which I guess, in a way, we are.

Mrs. Stephens' clicking heels lead me to the talk she wanted to give days ago. Her little ambush means she was expecting me, and I'm not sure what to make of that yet. I wonder how much of this was her idea or something planted in her head by my favorite life-ruining telepath. The very fact that I'm here when I was supposed to be suspended for a week and she hasn't mentioned a word of it tells me something is up.

Through the very same waiting room, I take a minute to pause and try to recall what I was worried about, back when small things seemed so big. What feels like a lifetime ago was barely two days.

The office Mr. Rhys popped out of now has its rightful occupant, Mr. Bernerd. He's been teaching since, like, the 70s. His cushy role as the wised old good cop to Mrs. Stephens' bad one seems dignified, but the last time I saw him, he was turning green and about to puke on himself. Anything seems more dignified than that.

"Ms. Kader. In. Now!" Mrs. Stephens says as the bell rings.

Sitting in her office, under her awards of academia, I don't find myself as worried as I imagine I would've been days ago. This place matches the waiting room. Same browns and taupes on everything. Same cozy and economic furniture. The kind of things schools buy to make you think this is comfortable. Everything from the wooly carpet to the "nice" big office chair she has.

More than cheap furniture, this place is full of well-intentioned promises. Keep your head down and fit in, you'll get this shiny life. It's funny; when they say that, they never account for life having its own agenda.

Mrs. Stephens leans against her wooden desk, the way Mr. Rhys did. She scowls down her nose at me, with a look similar to his then as well. Both of them no doubt thinking I'm something I'm not.

"We don't allow fighting at Blackburn, Ms. Kader. We don't like our young people skating from punishment either."

"I didn't skate from—"

"We don't like them talking back either."

"No free speech. Got it."

Mrs. Stephens gives me the look, and in record time too. Usually, new adults in my life take a minute to get here. This is the moment they try to read me like a book, their eyes squinting with hints of menace and uncertainty. I'm not doing what I'm supposed to do, because what I'm supposed to do is be afraid of her. She twirls her wedding ring around her finger before making her to her seat.

"Blackburn has a zero-tolerance policy about fighting. It was the first day, so I'm giving you a chance. Next fight, I'm expelling you."

That doesn't exactly say zero tolerance.

Mrs. Stephens has to get her point across, so she continues, "I asked around about you. Consensus seems to be that if you're lucky, she's a quiet girl. That you have no problem speaking your mind, if you feel you want to say something. Your middle-school teachers also said you're brilliant but lazy. That just tells me you're unmotivated. Have you thought about where you're going?"

"You mean after this meeting or like in general?" I ask.

"I was talking about your future. But you don't seem to want to discuss that. You also don't seem to respect authority."

She's two for two.

Why talk about a future I don't get to determine? It'll happen without my say anyway. I'm legally required to be here. You think that should give you authority? And you think I should respect this imaginary bullshit?

HA. No.

"We are going to fix that," Mrs. Stephens says. "When I'm done with you, you're going to be on the honor roll."

"Yeah, okay," I say before she's even finished, ready to get out of here.

Her face twitches. She seems conflicted about whether to be shocked or angry. If she could slap me, she would. Three times is too much, I guess.

"I'm not asking. When I talked to your mother, she was onboard with whatever it takes to get you where you need to be."

Ahh, there we go. There's the refreshing nose-to-the-grind-stone sort of threat I was expecting. Much better and more appropriate than being abducted by government gestapo.

Also, for the record, honor roll doesn't mean shit and special attention doesn't make me want to do things, it makes me want to stop moving like prey in front of a dinosaur.

Mrs. Stephens' voice cuts in. "Look here." She directs my gaze toward her personal hall of fame: letters and graduation pictures and ribbon-cutting photos sit in a shadow box in her office, on the same mantle as her degree; that should tell you something. In it, a dozen letters from kids she's personally taught. One went on to be an author, the others are successful business owners, realtors, or have been on local TV. Those are their big accomplishments.

"They all came in here just like you. Little hood kids fighting and cussing, and they all went off to college. Because they realize something you haven't yet. Ain't nothing out there in those streets."

No shit, Sherlock. I've known that for years. People say this like it's a revelation and it's not. No one chooses the streets; the streets choose them and they can't get away.

"They chose school," Mrs. Stephens says. "Got their GPAs up. Made better friends. Joined clubs. Volunteered and made something of themselves."

I lose myself in her little shrine, taking in all of the smallest details. Their smiles, haircuts, clothes. I take it all in, and it feels like there is something I'm missing. They all seems so happy, but I can't see why. It's not in the pictures. It's not in the letters. It's nowhere to be found.

My only thought: "That's it?"

If I somehow manage to graduate and, ya know, not die, that's the best that's waiting for me?

"That's going to be you one day," Mrs. Stephens says.

I hear her, but my focus remains on her pictures. Mrs. Stephens steps in front of me in all her pants-suit glory. "That's Jacob Shaw." She points to the dark man at a church cookout standing next to her with a big hat. "His uncle was a big-time drug dealer and Jacob used to be his number two. He was being groomed, but he decided he didn't want that life. So he chose something different."

They're standing in a field outside of a church, sweaty foreheads shining in the sunlight while they all smile. It's really not a good photo.

"Yeah, he was troubled; it's not something he advertised, but I could see it. Just like I see it with you."

"Yeah, okay," I say under my breath.

That doesn't take tremendous insight. Everyone has something they don't talk about; with me it's being homeless, with Yesenia it's her mom, and I guess for Jacob Shaw it was gang life.

But he got out. It's not seriously that easy, is it? Just choose school?

"I want you to think about where you are going in your life, and write me a paper on why you made that decision."

I'm reminded that people like her are the reason it's never been easy for me. It's not enough to excel; I have to do it their way. Whatever she's pitching, I already know I'm not cut out for it. School's not for everyone.

"Are we on the same page?" she asks.

We're not, but I nod anyway.

"I can't hear your head," she snaps.

She really has been talking to my mom.

"Yes, ma'am."

Forcing college on kids and, by extension, unshakeable debt should be considered a crime.

"Good. It was also brought to my attention that you and Alani have a history, so I talked to the registrar and changed your schedule. The two of you will have to do some peer mediation, but it's probably best to keep you separated for the time being."

That's something, at least. Mrs. Stephens whips a piece of paper from a folder and hands it to me.

"That's your schedule. Have a good day, and I will be checking on you."

Taking the schedule, I head out of her office.

"How bad was it?!" Yesenia asks, waiting for me in the hall, making me jump.

"Jeez! You scared the crap out of me. Not terrible. Apparently, I'm going to be on the honor roll." Both Yesenia and I laugh.

"What did she say about Alani?" Yesenia asks.

"They changed my schedule. I'm too dangerous to be around her."

"Duude. That sucks we have all our non-small-school classes together," Yesenia says as we make our way down the hall.

"Yeah, I don't really get the small school thing, still."

"It's just specialized learning programs geared towards careers. I'm in med small school, so I can hopefully get a leg up on a medical career."

I know that much. Her interest in medicine suspiciously came around the time her mom told her about the illness that eventually took her life. She's sticking with it even now.

"Okay, but I'm not in a small school. I'm just in general classes. What career are they preparing me for?" I ask.

Yesenia shrugs. "I don't know. Construction worker?"

Again, our shrill laughter bounces down the nearly empty halls. Yesenia's grades make up for her tardies, and me? Well, I just don't care.

At the end of the hall waits an almost frail-looking girl. At first glance, I can tell she doesn't fit. Something about her is wrong, but I can't put my finger on exactly what it is.

It's not her uniform; Yesenia and I are wearing the same thing.

Is it the sleek black headphones cupping her ears and tuning the world out? No, that's half of the Blackburn music department.

So what is it?

Every step gets us closer to her, but she doesn't move. Defiantly, she stands in our way, staring me down.

Only when we're nearly on top of her, when she's the sole thing stopping us from moving forward, does it hit me.

It's her eyes.

Wide, alert, lonely eyes so blue they almost seem violet. It's damn near unnatural, and I can't stop staring.

"You're late," she says to me, and her voice, it's so familiar. Why do I recognize it? I've never seen this girl in my life. Trust me, I'd remember.

"Hello? Do I know you?" I ask.

"I'm here to lead you to your new first period," she says.

"And so it begins," Yesenia says.

"If only it began on time," the edgy, frail girl says, and it comes to me like a lightning bolt.

"Oh! I heard you in my head!!" I blurt to the girl's dismay.

Right, shouldn't have said that aloud, but it is her. The voice in my head that told me to run from the cops belongs to this girl. Is she the one who was on the footbridge yesterday too?

"I meant ears. When we talked. On the phone," I say.

The girl's face remains unmoved.

We should call this whole thing off. Just let me die now, thank you. Why am I making an idiot of myself?

"Why did they send you an escort?" Yesenia asks.

"New small school," the girl answers. "Aeronautics and Engineering. We need to go."

"Cal's going to be an engineer?" Yesenia says in a sort of disbelief that hurts my feelings. "Okay, I guess."

I watch Yesenia's face drop. She's not happy we have to split, but ya know it's necessary.

"It's just like we said, construction worker."

Yesenia smirks.

"Talk to you later?" I say, hugging Yesenia.

The girl says nothing. She watches Yesenia leave, then turns in a huff and leaves. It's my job to follow. Rounding the courtyard, we find two doors; one leads to a classroom, the other into darkness, and down we go.

The stairs open to a smaller, narrower hallway. Air, thick with the smell of chlorine, greets us like an old, slightly toxic friend. I expect the pool before I see it, but somehow I'm still unprepared for the Olympic-sized majesty. Underwater lights give the room a trippy glow. Beige walls hide in the shadows.

"School within a school. You guys weren't kidding," I say.

"This is still a part of your actual school." She checks her phone.

"Oh." I guess I know where the money went.

"In here." She pushes her way into the equipment room where all manner of school-issued swimsuits live in huge boxes as well as pool toys and noodles.

What is up with this closet and why are we in here? Is this an attack make-out session or something? She's impatiently looking at her phone. Not even remotely interested in me. Up close, I can see that she definitely has a look. Our stupid Mary Jane school shoes have been exchanged for her well-worn black chucks. An old band T-shirt sits under her wrinkled uniform. It's like she dressed in a hurry and didn't care what she looked like on the other side.

Gum pops loudly. The girl stares at me, staring at her.

"So. I'm Cal, and you are?" I ask.

"Annoyed."

Look at me, making friends already.

The girl pushes past me through the door we just entered.

A heavy clunk behind us makes me look back as the door closes. And it's not the door we entered. It's heavy, dark mahogany. The kind of door secrets are held behind, and in front of me, an even bigger secret keeper. The boss level door.

There's no sign of the pool, not even the faintest whiff of chlorine. We're in reception of someone's office. There's this very dated look to the place, like they built it in the 70s. Lush red carpet and dark walls. Two doors, the one in front of us leading to what I assume is an office, and the one behind us.

DAMN IT! It happened again.

Every step the edgy girl takes towards the big door makes me cringe. Her dirty shoes on pristine carpet freaks me out. Though I guess my hygiene is nothing to write home about.

Her delicate hand rests on the door for a second.

Suddenly, she turns in a huff.

"I hate being late," she mutters again, pushing past me to exit.

"What's happening?"

"We missed them; now we have to catch up." She whips the door behind me open to a labyrinth of colligate hallways; each is long, uniform, and seemingly never-ending. Only about five feet between each door doesn't seem like enough space for an actual room. There are too many doors or too many hallways.

Something isn't right.

"If you get lost here, I'm not coming to find you. So for the sake of saving myself trouble later, keep up," the girl says.

"I have questions."

"If you wanted answers, you shouldn't have been late to the tour." The girl marches down the hall.

"There's a tour?!" I call after her, but too late. She's already taken off, blindly racing down the hall. I hate running, but I follow.

No little viewing windows on the doors. No signs of other people. What is this place?

A crispness in the air makes the hair on my arms stand at attention. A sharp, bitter smell like lighting in a thunderstorm lingers just enough for me to notice.

The girl stops suddenly, and I run into her and fall on my ass. She looks down at me with her vacant violet eyes.

In the quiet, the subtle pulsing of electricity coming from the hall almost sounds like breathing.

Hang on. What actually knocked me over? It couldn't have been her; I'm shorter than her, sure, but I almost definitely outweigh her. Also, I don't recall actually touching her. It's almost as if I got too close and an invisible hand just dumped me on the ground.

"Sorry," I say, unsure of why I'm apologizing, but the girl says nothing. Eerily, she stares at one of the doors, captivated. She lowers her headphones slowly and listens. Her eyes dilate as she slips into a trance. It's mesmerizing, but it feels wrong.

"Monet!" Her name and the bitterness of almonds still on my tongue. I realize I didn't choose to say her name. After all, how could I choose to say something I don't know?

The girl's eyes snap to me and fade back to normal.

"Today is not that day," I say again, not of my volition. What is going on?

Monet pouts, slips her headphones back on, and steps over to an adjacent door. She pushes it open with attitude and silence.

I sigh, follow her, and nearly run into the back of an older Korean couple.

Today is just not my day.

Behind me, the doors that close are big, expensive, and trimmed with brass.

Plaques and war medals line the thick brick walls lacquered in white paint. A very low ceiling makes me feel like I constantly need to duck.

Okay, damn it, someone needs to explain this.

<Imperceptible Movement Windows or IMWs. The world outside spins and lines up with places in this pocket dimension or even other places across the planet,> Monet says.

Uh-huh.

"That makes no sense," I say loud enough for the small Korean family to look back at me.

A proud but unsure mother and father stand with their dutiful son. He's not much to look at. I mean, sure, he's tall, muscly, and classically handsome, I guess, but his posture is the straightest I've ever seen, and the invisible but very apparent weight on his shoulders makes me tired just looking at him. He has a try-hard vibe, the very opposite of me.

"As I was saying, this is Fallen Hall," Mr. Rhys picks up as if he had been talking to us all along, standing ahead like he's leading a PTA tour group.

"Right, tour. I get it," I say to Monet. She returns a scowl.

"The history of what we do and why we do it is kept here," Mr. Rhys continues, gesturing to the place steeped so firmly in tradition you can feel it.

The six of us silently meander down the museum hall of war medals.

So far, other than the freaky doors, the most interesting thing is Monet. I've never seen eyes that color before. I find myself staring at them and then just at her. What's that about?

Only the boy's glare breaks my trance. Is he jealous or just an asshole? Wait, why jealous?

When I look back at her, Monet's staring at me. She gives us both the biggest eyeroll. Like, it's impressive. I should clap, but I think it'd be weird. No weirder than saying her name when I don't know how I would know that, I guess.

"There's no name on this plaque," the mother says with a flicker of worry she cannot hide.

Peeking over the tiny woman's shoulder, I read the plaque in front of her. "For Being The Line._______ ."

Mr. Rhys turns on a dime.

"They gave up their names. All of them." He gestures to the hall decorated in what I now know are tombstones. "Servitium Sacrificium, our motto in this Branch."

"The sacrifice of service," the mother says, but the father's face looks concerned.

"Not even your comrades know the depth of your sacrifice?" the father asks.

"Mr. Myung, you and your wife both know the risks involved in service. We're taking into consideration how hard and rare branch migration is, as well as your family's history serving in The Faction. Special accommodations are being made. One is that if your son were to lose his life in the line of duty, at the very least you will be informed," Mr. Rhys says.

"Unless it's something that threatens our national security," the man rebuffs.

Mr. Rhys doesn't take it as an insult, just says, "Unless it's an active threat to our national security."

So weird to hear them talk about losing their kid. They do it with expectation. The boy winces at the thought. Not enough for anyone to notice, other than me. There's something very caged about him.

Being here, I'm not sure I made the right decision, but looking at them, I do feel better about not telling my mom. No way she would just accept that I can die. She'd drag me out of here and fight Mr. Rhys to do it.

Our tour continues down the hall in a relatively uncomfortable silence.

Mr. Rhys pushes open a pair of doors at the end of the hall. I'm ready this time. I expect the most far-out setting I can think of on the other side of the doors.

As they open, the first thing to hit me is the smell: the perfectly distilled scent of freshly cut grass and dirt.

Looking out to the expansive field stretching before me, my jaw slacks; it's clear I wasn't as ready as I thought.

The swaying, bluish grass reminds me of the fields Mr. Rhys disappeared into yesterday. You couldn't imagine a more ideal landscape. Rolling hills, precise sunbeams, the gentlest of breezes.

There's nothing that would explain this. This can't be some weird artificial basement, because there's no way this place fits beneath the school. I doubt it could fit beneath our city.

Am I on another planet, and if so, how?

"I just explained this to you. IMWs," Monet says.

"Yeah, but... are Arcs aliens?" I whisper.

She gives me the look that everyone gives to their stupid friend. It's deadpan and disappointed in my intelligence.

Flatly, she says, "No."

Cool, that's informative. Really helpful. My focus returns to the setting.

It's like they have transported me to the moon. I feel lighter than normal; even the air is a tinge different, cleaner and thinner, I think.

It's all too much to take in. I never understood people fainting from being overwhelmed, but I'm just about there.

Behind me is a building that sort of looks like a library. No ominous elevator shaft to the heavens, just a sky fixed at sunset. Unknown stars wait behind the shades of fading evening.

Just how much this broke my brain isn't lost on Mr. Rhys as he watches not only me but the parents and the boy as well. Equally mesmerized as they take in every detail.

An amused smirk stretches across Mr. Rhys' face.

"This is I Small World," he says. "Special Branch Campus. Where we train. If you're cleared to be here, at the right moment you can enter from just about anywhere on the planet." Mr. Rhys talks directly to me, but it registers as little more than background noise. My mind hasn't fully embraced where I am.

"We've heard of the Special Branch's Small World campus, but seeing it is impressive. Nothing like Domestic's, or Foreign's for that matter," the mother says.

In front of us sits something that looks like a college campus: old-school-looking collegiate halls, winding stone walkways, timeless gas lanterns, and an actual bell tower.

All I can think is *how?* How is any of this possible? Who built this? Why'd they build it?

Before the questions can hit my lips, a soft, almost quiet voice like a song down a hallway plays in the back of my head. <Can you stop asking stupid questions long enough for this to be over?>

Well, someone's a bossy little asshole. Monet's head snaps in my direction with a glare. Right, freaking telepath.

When we are done taking in the sight, Mr. Rhys turns to us.

"Mr. and Mrs. Myung, my job here, as I'm sure you've heard, is to know things. In the spirit of transparency, I know about Kosovo."

Both parents reel back in uncomfortable distaste.

"I don't blame you," Mr. Rhys says.

"You don't have to be kind," the mom says.

"Kind isn't what we do here. Kosovo… was an impossible situation. I know what you lost personally, but your agent kept the principal alive. Your family has developed an incredible skillset over their generations of service to The Faction. I'm hoping it's something your son has inherited."

"Inherited? We've been drilling him since before he could hold a Hawk," the mother says.

"Then I guess it will please you to know I've already arranged your son's first assignment, and it's in your wheelhouse. Here is your son's principal. He will be in charge of keeping her safe and preferably alive."

This guy is my bodyguard? As I'm about to step forward, Monet beats me to the punch.

<Sigh, here we go,> her voice says in my head.

Monet's face doesn't let on what she's thinking as she forces a smile.

Mr. Myung salutes. She salutes in return.

"I appreciate your transparency, Commander Rhys," Mr. Myung says.

"No rank. It's just mister."

"Oh, I'm sorry. What you have pulled off today is impressive considering the security breach just a couple days ago," Mr. Myung says.

"Thank you, and there was no security breach," Mr. Rhys says.

"Oh, but we had heard—"

"From whom?" Mr. Rhys asks, with just a hint of his prior menace returning.

"Oh, I guess it was just a rumor then," Mrs. Myung says.

Mr. Rhys starts again. "Mr. and Mrs. Myung, I hope you understand Cadet Myung won't be able to share details of his missions with you."

"Because we've been all but ousted from the Faction," the mother snipes.

"No. It has nothing to do with how Domestic treats their own. It is about how we treat ours and ensuring operational security on our end. Monet will escort you to a meeting room where she and your son can discuss protection details and meet in my office in about ten minutes?"

"That works," Mr. Myung says.

Monet smiles and leads the way, leaving me with Mr. Rhys.

I overhear Mrs. Myung say, "Monet? So young to have your call sign."

"Glad you could make it," Mr. Rhys says to me.

"You didn't give me a choice. What are call signs?" I ask.

"We'll get to that. Follow me." Mr. Rhys leads me through the campus.

It definitely seems more like a college than a military academy. It's a very stately place, like Hogwarts came to life and turned a little fratty. It'd be easy to forget you're in a pocket dimension if you just look around. Downtime seems to be a very serious thing here. They work hard and play harder. You'd have no idea that everyone here is an Arc or that anything is out of the ordinary if you ignore the fact that all the kids lounging around wear black combat fatigues.

At the center of this place sits a massive building. Everything orbits it. People flow in and out. If this were a college, it would be the main hall, and it looks the part too.

It's the same sorta look you get from places in Washington, D.C. It has this important vibe coming from it, but with red bricks, tall spires, and huge windows. Our march through manicured annexes puts us on a crash course with it.

Mr. Rhys' pace makes him harder to keep up with. Catching my breath seems harder too.

"You'll get used to it," Mr. Rhys says. "The air is thinner here, the downside to atmospheric air conditioning."

Imagining what sort of monstrous technology this place must require leaves me feeling small. For all intents and purposes, this is a planet, designed to hide extraordinary individuals. Maybe I don't belong here?

"Since we spoke yesterday, I reviewed your transcripts and 'talked' to your former teachers." Mr. Rhys talks with his fingers in quotes, which makes me feel like he just pulled information from their minds.

"I did," he says.

Right, he can hear this.

"I can. Anyway, about your schedule. I know you are fluent in both Spanish and English. So, no foreign language necessary, but we encourage learning at least four. We have our own electives. Boot camp will take care of phys-ed. We'll keep you in science and math, shoring it up on our end. And according to you, there's 'no point in learning history when you can just Google that shit.' Which is fair, so we'll teach you what you can't Google. Did I miss anything?"

Not unless he's impressed by my people-watching skills.

"I've been listening, and I'm curious just how refined this skill of yours is," Mr. Rhys says.

Is he challenging me? The smug look on his face says he is. Fine.

"That guy is cheating on his girlfriend." I gesture with my head towards a couple standing in the quad.

"How do you know?"

"The way he's holding his phone means he probably doesn't want her to see who he's talking to, and sure, it could be a lot of things. But the girl pretending to study but obsessively staring at her phone and looking at him is probably who he cheated with."

"And how do you know the girl next to him is his girlfriend?" Mr. Rhys asks.

"She keeps touching him, is desperate for his attention, and they are familiar with one another. She keeps trying to look him in the eyes; he's avoiding that. He feels guilty maybe? To be fair, I think he just called her his girlfriend so they could fool around and now it means more to her than it does to him," I say, realizing that's not actually fair and is really incredibly dickish.

Mr. Rhys stops and looks at both sides for a minute. I think he's reading and confirming my hypothesis.

"All that from body language?" he says.

"Other people's lives are entertaining. Drama is fun when it's not happening to you."

"You see drama, I see a need to enforce barrack curfew more effectively," Mr. Rhys says, holding the door to the main building open for me.

"Barracks?" I ask.

"Like dorms. Full-time students live here on campus."

"Wait, they just get to live here, like, year-round?"

"Yeah."

"Must be nice," I mutter to myself.

I don't think I'd like living at school, but I've lived in worse places. And if the barracks are anything like this building, it wouldn't be half bad.

The chorus of a thousand clicking heels greets us as the skylight above bathes us in a warm glow. How is there sunlight in a pocket dimension?

I don't know snot about architecture, but this is a very pretty building. High, arched ceilings, beautiful wooden floors with slabs of geometric shapes lead down the endless halls. Above us hang chandeliers, really nice ones made of crystal. There's a faint smell of book musk and dust, I guess.

It's never been this easy to walk through a crowd. Everyone sort of parts around Mr. Rhys.

"It's a free period. Everyone gets to mingle for a bit. We're not just shuffling them off to the next class. What we do requires us to go non-stop. At least here there should be a couple minutes of peace," Mr. Rhys says.

"That's cool."

Slowly, people bump into us as if they forgot we are here, same as the abuelitas in the washateria.

Mr. Rhys is thorough when erasing where he's been. He doesn't even make footsteps. The only reason I notice is that I watch his hard dress shoes make their way up the stairs without making a sound. I've been here before. In fact, I just left. Back where I started: the room with the heave of electric breath and the doors of mystery.

As people forget, Mr. Rhys gets serious. "Callisto, there are things we need to talk about. First, the mission comes before everything. In your case, that means maintaining operational security. To do this, you mustn't volunteer information about yourself or your situation to anyone. As far as everyone else is concerned, you are a new recruit. That's it. Some of the first-years struggle to find their Arc. Your squad leader and I are your cleared points of contact. For logistics, there maybe a couple others added to that list as well, but that's it. Everything here is not what it seems. Not everyone will be your friend. This is just like high school in that regard. Except everyone here has the power to do actual harm to you if you aren't one of us. Understood?"

"How can I keep a secret with all these telepaths around?" I ask.

"We are fewer than you think, but in the meantime..."

"Yes, I will do everything in my power to not be extra."

If there's anything I can do, it's keep a secret. My best friend doesn't currently know I'm homeless, so I think I can keep important things from people. I've been doing it most of my life.

"I'm counting on it," Mr. Rhys continues. "Second, to answer your earlier question, a call sign is a point of emphasis and treasured in-program nickname that has to be earned. It's a requirement as your first earned rank."

"Call signs. Cool. What's yours?" I ask, realizing I'm now much more comfortable around him than I was at first. That makes me uncomfortable.

"I have many," he answers.

"What about Monet?" I ask.

"Monet. Though it's not common for someone to have earned theirs as early as she did."

"And when did she?"

"At three years old. For reference, people are usually teens and already running missions before they find it."

"Damn. Is that why she needs a bodyguard?" I ask.

"Part of it. Now listen, every student here who has yet to earn their call sign is referred to as Cadet. Understood?"

How easily Mr. Rhys navigates these hallways is impressive. Is this like a GPS situation or did he just remember every twist and turn?

"You're doing that thing again where you don't listen," Mr. Rhys says.

"Sorry. Cadet. Got it."

"I apologize for hijacking you earlier. Monet's in a particularly sour mood today. Powerful emotions can make her... distracted."

"I mean, I get it, I don't want to be here either," I say. "What was behind that door? What's behind any of these doors?"

"What's behind every door you've never been through? The unknown."

"Lame," I mumble.

Annoyed, Mr. Rhys stops in his tracks.

"That brings me to my last point, Cadet. Don't make enemies here. I only say this because you're prickly and you may end up in the field with someone whose job will be to save your life."

I can't believe someone described me as prickly. What does that even mean?

"It means don't be an asshole."

Wait, school officials can curse here? I think I'ma like this place.

"I know we have an arrangement, Callisto, but it would be unfair to hold you to it if, in the light of everything you've just seen, you've changed your mind. "

"Oh, um..."

"This place has many secrets, and now you're one of them. In order for us to remain safe, our secrets need to remain our secrets."

"Can I ask why?"

"Why what?"

"Why keep the secrets? Why do any of this?"

Mr. Rhys pauses for a second and thinks on my question. "We had a long history of just trying to survive. We waited for others to make our issues important to them, and it never happened. We were just left with bad and worse options. Until we decided to not let anyone make decisions for us. The secrets and all of this, it's a way for us to control our own destiny."

For some reason, that clicks with me. Everything falls into frame. I think back to the hall of medals. There were no pictures, no smiling faces. If anything, it was the opposite of the pictures on Mrs. Stephens' mantle. But it didn't feel hollow, and neither did his answer.

"Can I give you a piece of advice?" he asks.

"Um, sure?"

"You may only be here for a short time, but I want you to know this place is not about churning out graduates. We do have a great graduation rate, but more importantly, we are here to teach what you need to know to function out there on your own. So take this place seriously, learn all you can, and keep to yourself. Are we clear?"

"Yes, sir."

Chapter 5

M r. Rhys pushes the boss-level door open to an office made up of boxes and boxes of tape recorders on a huge stone bookcase that takes up one wall. It's not as much of a closet as I make it sound. It's actually an impressive room.

Wood-paneled walls, a desk that looks like it's only used for, like, meditation or pensive menace. There's nothing low-rent about this place.

There are only two windows, one large door, and a smaller one that probably leads to a bathroom. One way in and one way out. Unless you count the window, which would suck because, ya know, third floor.

"This is my office. My proper office," Mr. Rhys says.

A lithe, athletic girl with a single braided plait drooping over her shoulder waits silently in the corner. She's wild, distilled danger; it radiates off her, soldiery poise be damned. An entirely, distinctly different threat than passing dope boys on the corner. More lethal.

Every muscle is tense and ready to act, to fight. Her combat uniform like a second skin, bulletproof vest, combat boots and all. She seems both perfectly balanced and powerful.

"You missed the IMW," Mr. Rhys corrects me.

"What?"

"The bathroom's also an IMW. Do you case every room you enter for an exit?"

"No." Yes.

"Good instinct. Sit."

Across from his desk is a nice chair, like actually handmade nice, not the crap that sits in Mrs. Stephens' office.

Dropping my book bag, I sit and, as comfortable as the chair is, I can't get over the feeling of having my every move scrutinized by the quiet girl in the corner. Are we not going to talk about her?

Mr. Rhys clearly hears me and ignores my thoughts that are bombarding him. Instead, his gaze pops from me to the door as if someone had just walked up and commanded his attention.

"Just in time," he says as Monet enters with the Myung family in tow.

<Ugh, of course it's Feral,> Monet's voice says in my head as she looks at the girl standing silently in the corner.

"She's feral?!" I say in disbelief.

A low growl from the girl sounds like a jungle cat and nearly makes me wet myself. Everyone else ignores me.

"This is indeed Feral," Mr. Rhys says. "She will be squad leader to your son, his principal, and our newest recruit."

My attention, like the parents', turns to Feral, my squad leader. Mr. Rhys said that she'd be clear to know what's going on with me. How can she be this important and barely be, what, eighteen?

"She's very young," Mrs. Myung says, echoing my exact thoughts.

"In this branch, senior cadets only need three years to qualify for squad leader, sweetheart. It's mandatory for their graduation," Mr. Myung says.

"You're telling me like you're the one who worked on the Branch Head Liaison's security detail for six weeks," Mrs. Myung snaps. Her husband withers a bit.

"While Feral is a senior here, and this is her first squad, you should know she has three times the amount of experience as any of her peers. Your son is lucky," Mr. Rhys says.

Mrs. Myung looks over at her. "I understand."

The woman takes a brief pause, then salutes Feral.

"My soldier is yours to command."

"On line!" Feral barks.

The other two line up quickly. I guess I'm supposed to line up too? I waddle next to them, doing my best to stand up straight with my backpack still on.

<Why is she so embarrassing?> Monet's thoughts again reach me.

I'm not so sure she knows I'm listening.

"You two at ease," Feral says, gesturing to Monet and me. We step back and only Myung stands there.

"State your name, then repeat after me," Feral says.

"I, Chu Myung," he says.

In near unison, they continue with an oath that all feels very official.

"Solemnly swear allegiance to The Faction. We are soldiers of many. We are a goal of one. We are blood. We are fire. Together, we are rooted and strong. Upon taking this oath, it is my promise to follow the orders of The Branch head and superior officers. To work in defense of The Faction as a whole against threats both foreign and domestic."

It seems like bloated ceremony to me, but not to his parents. This is both their worst nightmare and everything they ever dreamed of. You can see it in their overwhelmed faces.

The room settles in reflective quiet when they finish.

...Are we supposed to say something?

"Will we be able to watch the first drills?" Mrs. Myung asks.

"Unfortunately, no, our training regimen is a trade secret. However, we have set up an exhibition. Feral will take the three to get uniformed," Mr. Rhys says.

"Move," Feral barks as she marches out of the room with the three of us on her heels.

Feral leads us down the stairs to a state-of-the-art locker room, unlike every area of this facility I've seen so far. Where the rest of the school seems older and classic, this place is cutting edge.

"You have sixty seconds," Feral says. A vague Latin rasp rattles when she's not barking... Shit, I should be careful what I think, everyone here is listening.

Monet and I head into one room. Cadet Myung disappears into the other.

Finding my locker takes no time. Through the metal mesh, I can make out body armor and lethal-looking tools hanging in adjacent lockers. Each fastened shut with biometric locks. Kits—somehow I know they are called kits.

"Filling in the gaps is easier than talking to you," Monet says from somewhere in the room.

Thanks for that, I think sarcastically, hoping she can hear me.

I pile on gear as fast as I can. I've had a lot of practice, since, ya know, fleeing from rent and squatting are things I do regularly. When I'm done, I look like an unstuffed scarecrow. Amongst the ill-fitting... fatigues, I find a pin, like the one on Feral's collar. It fits in the palm of my hand, probably no bigger than a quarter with a dull gold band around the edge. The design is one that I've seen around campus a couple of times already, including currently beneath my feet in the locker room. A thick gnarled tree, its winter branches naked and twisting like its roots, making it hard to tell up from down, but I guess that's maybe the point. Its outline sits against the off-white background, and a slick glossy overcoat hides the feel of the little details.

Weird.

I carry it with me as I walk out. I'm first, followed quickly by Cadet Myung then Monet. She's not happy about being in last place.

"Not bad," Feral says, "only ten seconds over. That means only ten extra laps."

"Wait? Extra laps? I have to run? No one said anything about running!" I say.

Everyone turns to look at me, fear in their eyes. I screwed up, didn't I?

"Monet, take Cadet Myung ahead," Feral commands.

Monet hops to it, both of them jogging down the hallway.

Feral focuses on my coin. She holds out her hand. As soon as I place it in her palm, she grabs my wrist. There's no squirming free. If she were to hold any tighter, my wrist would snap.

"This is your challenge coin. It's proof that you belong here," she says as she uses its pin and pricks my finger. My blood gets sucked inside like a needle. I watch it fill the inside of the tree emblem, weaving through every branch and root.

"Do I belong here?" I ask quietly, looking over her shoulder where soldiers stand at attention at the end of the hall.

Her eyes dart to me, heavy and unsympathetic. "I get where you came from. I understand that you're a visitor, but you're here now. I will not treat you any different. I can't. I'ma treat you just like I treat everyone else. It's up to you if you keep up."

For the moment it grounds me in this new reality. I'm in a program for super soldiers, and whether or not I belong doesn't mean a damn thing. I'm here, and they expect me to fall in line. This is going to be a problem. I don't do falling in line.

"Every Arc is stronger, faster, and tougher than a normal human. I mean, party balloon versus workout balloon tough. And that's before we get into using Arcs," Feral says.

"And if I don't have one?"

"Keep that to yourself," Feral says. "No more questions. Class is about to start."

Class is exactly where you're supposed to ask questions.

We wander out to the floor of a massive indoor training plaza.

Monet and Cadet Myung wait with his parents and Mr. Rhys. A small group of others I don't recognize make this a crowd.

A two-story training plaza awaits us ahead along with our group. All the lower floors are more high-tech retrofits. A dam repurposed for training these extraordinary individuals. This is probably the only place sturdy enough to take all the damage.

What looks like gymnastics training floor stretches to the far end of the room. The upstairs running track also sort of lends to the idea of Olympic training facility, but the crates and soldiers make me feel like we're a ragtag group about to go to war.

Okay, Cal. Don't focus on anything else. This is just a school. Fit in. Make friends, that thing you've been unable to do for nine years now. Talk about them, not yourself. Blend. There's nothing different about this place other than the people.

Muffled thunder comes from one of the many rooms dotting the surrounding walls.

"What's that noise?" I ask.

Feral listens for a second. "Gunfire."

Why is someone shooting?!

"The exhibition is starting," Feral says.

A pained roar of a wounded animal catches my attention, as well as the deep, odorous funk of what smells like cabbage.

My head snaps to the other side of the floor, and I have no clue what the hell I'm looking at. A six-foot-tall lagoon monster made of ... well, cabbage, grows as it charges a plain-looking teenage boy.

The vines, like puppet strings, dive into the ground and surface around a small, very sick-looking kid, like greener than he should be. He's literally planted, guiding the monster with his own hands.

The monster finally settles at around nine feet and hulking. There's a small whine tickling the back of my hearing. Where is that coming from?

The plain boy stands still. Unmoved. With no facial hair to speak of, not even eyebrows, he looks sick in his own way.

The closer the monster gets, the more nervous I become. Someone should help him, right?!

No one around me moves. Nor does he.

Maybe he's paralyzed with fear. Why isn't anyone helping him?!

As the thing gets closer, the whine in the back of my ears gets louder and louder, like a plane gearing up for takeoff until it's near deafening.

The monster trudges forward.

Bald kid coughs like he's hacking up something. His legs erupt into flames, singeing off the few buzzed hairs on his head.

This is so freaking cool.

Bald kid rockets forward toward the monster. As it swings, bald kid intentionally crashes at its feet, his jet stream turned up, and ignites the monster.

FWWOOOSH! The monster goes up like flash paper.

Oh, god, that smells awful. I can taste it, like charred spinach and sewage stew.

A pair of students rush over and extinguish the flaming heap.

That. That was amazing.

I really don't know what the hell I just got myself into. I can't do any of that. Crap. Crap. Crap, Cal.

As the vines retreat into the soles of the puppet kid's shoes, both bald boy and cabbage kid dap up.

A few people golf-clap.

The boys make their way over to our observing crowd. Both the Myung parents look impressed.

Cadet Myung has a more pained, focused expression on his face. Both the exhibition guys stand with their hands behind their backs. Even ten feet away from him, I can feel the fire feet's heat.

"I present to you Cadet Twigg," Mr. Rhys says, gesturing to the cabbage kid. "And Cadet Da—no, no. Lockheed."

Before Mr. Rhys finished saying it, I knew it. We all knew it. It was like overhearing someone's name being called in a crowd or having an answer on the tip of your tongue and suddenly remembering it. How? And what a weird sensation. But I'm certain the moment I saw him after his fight, I knew his call sign, and it is Lockheed.

Mrs. Myung can't hide how impressed she is. The woman is practically beaming. Any signs of hesitancy are gone. Mr. Rhys is a good convincer. He got me here, after all.

"Mr. Rhys, your soldiers are well trained, and it's not every exhibition that you witness someone get their call sign, and a freshman no less," Mrs. Myung says.

"Yes, Lockheed's parents are a long line of Special Branch Operators. He comes from excellent stock, this one. Just like your son," Mr. Rhys says. "Now would be the time to say goodbye, Mr. And Mrs. Myung. Once his training starts, he'll be on a strict regimen for the rest of the day. You won't have another chance."

"Right, thank you," Mr. Myung says.

"Stretch," Feral says to me. Both Monet and I watch as the son joins the parents in hushed conversation.

"How long is he going to be training for?" I ask.

"Four years before he gets to take leave," Feral answers.

"Four years?!"

The Myungs' goodbye is brief. A hushed conversation, followed by pained, resolute salute.

Cadet Myung comes back to us and joins in the stretching.

"Now, if you follow me, I can show you further accommodations that will be made for your son." Mr. Rhys leads the parents away, leaving Feral as the most dominant presence around.

"First, cadets, you need to understand that the exhibition was just for show. We don't go tossing our arcs around like jackasses," Feral says.

"Um, why not?" I ask.

"Look at them," Feral says.

I gaze at Lockheed and Cadet Twigg. Both boys are being cared for by medical techs. They can barely stand. Even breathing seems like it's hard for them.

"They're spent," I say, vocalizing my conclusion.

"Arcing burns up endurance. When you're done, you're done. And in the field, that means you're dead. Now, up and on line," Feral barks.

I do what Monet and Cadet Myung do. We stand there looking straight ahead and still. Both of their uniforms fit. I look scruff next to them.

"Your arcs will grow with training, but a stronger gift won't make you a better operator. Knowing the tactical situations that best suit your Arc and how to use them to enhance the chance of mission success is the reason you're here. For instance, Lockheed's ability is a jet engine—that roar of his could cover the sound of a firefight or an assassination without him having to light all the way up, or he could've hit Cadet Twigg directly and neutralized the opponent with minimal effort. It's not just about your ability, but the situations in which you use them."

I raise my hand, unsure if this is still like an actual school.

"Cadet Kader," Feral says.

"How do we learn that?"

"I'm glad you asked. New cadets means we start with the Room," Feral says.

Monet looks suddenly determined. Damn near excited.

"What's the Room?" Cadet Myung asks.

"Good question. Foreign Branch fights in war zones; their arcs are specially recruited for that purpose. Same with Domestic, who polices, investigates, and legislates. So what does Special do?" Feral asks.

After a few moments of silence from me and Cadet Myung, Monet answers, "We adapt."

"Yes, Monet. We adapt. We have all the wild Arcs that don't fit neatly in other branches. So our battlefield tactics require us to be in an ever-fluid situation. The Room tests your ability to deal with that. Follow me."

Feral marches us to one room off the main floor.

"Every completed room leads to a progressively harder and harder one."

An old vault door buzzes open, and she ushers us in. Before we realize where we are and that she has not followed, the door slams shut.

"Shit," I say.

"It's just a test. We'll be fine," Monet says.

Looking around, we might as well be in detention. It's a very ordinary classroom. Twenty-one desks, including one for the teacher, windows and two doors that lead out to the hallway.

Feral's voice booms over the PA system.

"Each of you has a mission. Your task is simple. Don't compromise your mission and escape the Room. You have ten minutes."

All three of us look at one another.

"It... it can't be that easy, can it?" I say.

Monet takes a second, like she's sensing or hearing something. Quickly she moves to the center of the room, panicked.

"What's... What's going on?!" I ask.

"Geigers on every window and door," Monet answers.

"So why are you standing in the middle of the room?" Cadet Myung asks.

"Because I have a tendency to set them off at a distance," Monet answers.

"Oh, you're like super radioactive," I say.

Monet frowns at me.

"I think the first question we should've asked is how she knows they're there," Cadet Myung says.

"It's complicated," Monet answers.

Cadet Myung approaches the door carefully. He peeks through the partition and sees something that causes him to back away just as carefully.

"You're right. Every exit rigged with geigers."

"If we trip them, no doubt fire teams will be on us in minutes," Monet says.

"I need to get her off the X," Cadet Myung says.

"What's the X?" I ask.

"Area of danger."

"Cool, that's your mission. What's yours?" I ask Monet.

Monet speaks softly, as if sneezing will set off the trap.

"Mine... I'm... I'm your shadow."

Wait? What?

"You're the person they're having watch me?" I say.

"You have a problem with that?" she asks.

"No, I mean, you didn't exactly make a good first impression, but sure."

Great, my bodyguard has a bodyguard and likes to say bitchy things in my head. A teen with a bad attitude following you around all the time can really be a drain.

Oh god, is this what my mom feels like?

"Probably," Monet says.

"Don't do that," I warn.

Cadet Myung looks confused. Right, I guess he didn't hear that.

"What is your mission?" he asks.

I shrug.

"I was told not to be an asshole," I say casually, strolling to the door. "Do either of you know how to unplug a geiger from the alarm?"

"Geiger is the alarm," Cadet Myung says.

"So that's a no?" I say.

"Our best option to get out is either up or down. You choose and let's get to work," Monet says.

"You're wrong," I say.

Opening the door, I stroll out into the hall. I turn around and look at both Monet and Cadet Myung. They gawk at me with slacked jaws. No one told them, or maybe someone did and they didn't believe it. Somehow, I don't think this is playing it close to the chest like Mr. Rhys and Feral insisted, but if they are always going to be around me, they were bound to find out, anyway.

So I'm in the hallway. Now wh—

I duck just as Feral's fist dents the locker where my head just was.

"Are you crazy?!" I scream.

Feral says nothing, just keeps swinging. I dodge a couple times and then say screw it. If she wants to fight, I'll fight.

I throw a punch, but it hits nothing but air.

Feral dodges.

Fighting back gives her sick pleasure. Her face remains unmoved, but now I get the sense this is more her missing and less me dodging; the more time that passes, that margin shrinks. Each blow I throw misses wider and wider.

Lefts, rights, hooks, crosses, it doesn't matter. They all hit air.

Oh, shit. I think I'm in danger. I was barely missing, but I'm watching her watch me. She's opening it up. My near-misses are now like baseball fields away. How is she doing this?

Feral's eyes never leave me; she just keeps moving around me. She doesn't throw a punch, and I wish she would at a certain point. The anticipation of it is somehow worse. I'm flinching mid-fight, terrified of being hit.

But she doesn't do it. Her face is so still, like she's comfortable. Meanwhile I'm gassed. I've thrown everything harder and faster.

Finally, she cracks a smile. I know she only does it to piss me off. And it pisses me off even more because it's working. Throwing another punch, Feral ducks, this time ramming her fist into my stomach.

AHHH!

My entire body wraps around her fist. I've been in car crashes that hurt less. It feels like everything I've ever eaten wants to come back up. I barely manage to hurl water. My vision blurs, and my legs are piles of sentient goo, doing everything but holding me up straight.

If you get hit, you make sure they look like they've been in a fight too. I swing, but there's nothing really behind it. I'm not shocked when I miss, but this time I grab the plait hanging off her head and pull back.

Feral smirks, unfazed, grabbing my hand. She does some sort of kung-fu magic and flips me upside down. Next thing I know, I'm lying flat on my back, my chest hollow as all the wind rushes out of me. The rest of me aches somehow. What the hell was that?

Feral looks down at me.

"Don't you wish you had a team to help?" she chides.

Anger numbs the damage she did now that I know I lost, and that's some bullshit. It urges me to my feet. Instead, Feral puts her foot squarely on my chest, pinning me down like a heavy box just sat on my entire body.

In her eyes, all I see is death. Bloodlust that makes me shiver uncontrollably, all of me shrinking, feeling smaller and insignificant, like I need to hide.

Her pupils narrow into slits, like a cat, and fangs in her mouth enlarge. Without a doubt, she's going to kill me.

"This feeling right now. Remember it. Know that every order I give is to stop you from feeling like you do at this moment and you may just make it out of bootcamp. Do we understand each other?" Feral says.

A deep, primal mix of fear and anger forces me to say, "Yes, sir."

Taking her foot off my chest, she turns her attention to Cadet Myung and Monet.

"You acted on your own and got killed. So Cadet Kader, you failed. Monet, you spotted the geigers but not the enemy guarding the door. This oversight leads to a tact team being called. The two of you fight bravely, but ultimately, you both die. That means Cadet Myung, you fail. And since the dead can't report on their shadows, Monet also fails. Congratulations. You won't always have all the information you need. Operations are done in steps. Solve what's in front of you and, if you can, anticipate what's next. Actions inform actions," Feral says.

Monet deflates and petulantly stomps out of the room, followed by a solemn Cadet Myung.

"How were we supposed to escape?" I ask.

"Right and wrong don't matter as much as results. No results equal failure," Feral says. "Get changed. You have Bio-Chem."

Right, it feels like we just started, but between homeroom, the tour, the exhibition, and this, we're halfway through the school day already.

Minutes later, Feral marches me through the Small World annexes towards where we first met, Mr. Rhys' office. The corridor outside his office is lined with doors to ensure whenever and wherever they needed a window, they could find one. It's hard to find my bearings here. It's not just a school for incredible individuals. It's, well, I'm not really sure what it is. That's the problem. I'm not sure I belong.

"It won't always be this chaotic. Blackburn has block scheduling. Block A will be spent here. Block B will be spent at Blackburn."

That answers a lot of questions I had about how this is going to work. Still, going to two different schools seems unnecessarily complicated.

"You're a liar," Feral says suddenly.

"Excuse me?" I snap, offended.

"It's a good thing. Use it to your advantage."

"Thanks?" I say, not sure if that's a compliment.

"We did as good a job as we can building your legend, but there's sure to be a few oversights. Monet and Cadet Myung are in a majority of your classes. Look at your schedule."

I glance at the paper in my hand. There's nothing remarkable about it at first, except I'm taking two government classes.

"Hold on?" I start.

"Shut up. Let me talk," Feral says as we get nearer to the IMW. "All your classes read normal in case someone gets a look at your schedule, but we tried to make this as simple as possible for you. If you start your day in Small World, you will end your day at Blackburn and vice versa. Switching out after lunch. We will eat at Blackburn as much as possible. People can see you. The most exposure you'll get is there."

"Okay."

"There are other minor hiccups to account for."

"Like why I'm taking two government classes?"

"Yes. One for our government and one for theirs. It's a senior class, so instead of transferring three freshmen into it, we got you and me. There's no proper explanation for this, but Mr. Rhys assured me that if it comes up, your brand of creative storytelling will ease everyone's mind. Can you do it?"

This feels like a test. There's no way they'd leave something like that up to chance.

"I asked you a question, Cadet."

"Yeah, lying to teachers is kinda my thing."

She doesn't flinch. She doesn't find me funny.

"On this side of the window, save all your questions for me or Monet."

"Monet doesn't seem like the question-answering type."

"She's been ordered to answer. It's imperative you know as much about Arcs as every other cadet. We don't want to draw attention to you or your arrangement with Mr. Rhys. Is that understood?"

"Why? Isn't Mr. Rhys head honcho?"

"No power is absolute. Even the ones in charge answer to someone."

"Got it, boss," I say.

Feral glances at her phone as we stand in front of a classroom door. "Thirty seconds. Questions?"

"Yeah, the doors. How do they work? Like how do you know which door takes you where you need to go and the time you should be there?" I ask.

"Open it." Feral gestures to the door in front of us.

I hesitate.

"I'm answering your question, so do as you're told."

I whip the door open. There's a narrow hall leading into a classroom.

"Okay," I say.

Feral closes it, looks at her phone, and opens it again. This time, waiting on the other side, a classroom in Blackburn. It's miles away from everything on this side of the door. It's more than just the time of day, but here, everything is so labored over and meticulously kept up. There feels, I don't know, cheap and mass-produced?

"IMWs are calculated through a complex algorithm. They have to be opened at precisely the right moment and will stay open for one minute," Feral says.

"Okay, but how?"

"There's an app for that," Feral says, showing me her phone. It looks sorta like a GPS app.

"Oh, that. I guess makes sense."

"Your challenge coin is DNA coded and gives you access."

That explains why I haven't randomly opened doors to the Small World at any other point in my life. And I'm sure there's some other super tricky answer about why we don't accidentally open doors to places now that we're in the program with the coin.

"Any more questions?" Feral asks. "Make it quick, window's closing."

"Yeah, I can't exactly call you Feral over there, so..."

For a brief moment something shifts in her. Something that makes me think maybe my schedule screw-up was actually an oversight. It's just a peek, but a window in its own right to a life lived and forgotten. Well, maybe not forgotten that has different context here, but definitely repressed. Her resolute postures melts for a second as she softly says, "Charlotte. You can call me Charlotte."

CHAPTER 6

Damn it! I forgot to do my homework. Even before a cold wind cuts through the car and my blanket and Mom turns over, jostling the vehicle, I'm awake.

To be fair, it doesn't take much. Even if I weren't crammed in the back of a Volvo with ripped vinyl seats slicing at me like tiny knives, sleeping would still be difficult.

The only time I can reliably fall asleep is in class, and Monet has ruined that. One more way this Arc business is butting into my life. Monet is constantly chirping in my head, "Wake up" and "She's such a terrible student." She doesn't get that I don't need to be awake in order pass tests. Seriously, if it weren't for homework, I'd never fail a class. It seems, however, the better that I do on the test, the more homework I'm suddenly assigned. It's like they want me to fail. And I'm not interested in playing this stupid game with teachers and their institution. Then Monet had to go and make a good point. My homework has to get done, because it's the only way to keep my mom off school grounds and to keep her out of it. We'd have a real problem if she came to school and wanted to meet all my teachers. Sigh, but even if that's the case, there's no way I'm waking up in the middle of the night to do Blackburn bullshit.

Arcs don't give much, if any, homework, but Feral saw to it that I get encoded papers to learn about basics of Arc life under the cover of taking a humanities class. Which should probably be called Arc-anities? No, now that I've heard it, that's stupid. This is the only chance I have to not suck on that side of things. I don't think I've really wrapped my head around how I'm even allowed amongst these people. Arcs are one of the biggest secrets of modern civilization and I'm just walking around amongst them, with no clue if I'm really one of them. I get none of the perks, either. No cool gifts, like cabbage boy or Lockheed. No barracks to sleep in. Nothing.

For the most part, all we do are fitness and tactical evaluations sprinkled with military history. Which is boring. It's like they aren't teaching in English, which in the case of my homework, they aren't. I had to pass a test on substitution ciphers and learn one just to be assigned actual at-home reading.

From my backpack, I slip out a humanities book and the small scroll cheat sheet I'm allowed. I do my best to be quiet and not kick the dry cleaner bags hanging over the back window like homeless curtains. If they move, it kind of ruins the illusion that the car is just parked. Striking the balance between being parked, not abandoned or lived in, is crucial. It can be the difference between being left alone, being towed, or having the police called. Those are the best options, honestly, and they're not great. Not seeing is a sort of two-way street, and the not-distant-enough gunshots serve as an all-too-real reminder that danger is out there.

At least we aren't at a rest stop. They're too conventional, and people sometimes will wait there to prey on a mother and her young daughter. Getting robbed at knife point really puts things in perspective. I don't really recall being scared, just worried for my mother, but over time the image of this slobbery man in flannel wielding a knife at my mom came to define fear and everything I worry about. Remembering her placing herself between me and him still makes me shudder as if it were happening all over again.

Putting the thought out of mind as best I can, I focus on the text. The reading is, like, so dull. Like, do I really care about Arc assignment camps where their civilians live, or the "There's an Arc amongst you" campaign in the 40s as the reason there are geigers everywhere, or that their entire society started off as one military base until the State of Standards 1952 treaty?

Absolutely.

No one on this side of the window knows any of this. I still don't know how Arcs happen or how they get their gifts or how I set off the geiger. All of this is very interesting stuff. There's seriously a whole freaking section on the founding of those goofy-ass doors and how they evolved from hidey holes in the second great war, but it's written in the most boring way ever. Maybe because it's ciphered out of a textbook.

As I read for a second, I think about my life—hunched over in the backseat of a car and reading by streetlight slipping through the window. Sirens and helicopters, the inner-city lullaby tempting me with sleep I know will never come.

I'm up for at least another hour. Right as I'm getting ready to doze off, Mom's alarm rings.

This is going to be a long-ass day.

"Cal, what you doing up?" Mom asks, still trying to shake off sleep.

"Homework."

"I must still be asleep."

"Funny."

Mom chuckles to herself a little bit and sits her seat upright. As uncomfortable as sleeping in the backseat is, sleeping while sitting up seems worse.

"Alright, here we go," Mom says. She starts the car. It screeches like a stuck pig or something. The sound booms through the entire parking garage.

"Sounds like the timing belt," I say, closing my book to listen. It doesn't make any sense to me, but we all do it.

"No, girl, that's the alternator," Mom says.

"Which one is more expensive?" I ask.

"Why you always gotta be a smartass?"

"You raised me," I say.

"Either way, it's going to have to wait."

Mom scans the parking garage to see if anyone noticed our car's plea for a merciful death. I take down our homeless curtains. Mom puts the car into gear. Up the ramp and around the cement pillars until we find ourselves two floors up. It's identical to the floor we slept on except for the number five spray-painted in orange. Greenish lights make all the cement walls and floor look sorta sickly, like that cabbage kid.

"We're going to leave Brenda here today. You going to have to take the bus to school," Mom says.

That sucks. It's almost six am and, given how buses run in this city, I'd need to leave like now.

"Mom, I don't know if you realize this, but we're in a car. It can go places like work and schools."

"She needs less stress," Mom says.

"I need less stress," I mutter.

"What did you say?" Mom asks, staring bullets through me.

"Nothing."

"I don't need your attitude right now, Cal. What I need is for you to get dressed and get to school. I will meet you at the Jack N Box on the corner when I'm done with work, and you better be there. Do you hear me?"

"Yes," I say through gritted teeth.

"Yes, what?"

"Yes, ma'am."

More of this shit. Angrily I stuff my books in my backpack. No time to shower. Just have to put my uniform on and go.

"You mad?" Mom asks.

I don't respond. I just get dressed.

"It's not always going to be like this, Cal. Just things aren't goin' our way right now."

Have things ever gone our way? I'm honestly asking because I can't remember a single time where that has been the case. But I don't get to ask questions like that. Not without quickly being reminded that I'm a child and I'm not supposed to. Fine.

No sleep. Taking a bus to school. I'm grimy and now pissed. What a lovely way to start a long-ass day.

CHAPTER 7

S *tttrrrrp!* My chair jerks forward abruptly, waking me. Angrily, I lift my head and a string of drool off my desk.

"Bruh, who's kicking chairs....?"

Piercing eyes glare at me inches from my face. A very handsome mid-twenties man with a flowing dark mane looms over me, soot still clinging to his uniform. Honestly, he looks a bit like my Algerian cousin if my cousin took facial hair advice from a musketeer.

Disciplined Arc students keep their snickers muffled.

"Don't sleep in my class," he says.

"Don't be forty minutes late to your class," I respond, wiping slobber from my face.

All twenty very impressive-looking freshmen, dressed to the nines in our combat uniforms, are suddenly silent, looking to our teacher to set an example. My first impression of guy: he seems almost gentle for a soldier, doesn't seem like a screamer.

"On line, Cadet!"

But I've been wrong before. Groggily, I pull myself out of my chair and stand at attention.

"Burpees until I say stop," he says.

I've only recently learned what a burpee is and, well, it's cool to learn new things you hate. When Feral has me do these, she chants, "reach for the heavens" on every jump and "kiss the ground" on every push-up.

"Now, Cadet," he says quietly; no need to yell when he's this close to me. It's more menacing this way, and he knows it.

I do what's asked of me as begrudgingly as I can. You'd think there was more to this stupid program than exercise and logic puzzles.

"As your fellow cadet pointed out," the teacher starts, "I am late. We missed our window and had to hoof it to catch the next one. Let's just say thirty klicks through sand is a lot farther than you think. For that, I apologize. I am First Lieutenant Djinn, but for this class, you may call me Mr. Kahn. Because of my assignment running over schedule for a couple weeks, we won't have as much time to get you where you need to be, but you all look capable." He pushes my seat in.

From here I can see it was Cadet Myung who kicked my chair. What's his problem?

Classrooms aren't meant for exercise, I realize as I bump one of the desks. This is a very modern classroom, but not much different from what you would find on the other side of an IMW. White board, desks, chairs—not much innovation in the way of classroom technology.

That is, until you look out any window and see a man-made constellation projected in the sky. I've learned the sky is fixed into position depending where you are in Small World. It's a matter of convenience. This way there's always a beam of sunlight where you need it and night where you need it. This places an even greater importance on the clock tower and bells. It's the only way to tell what time of day it is, and since these people travel by doors that only open at a specific time, that seems to be important.

Mr. Kahn makes his way to his desk and sits on it. Everyone here apparently has something against chairs.

"My job is very simple. I only have to help you answer one question, and that is: who are you? I'm not talking about your favorite color or which song makes you cry. I'm asking what makes you. Does anyone know?"

The class remains silent. I look around, and no one even hazards a guess.

"So we'll start at the beginning," Mr. Kahn continues. "After all, how can you use something if you don't know what it is or where it comes from? Welcome to Arc Development. This is a broader, encompassing class. We'll cover bits of science and biology, pieces of history, pop culture if necessary. Because the subject of the class is you. So wherever your Arc takes us, that is where we'll go. And if we're lucky, a few of you may even earn a call sign."

That gets a rousing whoop from the class. Mr. Kahn looks back at me to make sure I'm still exercising.

I am, but poorly.

Monet seems bored out of her head; she doodles in her notepad. Cadet Myung couldn't seem more excited. Though anything other than his "I'm over this" scowl is new.

"So, here I am Mr. Kahn. In the field, I go by Djinn. The western world thinks of them as genies, but you know what... I'll show you."

Mr. Kahn closes his eyes.

A moment later, a flutter of wind tosses papers everywhere, and heat burns the moisture from the air, making it hard to swallow. Even the sweat pouring down my forehead evaporates.

Smoke, gray and dirt green, pools at his feet before stretching to his chest. It settles there and forms a person-like thing, a shadow made of clouds. That was weird enough, but the sweet smell of pastry and the beam of light from outside shines on the thing and just ends right where the thing's skin starts, making it downright confusing. Its eyes are ominous holes that peer into the universe, a void lit by suns. It's terrifying and awe-inspiring.

Clutched in its grotesque little bird claws, a book.

"This is why I'm called Djinn. My dark passenger brings me random items that may or may not be useful in battle. I'm sure being a man of Arabic descent also played a part in the call sign," Mr. Kahn says with a laugh.

The class joins in like a laugh track.

Suck ups.

"But which really came first?" Mr. Kahn asks, taking the book from his friend. As soon as it leaves its grasp, its head creepily turns and looks at me.

A pained gaze fills Mr. Kahn's eyes, something making him worried. He steps in front of it and utters what I assume is "thank you" in Arabic. Then his shadow melts into the ether. Mr. Kahn takes a second to look at me before for starting on his next spiel.

"My mother makes clouds. Not storms or rain or even fog, really. Just clouds. My father is a basic, typical Arc durability uptick. Though, my mother believes he has a knack for knowing exactly what she wants, but it never tested as an Arc. Neither one's arcs lead them to active duty. Which brings me to my next point. You are the weapon, not your arc. How you use it may help you in battle, but that's not all they are for. Life echoes define them. How you live and carry yourself through life. How you've been taught to carry yourself. Remember that. Arcs require triggers. The few of you who can wield your arc know this. When you find that trigger, whatever that sensation is, every cell in your body will fire in unison, giving all the energy they have in order to make you what some of our enemies call five-minute destroyers. That's why we have such an emphasis on conditioning." Mr. Kahn gestures to me, now sweating in the corner. The class has a chuckle at my expense.

"My arc evolved from my parents in some way. Tapping into it requires a sense of stillness. Almost like meditating or the eye of hurricane. I create a void deep within myself and the passenger fills it. When your arc is in place, it's up to you to know how you are going to use it. That's what defines you. That's when you are close to earning a call sign. Some of you have a very long way to go. Now, I rarely get a chance to ask freshman at the beginning of the year about their call signs, but I have the opportunity now. Lockheed."

The bald kid from the exhibition stands up immediately, like I guess a soldier should. He's eager to please.

"At ease," Mr. Kahn says.

Lockheed relaxes.

"What was it like to get your call sign?" Mr. Kahn asks.

The kid with the phlegmy, ragged voice doesn't hesitate. "It was a moment of completion, I guess is how I would explain it. It was like it could be nothing else. I sort of always knew who I was. This was just the stamp of approval."

"That's interesting. You come from a family of people who've served, so you knew you'd serve. You've been preparing for this all your life. It makes sense you'd be quick on the uptake. Sort of honing in on what your mission in life is," Mr. Kahn says.

For no reason at all, I look over at Cadet Myung. His glee has dulled to an intense glare. He watches Lockheed like Feral once watched me, studying every mannerism to see if there's something off about him, to see if there's something he might learn. Cadet Myung's eyes dart in my direction. I want no part of that, so I immediately go back to my exercises.

"Do you mind if I ask who named you?" Mr. Kahn asks.

"No, sir. My father gave it to me; he was at the exhibition. He told me the way I took off was like a rocket and the name was just the first thing he thought of when he saw me in the fight," Lockheed says.

"You lucked out. The person who gives you a call sign usually becomes a cherished person to you. But your father is already that, I assume?"

"Yes, sir. He's the reason I'm here."

"One last question. The sensation. What is it like?"

For the first time, Lockheed hesitates. It's almost as if he doesn't want to speak, but orders are orders.

"Breath control," he mutters. "A cough usually ignites me. Except there's more power like diesel in my lungs, and when it catches, it's more of a car being turned over."

Mr. Kahn nods and gestures for him to sit while saying, "Monet. What about you?"

She perks up, already annoyed. Monet knows what he's about to ask and doesn't get out of her seat. Hell, she barely looks in his direction.

"Tell us about your call sign. What cherished individual gave you your name?" he asks.

"I don't want to talk about it," Monet mutters.

Mr. Kahn doesn't relent, though.

"That's fine. Not everyone wants to. The name itself, though, comes from the"—Mr. Kahn flips open the book his shadow friend gave him, skimming the pages until he stops and reads aloud—"nineteenth century French painter, correct?"

"Yeah," Monet says, clearly not wanting any part of this conversation.

"How does that speak to you and your abilities?" Mr. Kahn presses.

"I said I don't want to talk about it," Monet says.

"I get that, but I think it would help your peers better understand—"

"I have no peers and I'm under orders not to talk about it," Monet clarifies.

Mr. Kahn is stunned into silence. It'd be weird if there were orders like that and a teacher didn't know, right? The class bell rings.

"Monet, stay. I want each of you to work on a project about you and your family bloodline since engine ignition. Where do you come from? Whose abilities did you inherit? How can how they use their ability to teach you something about how you can use yours? Or if your ability is morphed from your parents, how did they combine to make yours? Projects will be due at the end of the semester!" Mr Kahn says as everyone piles out. Monet walks over to me, now knee-deep in sweat.

Mr. Kahn gestures for me to stop. "I will not tolerate insubordination in my class."

"Yes, sir," I say through gritted teeth, but Monet just stares at him.

"Cadet, do you understand me?" he repeats to Monet.

"I don't know who handled your transfer from Foreign, but when I don't answer your questions, it's not insubordination, and if you don't understand that, talk to your recruitment officer."

"Oh, you're—" Mr. Kahn starts.

"Yes." Monet cuts him off and then goes silent.

"Are you waiting on something?" he asks.

"It's your classroom."

"Right, you're dismissed," Mr. Kahn stutters.

I follow Monet into the hall.

"What the hell was that?" I ask.

"Where do you think we are?" Monet asks. I stammer, unsure of how to respond, but she continues. "Okay, this is a military school. The only thing that matters here is the chain of command. How people treat you, the reputation you build for yourself in these halls, will follow you into the field. Better to let people know who you are now."

Huh, I sorta get that. It's the same on my side of the window, why Alani thought she could continue pushing me around. I let her get away with it for three years. As we catch up to her guard, Monet's advice suddenly strikes a real chord with me.

"What's your problem, asshole?" I ask, loud enough to draw attention to us in the hall.

On the other side of the IMW, this would probably go unnoticed. Here, where everyone marches in tidy little lines to and fro... Where running in the halls is strictly forbidden because it can mean the difference between life or death... Where it seems like every beam of light from the computer-generated sky lands exactly where it needs to...

This is out of order.

"What did you say to me?" Cadet Myung responds, now posturing towards me.

"I called you an asshole. Why'd you kick my chair?"

"Because you're lazy and we're in class to learn, not to sleep."

By this time, we've gathered a nice little crowd. People expect students here to be disciplined.

They are soldiers.

I am not.

"You don't know anything about me," I say.

"I know that you're just like every other n—"

Look, I've been on this side of slurs enough to sense when they are coming. I don't need him to finish his sentence before I punch him in the mouth.

CRCK! Something in my hand snaps. Hitting him is like punching a statue. No oohs from bystanders. You can hear a pin drop.

In Cadet Myung's eyes, I see bad intentions, as if I just gave him permission. He makes his way towards me, about to unleash.

"Cadet Myung, stop!" Monet snaps, getting between us. Her voice more forceful than I've ever heard it.

"You three at attention," Mr. Kahn says, stepping out of his class. He stares at me first. "Brig. I'll make your squad leaders aware."

"Squad leader," Monet says.

Mr. Kahn looks at her as if to say, *repeat yourself.*

So she does. "Squad leader. We have the same one. Feral."

Mr. Kahn's musketeer stache curls along with his lip in a devious smile.

"I do not envy the three of you."

A short while later, we are Breakfast Clubbing it in another far-off classroom, this one duller than the last. My hand packed in ice. The brig in this case isn't prison, just detention, a.k.a. prison for children.

A teacher, an older man easily in his 60s, develops his lesson plan and guards us as if we were neighbor kids and our parents had to run out for an emergency. Other than, I guess, Mr. Rhys, this guy is the first person I've seen in The Faction who's not a kid or in their mid-twenties. It's sort of odd when I think about it. They gave no time limit to us when we were stashed here. So we wait, sharing glares as if we're dueling at high noon.

Monet is the first to speak, err, em, think. <You can't call her a null.>

< Wait, that's the N-word you were about to call me?? What kind of insult is that?> I think.

<In other pockets of Arc culture, your value comes from your arc. If you are null, you have no value. You are worthless.> Monet answers.

If my fighting hand wasn't hurt, I'd hit him again.

"She's a burden and an idiot," Cadet Myung says.

"That idiot just saved you from being dismissed," Monet chirps.

"The three of you, quiet!" the teacher says.

<What are you talking about?> Myung thinks.

<I don't know how they did it in your last branch, but in this one, we don't go around yelling classified secrets in the halls,> Monet thinks. The way she says it comes with a hint of distaste, as if she's also trying to remind him that here, we're better than they are.

<Her?> Cadet Myung thinks.

<Just like me. Classified. No one knows she can walk through geigers and you were just about to tell the world. Exposing classified material is grounds for dismissal at the very least, but more than likely you're looking at a court martial,> Monet thinks.

<Oh, I...> he stutters.

<Who's the idiot now?> I snap. Neither of them focus on my input.

Monet scolds him. <Arc-less are called civilians or non-combatants. If you're going to continue being my bodyguard, keep your Domestic Branch programming in check.>

<Yes, sir,> he thinks pitifully.

<Why'd he call her sir?> I think to myself, realizing too late that I'm broadcasting. It's hard because you can't really tell. Everyone else's thoughts in your head sort of feel like intrusive thoughts that aren't your own. Quiet whispers. <I'm impressed Monet can do this.>

<Thanks, because what you think of me means so much. He called me sir because I'm not a cadet. I've been in the service since I could walk.>

That's right, Mr. Rhys mentioned she got her call sign at three.

<So what is your rank?> I ask.

<Classified,> she answers.

<I thought you were under orders to answer my questions?> I ask.

Monet lets out a dramatic sigh.

<My rank is tied to my arc. Telepaths are rare. Once in a generation rare, because it's not passed down genetically like other gifts. We don't know why. But I'm told not to disclose it if I don't have to. I'm named after an impressionistic painter, because I get impressions of things like people's thoughts. It's not exactly telepathy, but it's close enough on the spectrum of mental gifts.>

<Oh, and here I just thought "I'm classified" was a dope lie to get people to leave you alone.>

<Most of the time, it is. When they're smart enough to stop asking questions,> Monet says.

<That was a shot at me, wasn't it?> I ask.

<Cadet Myung wasn't wrong about you being dumb and lazy.>

I've heard that all my life. I care very little about what a pair of sheltered teenagers think about me.

< You should care more,> Monet thinks.

We've been going to school together for days now, and this is the first time any of us have really talked. It only took five minutes to know Cadet Myung is a racist douche and Monet is some super-secret soldier princess who loathes being here. For the most part, I've avoided talking to them, because Monet has made it very clear she doesn't want to talk to me and I have no idea what to call her bodyguard in mixed company.

<Are we still doing that? Calling him Cadet Myung? Like, what if we have to be in public together?> I ask.

"Good point. What should we call you?" Monet says.

Begrudgingly, he mumbles, "Chu."

"Now that that's out of the way, your phone," Monet says.

"What?"

"Hand me your phone," Monet says again, holding out her hand.

Tentatively, I hand it to her. Monet types something in it and hands it back to me.

"Did you just give me your number?" I ask.

"Yeah, don't make it weird. And I programmed five as your emergency speed dial. If you find yourself in trouble, speed dial five. Feral will find—shit."

Feral opens the door calmly and salutes the teacher.

"Can I have the room, sir?" she asks in a sweet, almost quiet voice, which is unsettling. Her rage echoes like tremors, but visibly she's so still. Do you know how terrifying it is to know someone is pissed but for them to have the composure to not like throw crap and scream? I don't like that. I don't like that at all.

<Oh, god, we're all going to die.> Monet's thoughts leak into my head.

The older man scurries away quickly, like a rat fleeing a sinking ship. He even leaves his lesson plan behind.

Feral waits until the door starts to shut.

This feels like an older sibling coming to get you out of school when you've gotten in trouble. From the people I've talked to, older siblings can be worse than parents in this department. They have no problem hitting you, and Feral looks like she may actually kill us. Her always-tight muscles and wild eyes look like a dam bursting at the seams with violent intentions, but when she speaks, she's calm, quiet even. Instinctively, we all lean in to hear her, even though we're closer to danger. I wish she would just yell.

"If anyone ever has to talk to me about my squad's behavior ever again, I'm going to bury all three of you. Literally. I don't give a damn how precious you are to anybody. You're my responsibility. Your lives are mine. Do you understand?"

You can feel the tension in every word. Every movement makes me want to flinch, but I steel my nerves. I can't help but remember the moment of knowing my death from our first fight when I look at her.

Our in unison and immediate "Yes, sir," tells me I'm not the only one feeling it.

"You're going back to the Room, and if you don't get at least six rooms in, I'm breaking something in or on one of you. Now, go."

We scurry for the door, but Feral snatches me by the arm.

"I need you to understand something more than the other two. You chose to be a guest here. Guests don't get to raise a hand against my operators."

"But—" I start, but her eyes suggest it would be better if I didn't finish that sentence. Her patience is wearing thin, and I think it may be a record for the shortest time I've pissed someone off.

"Yes, sir," I say.

What does she mean, I chose to be a guest? I'm not one of them. In a school full of outsiders, I'm somehow more out of place than ever.

"I don't belong here," I say.

"But you're here, so what are you going to do about it?" Feral says.

"What can I do?"

"You have two options."

"I know my options," I snap, frustrated, fully expecting Feral to lash out at me, but she doesn't. Instead, she takes my hand and looks at it. She's upset but gentle.

"Mr. Rhys told you your options. But what he didn't tell you is that at any point you can pull the ripcord and you'll be out. Just Blackburn, no more Small World, and you'd be oblivious to the threats acting against you."

"Why would I do th—" *CRRRRCK*! My hand pops in four different places as Feral suddenly yanks on my fingers. She covers my mouth with her other hand.

"Breathe," she says calmly like she didn't just send lighting down my hand. Seconds after the sharpness, there's relief and no pain.

"Your knuckle was slightly dislocated. I just reset it," she says.

"I wish you would've warned me," I say.

Feral turns to leave as I flex my hand. It's already feeling better. She stops in the doorway.

"To answer your question. Not everyone is cut out for this program. There's no shame, Cadet. So anytime you want to quit, let me know. Right now, Room."

Chapter 8

L ast school bell of the day rings—my favorite one.

Yesenia and I sit on the school's stoop, watching kids flood around us, pooling into cars and buses. There's a small traffic jam in front of us as some cars idle waiting for their kids, their air conditioners humming in chorus. Others are trying to pull off, and their horns blare on a dying summer breeze.

Yesenia's head on my shoulder makes it hard to eat honey buns. A well-deserved snack, after this morning's torture chamber. Room drill until we were sick. It required problem solving, working together, and running. We only got three rooms in. After lunch, more things I hate in the form of math homework review and tests. Huzzah. Two schools in one day should be criminal.

"When's your tía getting here?" I ask, biting at the pastry with all my frustration.

"Later. I have labs. Is she your guard dog?" Yesenia asks, looking back at Monet, who's firmly camped inside the building. I may have walked out only after she told me not to.

<If you get abducted or shot, I'm going to be pissed,> Monet thinks.

<That's not going to happen. Calm down.>

<For all you know, there are a dozen gunman waiting in the wings right now, looking for you.>

Whatever. I try to put Monet's fit out of my mind, literally.

"No. Just a new kid without a lot of friends. Kind of a loser, honestly," I say.

<Bitch,> Monet thinks.

"Mm hmm," Yesenia says suspiciously.

"What?" I ask.

"Nothing. Just. We're hardly into the new year. You've already got a new best friend."

"Not my best friend. A necessary evil is more like it."

"Sure, but we don't have lunch together. I never see you in the hallway. And you haven't come over once to talk about school or crushes or any of that stuff. I was really hoping we could maybe talk about colleges."

Normal life is slipping. I hadn't noticed, really. It's exactly what I was scared of. Maybe I should pull the ripcord and be the friend I'm supposed to be? No, Yesenia'll forgive me if I just stop being absentminded. I can do both, be her friend and go to super-soldier school. Free time is a bummer; my weekends are spent in Small World. I'm told it's the safest place for a kid being hunted by whoever the hell I'm being hunted by. Where I go, Monet goes. Until shift switch when their night unit takes over. It probably means they all know I'm homeless. Hanging out with Chu and Monet isn't top on my list of priorities. The only thing worse would be doing it at Yesenia's or in the backseat of my car. Whenever Mom finds a new place to stay, I'm sure they'll invite themselves.

"Cal?!" Yesenia asks forcefully.

"We both know I'm not going to college and that's like four years away. Also, that stuff is really just me listening to you talk about schoolwork and your crushes," I say.

"Right, cause Callisto likes nobody."

"Yerp," I respond, taking another bite. "But if it makes you feel better, I'm sorry I missed it."

"I don't like it when you say you're not going to college."

"We both know it's true."

"But I don't like it. You don't know! What are you going do instead?"

"Literally anything else." I watch the traffic in front of school get worse because the crossing guard is just a PE teacher.

Yesenia gets really quiet. She normally doesn't like talking about the future. The fact that she's doing it now is kinda brave. And I just stepped on the moment, didn't I?

"Where are you thinking about applying?" I say too late.

"Just forget it. How's your small school?" Yesenia asks.

"I don't really know what to make of it. My TA is kinda a hard-ass, and my teachers are assholes."

Feral's pseudo revelation about leaving bugs me. If I can leave whenever I want, does that mean they already know what I am? If so, why am I still here? Or is she lying to me? How much easier it would be if I could just tell Yesenia everything. Someone outside this entire thing to help me make sense of it, but she has enough on her plate already, and protecting the ones I care about includes her. It sucks that this has become just another thing I have to keep from her.

"Radical thought. If everyone is an asshole, teachers, bus drivers, maybe you're the common denominator. Maybe you're the asshole," Yesenia says.

"Hey!" I respond, slightly offended.

"Just saying."

"There's a hole in your theory, miss. Get it. A hole?" I say finally.

"Boo. Boo you. And my logic is solid."

"What about Ms. Washington?" I say with a knowing smile and caked sugar on my chin.

"Ugh, Ms. Washington," Yesenia whines, suddenly reminded of the bane of sixth grade.

Ms. Washington was our middle-school keyboard teacher? We don't really know what she taught. Everyone today can type. She hated kids but still decided to be a teacher and take it out on us. Yesenia got the worst of it. That may have been the first time I thought about fighting a teacher.

"I should've let you beat her up," Yesenia says.

"I think your mom did a pretty good job," I say without thinking. Recalling Mrs. Barros giving the woman what my mom would call a tongue-lashing in both Spanish and English after she tried to flunk Yesenia... Ya know, the girl who would eventually be middle school valedictorian.

"Yeah, she did. Didn't she?" Yesenia's voice suddenly matches the day: gray and gloomy.

"I'm sorry."

"You don't need to apologize. I enjoy thinking about her. Sometimes even when it's hard." She tucks her hair behind her ear like she's trying to tuck away her worries. I know this person. I know when she's hurt. I know when she's lying. And right now she's both.

"No one expects you to be okay, Yenny." I wrap my arm around her.

"Dad says the same thing. Even tía, but the thing is, I want to be okay. I don't want to forget her, but I don't want thinking of the good things to hurt too." She wipes a few tears from her eyes. "I'm such an embarrassment crying in front of everyone." She sniffles.

"Don't worry about anyone else. I got you. I will literally fight all these kids, their parents, and Mr. Powell in the short shorts if that's what it takes."

Yesenia smirks. Maybe I should give this ripcord more thought. It's hard to see her hurting. It's hard to put her back together again. Her eyes and nose are so red. She pulls her hair tie out like clockwork. She'll hide her tears behind curtains of hair.

Yesenia's phone goes off.

"That's my lab alarm." She pulls the phone out. She turns it off and then clicks around.

"Your mom says to remind you that you're taking the bus." Yesenia shows me a text from my mom.

I've been doing this for days now and I still forget. Immediately, I check my phone, and of course it's dead. It's not like I have a place to charge it at night.

"Son of a bi—"

Mrs. Stephens, walking down the stairs, glares at me.

"—iscuit," I continue and smile sheepishly while the overlord of our school continues down the stairs.

"If you're taking the bus, does that mean your new place is close?"

I never really explain why we move so much or where we live between places. She doesn't ask, but I think she has an idea. Before her mom passed, I practically lived at her place for a summer.

This is how people get good old days, I guess. It's not even a debate that frolicking in my best friend's apartment complex beats my "new place"—a 2004 Volvo S20 parked in a garage just outside the financial district. But I can't tell her that. Everyone has their thing. This is just another one of mine.

"No, I'm going to my mom's job and ride home with her," I say. The downside of being good at lying is that no one knows how good I am at it. But how flawless, quick, and natural it was, ugh. That's art.

"Kay. I gotta get back. I'll see you later." Yesenia hugs me. "Thank you," she whispers.

"You never have to thank me."

We go our separate ways. She disappears into the halls of Blackburn while I forge forward past traffic and through the field of dying grass in front of our school. The bus stop is on the other side of the street, next to the house that decorates their yard for every holiday. They've already started to sprinkle out their Halloween stuff.

<Night shift is taking over,> Monet thinks.

I must be imagining things. Her voice in my head almost sounds sad and even more distant. I stop and look back at her—I don't know why, but I do. Blackburn is just a row of brick houses and barbed wire fence. It looks like a prison and not a stylish one either. For the briefest second, I see Monet and Chu, already turning to leave.

<Later,> I think in a whisper.

Chapter 9

Very few things in the world feel as vulnerable as balancing on flip-flops in biker shorts and a ratty bra while you take a washcloth to your pits. The key is to not looking in the mirror while you do it. Then it's like it's not happening. You don't have to process the shame and anger. So you look anywhere else if you have to. There're so many options in this rest stop bathroom. The graffiti etched in tile, broken light fixtures, or any of the stalls missing doors in this dingy beige room wreaking of piss. Like I said, options.

Rest stop bathrooms aren't great, but there's low foot traffic. As much as I hate them at night, during the day they're ghost towns. Still a foul place to be, but at least no one really hangs out here. Most are off to their jobs or panhandling.

My morning sink bath is interrupted when the door opens. Scrambling to cover up, I hold my uniform shirt against my chest.

"Girl, you ain't got nothing I ain't got, I ain't seen, or I ain't gave you," she says.

"Mom, you're supposed to be watching the door."

More humiliation and discomfort. Yay.

"Cal, I'm standing right here in the door. What do you think is goin' to happen?"

"I don't know. I—"

"Look, don't put your uniform on. You ain't goin' to school today."

"What? No. I have to go to school."

Mom steps back, her eyes large with surprise.

"Who are you and what have you done with my kid? The Callisto I know would be looking for any reason to not go to school."

Well, that Callisto didn't sign up for secret super-soldier school to keep her mom safe. Mr. Rhys and the gang never covered absences. What do I do? Is this only happening because it's something I want to do? Wait, school is something I want to do? I'll unpack that later. Right now I have to do something I thought would never happen: I have to make my mom let me go to school.

"Mom, please."

"Cal, the car won't start. We have to take it in. What do you suggest I do?"

"I've been taking the bus anyway. I can go to school and meet you afterwards."

"Where you going to meet me, Cal?! Hmm. Think about it for a second! Do you know how much it's going to cost to fix?! Or when it's going to be done?!"

"No."

"So if it's in the shop…" Mom lowers her voice, looking around as if anyone is close enough to hear. "Where are we sleeping tonight?"

Her words just sorta hang there, washing over me, pissing me off. Damn it. Why is it always like this? We certainly can't ask Ms. Arnaud or one of her other so-called friends for a place to say tonight. They would think less of her and that's what's really important.

"Cal, I need you," Mom says sincerely.

Everything in me wants to scream no and slam the door in her face. You know what? Screw it. She deserves it.

My mouth opens to scream, but out comes, "Fine." instead. I'm such a coward.

"Do we need to have a talk about why you're so anxious to go to school nowadays?"

Seriously? All she does is complain about me going to school and when I actually want to do the shit she's asking if it's a problem? I roll my eyes so hard I get dizzy.

Mom decides to not press me on it. "Make sure your phone's charged. I need you to look for places to stay if Brenda's in the shop."

Before Mom is even completely out the door, I'm dressed and texting Monet. I expect her and Feral to make my life hell when I get back to school. Or worse, tag along. How would we explain that? How would I live that down?

"Family shit came up. I'm not coming in today." I wait anxiously as Monet types back. She texts so hella slow, you'd almost think she wasn't a teenager. I watch the three dots go for what seems like forever. In my head it's a race between the text and Mom butting back in.

My phone rings instead. The generic tone bounces off the tiles around me. Is she using her phone as like a phone? What?!

"Yeah?" I answer.

"It sucks," Monet says. "But you're good. We have contingencies in place. Night team will watch you through the day, but they'll have to hang back. So you for the most part have to keep yourself safe. Don't be stupid. If you suspect something, call Feral."

"Aww, you care."

"I do," she says earnestly.

"Oh ...uh," I stammer.

I wasn't expecting that. Wait, are we cool? We've never really talked outside of assignments and bitchy barbs at one another.

"You're my assignment," she says, killing any sorta vibe we may have been having. "Now I have to go to your freaking school without you so our absences don't look suspicious. Bye." Monet hangs up.

"Cal, hurry up. The tow truck is almost here."

It's been hours of siting in this stupid little waiting room, Googling anything that might give me a roof for a night. An oversized coffee table covered in magazines and a small television playing daytime judge shows—exactly how I wanted to spend today. If this were a Room drill, I'd be worried about what the smell of fresh tires and the constant whirring of power tools are really hiding. The problem I'd be trying to think myself out of would be less personal and probably less dreadful, but shortly into hour four, Mom walks in and puts me out of my misery.

"It's the transmission. They need to keep her for a couple of days," Mom says.

So we are officially without a place to stay tonight and any hope I had of convincing Mom to get a hotel and maybe a hot shower goes out the window.

"Have you found a place?" Mom asks. The day is already wearing on her. Her face is red from yelling at someone. I'm all too familiar with her fresh yelling face.

"Not yet," I say, still scrolling.

"What have you been doing out here all this time?"

"Searching."

"I have to do everything myself." Mom snatches my phone. "We can't afford a hotel."

"I know that."

"What about this place? It's right down the street," Mom says, suddenly angry.

She shows me a logo, a pair of open hands holding dual S's with sunlight shining. The Samaritan Society. There's something very Ned Flanders about the whole place to me.

No one is interested in helping everyone, not without a price, but I've never been close enough to find out what it is.

I guess that changes now, since a short while later we are walking up to their building.

From the street, you can only see the side, and it's unimpressive.

A single driveway through the gates gives a look at what I guess is the front of the building. It almost looks like a YMCA with apartments shooting out the top.

A placard etched in metal tells me where we really are. A Samaritan Society Sanctuary. That's what they're called.

"This feels like a church."

"It's not a church, Cal," Mom says. "Samaritan Society is a non-denominational patronage. They help people in need. Right now, we're in need. So will you not be a brat and do this for me?"

Second time today she's brought out the do-this-for-me card. Maternal guilt is a weapon of mass destruction. What am I going to say, no? "Do this for me" is basically an ATM card for favors that you can't refuse because she, like, gave me life. And to be completely honest, this far in the day, I've given up. We're going to do whatever she wants us to. That's very clear.

"So what exactly do we have to do?" I ask.

"This is a women's shelter, Cal. If they have beds, we'll try and get one for the night or until Brenda is fixed. We don't have to stay if we don't want to, but we don't have a lot of other options."

Not exactly what I thought when she said we were going to look at a place, but whatever.

Soothing air conditioning greets us with a weird funk. Loud construction sounds in some far-off part of the building give the distinct impression that we should be wearing hard hats. Faint pulsing is something I realize that I can alone hear, and I've been hearing it more and more since entering the program.

I know it's there before I look: a geiger. Some things up and running apparently.

Remnants of lush fixtures and concessions stare at us in a badly repurposed interior. The carpet still has stains from what I hope is just liquor, and all the wood trim is from a bygone era. It's like a 70s playroom vomited in here and someone halfway cleaned it up.

A heavy-set Black lady makes a beeline for us. She looks like the kind of woman who pinches cheeks and says shit like, oh, ain't you precious.

"Don't embarrass me, Cal," Mom says with a harsh whisper before putting on her polite smile.

"I'm Kim Cooper. The facilities coordinator. Can I help you?" the woman says.

"I am Adena Kader," my mom answers. "And this is my daughter Callisto."

"Hello," I say, trying not to make it apparent I don't want to be here, but...I don't.

"Oh, ain't you a sweetheart. You look just like your momma," she says.

"Thanks," I mutter as my mom's sharp elbow not so discreetly digs into my side.

Mom can't bring herself to ask for beds for the night. The woman can kind of see it, so instead of pressing on this very exposed nerve, she asks, "Would you like a tour of the facility?"

Mom is still pulling herself out of the funk. "That would be cool," I say.

Ms. Cooper smiles at me. "Right this way."

Her outfit is part church lady, part real estate agent, and all of it bright pink. Her tight skirt forces her to sort of shuffle along in kitten heels.

"So we just got this space and are still renovating. We have a rescue mission a couple blocks away, but it gets so crowded we really needed the extra space. We're already able to provide some dinners and daycare services. We have a few teenagers, so they double up helping us with drop-off care if they don't mind." She holds the doors open.

"Volunteers are helping the contractors and all work stops well before lights out," Ms. Cooper says.

The lady continues our guided tour. I sort of imagine we're like the Myungs being shown all the bells and whistles.

First stop is the sleeping arrangements. In a room that looks to be several VIP suites with the walls knocked down in order to make one massive area sit about forty twin beds with foot lockers next to them.

"This is the drop-in general sleeping area. Beds open at eight normally, but if I'm being honest, we know we're full around three. Everything you bring is yours. Just lock it up. Everyone has to sign in and out of the sleeping area just so we can keep track of who's coming and going," Ms. Cooper says.

"By three?" Mom says, checking her watch.

First time I've really looked at the clock. It's almost four. School's been out for an hour.

"Yes, unfortunately we don't have any beds tonight. I'm sorry," Ms. Cooper says.

I wish she'd started with that. In the meantime, I guess it's been nice to walk around their air-conditioned building.

"Okay, well, can we see the rest of the building?" Mom asks.

"Of course. Our mission is fostering a community of people who lift up one another. We encourage volunteering. We're really just looking for the world to be how it was when we were kid. When everyone knew their neighbors and could trust one another."

"That sounds nice," Mom says to my surprise.

Why we didn't book it after they said they don't have beds, I don't know. Mom stays on the tour. Ms. Kim shows us where the bathrooms are and tells about their plans to expand the upper and lower floor decks into some kind of activity center. She talks about how private rooms are still under construction, the daycare for young and working mothers, and their nondenominational worship space. This makes me worried. Normally, this stuff makes Mom and me beeline out of there, but Mom is chugging the Kool-Aid. The line between her polite smile and her genuine one is almost indistinguishable, but I know what I'm looking for. Usually it's all in the forehead. Your face says one thing, but your eyebrow area is completely still. In a lot of ways, looking at her face is like looking at mine, and I can see that she's genuinely taking it all in. Why?

"Oh, hey, Dylan," Ms. Cooper says, calling over a sweaty skater kid with shaggy hair and a muscle shirt. He's scrawny, and the tool belt hanging off of him damn near looks like a hula skirt.

"This is Dylan, one of the volunteers. This is Ms. Dena and her daughter Callisto."

"'Sup," the guy mumbles.

"We have all kinds of kids around here, so we try to give them a space. You wanna show Callisto to the entertainment room?"

"Cool." Dylan waves his arm for me to follow him.

Against my will, but still playing my role, I follow him.

"This place used to be a private concert lounge. Hella artist used to perform here back in the day." He leads me down narrow stairs, knowing nothing of the vindication I have for people who say "hella."

"And like they all had these greenrooms that already had internet hookups and stuff. So instead of ripping it out, they made it a chill entertainment room slash business center."

Behind a thin wooden door sits another room with hastily knocked-down walls. I guess it's cool. It's more than I have. A foosball and pool table in the center. A couple of arcade cabinets and an air hockey table. There's a nice TV with a big old couch and top of the line computer from like twelve years ago. Overall, not bad. Definitely not enough if all the people who have beds up there also want to be down here.

"Is your mom a junkie?" Dylan asks, catching me off-guard.

"What?" I say, mostly as a reflex to someone asking me something dumb like that.

"She looks nice, but, like, you never know, and you guys are looking to stay here, so there gotta be a reason."

"Bruh, look, you don't know me. Don't make assumptions. I want to be here just as much as you do," I say. It takeseverything in my power not to break his face in places where faces don't break.

Dylan holds up his arm to show a tattoo of the SS logo on the placard out front.

"I'm all in Samaritan Society. Don't make assumptions," he says smugly. "If you are going to stay, you need to bring your own locks for the lockers. Get something pretty heavy-duty. Junkies will sometimes slip past screening. When they start to dry out, they get pretty desperate," he says as he leaves.

Upstairs, near the main entrance, Mom waits with Ms. Cooper.

"How was it?" the woman asks as she looks at me.

"Pretty neat," I say.

Did I really just say "neat?" Who am I? My mom's eyes widen as she both tries not to laugh and tries to scold me silently from afar.

"Oh, I'm glad, baby," Ms. Cooper says, apparently none the wiser. "I can't guarantee you beds, and I'm sorry that we don't have any for you tonight, but I can tell you if you're here by two or three, then I can get you in."

"Thank you, Kim. I'll keep that in mind. I think the space is going to be great," Mom says.

What the hell just happened? And more importantly, where the hell are we sleeping tonight?

Metal grates on un-oiled chains like shrieking thunder. Mom and I struggle to roll up the doors to our storage locker. Inside waits a palace of unused, out-of-date furniture and clothes, complete with collapsing boxes that are worse for wear. Immediately, the musk of dirty laundry, mildew, and rat droppings washes over us. This is where all my mom's money goes: a keepsake for memories she doesn't have the bandwidth to deal with and, unfortunately enough, where we'll be sleeping tonight. It only took two buses to get here.

Obviously, you're not supposed to live in your storage unit, which is terrifying enough, if we get caught, but it's a twenty-four-hour facility and they are big enough to drive a truck, and no one saw us enter.

"I don't like this," I say.

"Cal, it's our only option."

"I'm aware."

"Cal, I don't have time for your attitude," Mom snaps.

She never does.

Mom makes herself a pallet on our old couch. "If you're so against staying here...I don't want to be here either, but it's what we have to do for tonight. So I'ma need you to start going to the shelter to save our space."

"Mom. I have school."

"Don't act like you want to be there now. And I have to work until six. So it's either you do it or we sleep here."

"I don't understand you. I'm at school. I have school. I can't be somewhere at two when school doesn't end till three."

"Raise your voice at me one more time."

We can't fight. Our voices in here are creating havoc. Someone's bound to notice soon. I'm trying to keep her safe. I can't dip out of classes because my mom wants me to save beds at a shelter. Especially when those classes are my only leverage to keep bad guys from killing us.

"Stop standing there," Mom says, remarking that I haven't moved since we stepped in here. "Clear off that couch and grab a blanket." She gestures to the couch across from her.

No, I don't think I'm going to do that. I don't want to be anywhere near her. This is dumb and it stinks. It feels low. It feels dangerous.

Instead, I clear a box off a loveseat near the opening door. Mom looks at me, exasperated.

"Someone has to listen for people coming," I say.

"Whatever, Cal." Mom rolls her eyes and rolls over.

This chair is broken. I don't know why we kept it and why we only seem to collect bad things. Tucked in this broken chair, I crack the Intro to Biochemistry textbook open—a fantastically thick piece of literature with a glowing DNA strand on the front and some bright-eyed kid that's apparently never seen DNA before. Harsh white light from my phone screen illuminates my face and textbook as I attempt to write this paper on cell life cycles. They did not design phones to write essays.

Our unit door is thin, corrugated sheet metal that offers nothing in the way of sound proofing. Down the halls next to me, I can hear people's footsteps and lockers opening even at this time of night. There's not much foot traffic, but enough to cause me to worry. Danger used to be imagined, but I know it's out there.

Monet's threat comes floating in my head like she planted the thought there. "A dozen gunmen in the wings looking for me right now."

Vividly, I imagine a gunman dressed like he just left a ball game. Casually strolling by, then stopping and firing point-blank through the door. Or worse than that, imagining my mom waking terrified that I'm no longer here where she saw me just minutes ago. Just gone. No body. No sign that I left or was even there.

The tears and the quiver in her voice are so real.

It consumes me. Eventually, I close the book and stare, waiting. I can't see; all I can do is listen. Listen to every footstep, every creak, every nuance that happens outside the door and wonder if someone is coming for me. I examine the shadows, each growing darker as anxiety, like an invisible hand, slowly squeezes my chest till it's hard to breathe.

Something is coming. I can feel it.

CHAPTER 10

Sleep is an afterthought, whether it's in our storage locker, or, most days, the shelter. Patron's muffled sobs interrupt eerily quiet nights, along with their contented snores and night terrors. I guess I didn't know how good I have it or how much I'd really miss Brenda.

The lockers are for overnight stays. So we're forced to take everything with us when we leave. I trudge to school with two bags, one for books and the other for everything else I own.

My first stop: the cafeteria. School breakfast isn't great, but it's cheap, and if I don't eat here, I won't eat until maybe lunch. My first window to Small World opens fifteen minutes after the cafeteria. I take my breakfast, a burrito and juice, and head down one of the hallways. Blackburn is so big and new, not all of the classrooms are occupied all the time. Other than me, the only people roaming around this vacant wing are students looking for privacy to do their... extracurricular activities. I make sure they don't see me, not that they would care. I have to be quick. Because of me, there are multiple windows into Blackburn a day.

I make it to the locker room with ten minutes to spare. My first class is government with Feral. Chu and Monet have a free period, I think. Stashing book bag two own into a locker is exhausting, but at least these are made for holding weapons and bulky items. This would never fit into anything regulation.

After that, I eat in peace for a few minutes. It isn't hygienic, but it's quiet. Feral, or, as I'm supposed to call her on the other side of the window, Charlotte, waits for me at the entrance. She doesn't say anything, just watches me with knowing eyes.

Her Blackburn uniform fits the way it's supposed to, better than the tailored one that I'm wearing. The wrong assumption would be that her body is model-like. I know better.

The teenage girl in front of me, casually wearing her chestnut hair down, is not skinny but a lithe athletic cat woman who could, at the very least, make everyone exercise until death is a better option. Her appearance seems labored over. She's well put together, very tidy, not like the soldiers who shadow me. They don't quite blend in, which sorta works because freshmen are chaos anyway. Charlotte, on the other hand, blends beautifully. All the small things that Monet and Chu don't know about this side, like vending machines and casual conversation, Charlotte can do effortlessly. She's really good at her job. She'd otherwise be invisible if she weren't so goddamn beautiful. All the boys in our class would certainly agree. There's practically a pool of drool on the ground. But then again, dudes are gross. If she walks, talks, is quiet and new, that's what really interests them. The way they looked at me, the only freshman girl in this class, would be unsettling if I weren't used to being leered at by older dudes since I was uncomfortably young.

Charlotte and I act like we don't know each other, which is easy because we almost never talk. It's strange that I spend so much time with this person and never know where I actually stand with her.

We enter class together, and no one thinks twice about it. She does sit right next to me. It would be hard to stop me from dying if she didn't.

The bell hasn't rung, but I'm already fading, fighting a losing war against sleep.

Mr. Dibiase, our teacher, a portly man with a caterpillar for a mustache hanging beneath his nose, enters quickly. No greeting or anything. As the bell rings, he gets right to it.

"Last class we discussed laws as they pertain to a government's ability to effectively rule. You were supposed to do the assigned reading for today. So pop quiz."

Shit.

Our teacher hands out worksheets as I try my damndest to keep my eyes from blinking. Every time it feels like they may never open again. Like an instinctual countdown to sleep.

On my best days, I wouldn't do the reading, but I'd have enough in the tank to maybe wing it. But this class is a little different. With the combination of sleep deprivation and it being a senior class, I have no clue what's going on in here half the time. Point is, I'm screwed.

As he finishes handing out the papers, Mr. Dibiase calls into his smartwatch, "Set a timer for fifteen minutes."

The sound of scribbling on paper takes over as our teacher scrolls on his phone. I look around with drooping eyes. If I'm not going to pass, I guess I'm gonna nap.

I fold my arms and lay my head down.

"No sleeping," our teacher says as soon as my eyes shut.

Err.

He stares at me a minute and then back at his phone. Well, this now really sucks. If Yesenia was here, maybe I could copy and not get a zer—OW! A small piece of paper flicks my ear and hits the floor. I look over, angry. Feral, or, umm, Charlotte, is just looking at me. She's probably mad I brought even the smallest attention to myself, but then she surprises me. Subtly, she slides her paper forward. Oh, shit yeah.

I can't write fast enough. I'm weirdly aware of how heavy I'm breathing as I scan the room trying to keep a read on our teacher, but recon is Monet's job. I suck at it, like most things I do in The Faction. A fact that becomes even more painfully clear when Mr. Dibiase snatches my paper and tries to snatch Charlotte's. She catches it and stares at him. Her deep, bassy growl is quiet enough to not disturb other quiz-takers, but our teacher certainly feels it. Her eyes forget he's not a threat, and he's suddenly reminded that outside this classroom, outside of a society that confuses age for experience, he's a very small man with no authority.

Charlotte's eyes suddenly dart to me, and she lets go of the paper.

"Zeros for the both of you," he stammers, trying to regain his composure. The rest of the period, he drones on carefully about laws and such. All under the careful eye of Charlotte.

When he made a dismissive barb about the S.O.S. Treaty and how it should be voided due to the illegality and precedent it set—ya know, The Faction—Charlotte almost took his head off. She at least very seriously considered it.

After class, I catch up to her in the halls as she fends off approaches by the awkward and the douchey.

"Thanks for that back there. Sorry you failed the quiz," I say.

"I'm responsible for you. And I don't leave people behind."

"Still, I appreciate it."

"You're not the only one who can't sleep in new places."

"How'd you—"

"I get your reports from the team watching you."

"Oh."

When people try to relate to me, I hate it. I can feel how false it is a lot of the time. They know this thing about me, and that's what they talk about, but this isn't that. I get the feeling the reason she can't sleep and the reason I can't sleep aren't the same, but they are close enough that she actually does know how it feels to be an exhausted, dingy mess ninety percent of the time.

Charlotte pulls me into a classroom and sits me down. There's little I can do to resist her; she's very, very strong. She locks the door and listens for a second. She has enhanced hearing—I learned that the hard way, in the form of stadium stairs. When she's satisfied no one is in earshot, she looks at me.

"You can't keep doing this," she says.

"What are you talking 'bout? Is this about the quiz? I—"

"No. It's not about the quiz. It's about you fighting a war on two fronts."

"Umm, what does that mean exactly?"

"You've had to leave school early every day to get to the shelter for beds. It's stretching our protection detail thin."

"I'm sorry. I guess now wouldn't be a good time to mention I'm being dragged to a donation drive for the shelter this weekend."

This is going to suck. Not only am I Arc-less, I'm also homeless and living at a women's shelter. Details of my private life are about to be exposed to their entire company and there's nothing I can do about it. My face must've soured, because Feral lifts my chin and looks down at me.

"I'll handle it, but it would be easier on everyone if you just tell your mom about us."

"I... I don't know."

"We've opened additional windows for you; I'm sure Mr. Rhys would find you guys housing too."

This is so weird. Having a candid conversation about my life with someone. I don't like it, but there's something about her. She's not talking down to me; she talking to me. It's like she's talking to me about a life she's also lived. Like she's the one who has to catch buses at six am. She's wildly better at understanding this than any Arc.

"How much time have you spent on this side of the window?" I ask.

My question catches her off guard. Which is the only time I've ever been able to do that in any capacity. It's not much of a tell, but she shifts her weight to her back foot.

"Why do you ask?"

"You're seamless in a way no one else is. You get this side of the window."

Charlotte stares at me. She says nothing for long moments before finally saying, "You think not asking for help means you don't need it and it's easier to fail intentionally than really try."

"Uhh."

"It's why you gave up on the Room exercise before it even began."

"That's not—" I start to lie, but Feral once told me she can smell the truth. I don't know if that's really true, but I don't want to find out.

"You're good at watching people, but never forget people are watching you too. You're also trying to deflect from what makes you uncomfortable."

Busted.

"My mom. She has a lot to handle already. I don't know if she could take this," I say honestly.

"If you can forget, she can forget."

She has a point. Life would get easier. We'd have a place, we wouldn't have to go to this thing this weekend. Charlotte isn't telling me anything I don't know. So why don't I want to tell my mom?

"I don't know. She would put herself in danger. I would be doing that to her."

"I could order you," Charlotte says as if she too is a telepath. There's some weird insight she and Mr. Rhys have about me, and I wish I could see it. I wish I knew what they knew. Right now, I should be thinking about consequences. If she orders me, I'd be forced to comply. There's a whole section of text that I skimmed over about punishments for disobeying direct orders.

"But I'm not going to do that. If you're going to choose to be here, you're going to choose to tell your mom or not. I'm not going to give you the easy way out."

Is this what people mean about feeling seen? Because if so, it sucks. It's like squirming away from someone who has the same playbook as you.

"In the meantime," she says, "there's an early morning window. Our guys come in and sweep the school. If you're here, you can eat on our side. Mess hall is free and better for you. Also, our locker rooms are empty. Everyone showers in their barracks. You'll be alone. Showering is the scariest part, right?"

Even with my mom standing outside the door, I've been opting for sink baths. It's not the most hygienic, but it's what I can manage. The self-conscious part of my brain thinks she can probably smell me. Then the other part of my brain remembers she's a cat Arc—she can definitely smell me.

"Umm thanks."

"You don't get to thank me. You're my responsibility. And on that note, do your homework or I'll kick your ass." Yesenia always says something similar to me, but it's a hell of a lot scarier coming from her.

Charlotte puts her hand on the top of my head the way someone might do to a little kid. She leans very close to me.

"Operators need sleep. Even me. Whenever I get leave, I head home and conk out. You're here until you either choose not to be or we find a reason to dismiss you. It may be a while, so you need to find a way to rest."

It's the first time someone actually acknowledged the length of this arrangement, something I conveniently forgot to ask about. But she's right. I'm dead on my feet, and I guess with everything else we do, that's going to be literal soon enough.

"Home is a foreign concept to me. I've never had a place that I—"

"I didn't say it was a place," Charlotte interrupts. "Now, get some sleep."

"I can't I have a full day of classes and—"

"You can sleep. Or I can put you to sleep."

"No. No," I say, remembering being slapped awake by Monet after Feral choked me out in a Room drill. She's such an asshole. But at least she's an asshole that cares.

Tomorrow will be the first weekend of Monet actually shadowing me, and it's in a super public place with my mom and a bunch of others. We've been spending our weekends in Small World doing absolutely nothing. But the donation drive will be different.

We're back at the storage unit, this time searching for something to give away. Normally, we'd donate and dip, but Mom wants to stick around. She doesn't want to feel like a mooch since we're living in their facility. Naturally, I've gotten roped into helping too.

A couple weeks into this cloak-and-dagger crap and it's nothing like I thought. Feral's advice about telling my mom has been rattling around in my head for days. She may be right. Hell, Mom might even understand why I'm doing this. So, to make things easier for everyone involved, I've decided to tell my mom about the program.

"Cal, we have to be up early. Don't just stand there. Help me look, and be careful," she says.

The sun has already set, and it's cool out. I imagine amongst the other storages are an Arc team monitoring me and being bored, like a stakeout where the guy falls asleep in the truck.

"Come on, girl," Mom calls again.

Moving through boxes of what feels like past lives, I struggle to start this conversation.

How do you tell your mom that you are a teenage super-soldier? No emphasis on the super part.

A bedside table blocks the walkway leading to the back section, probably left here by someone who was too tired to carry it to the next one in the corner.

"Cal, that's heavy. Wait, let me help you," Mom says, closing her armoire to scuttle towards me.

This is heavy? I second-guess the weight of the awkward, longer-than-it-should-be wooden contraption. I hoist it up and over my shoulder with relative ease and put it on the couch. Mom reaches me as I set it down.

"Oh, look at you, mighty man," she says.

Benefits of push-ups every day, I guess. God, I hope that doesn't become my call sign. Mighty Man? That'd be horrible.

Mom pulls out boxes of my baby clothes. Most of these things were in storage before we got evicted the first time—that's why we still have them. Notebooks of crude drawings from my childhood and crayon-scribbled coloring books spill from the bottom of a box. Shredded corners and gnaw marks reveal that something has been snacking on it. It takes a few more glances in boxes before I confront myself about what I'm doing. I'm stalling. I have no way of knowing how she will react, but putting it off is only going to make it worse at this point.

"Mom!" I call. My voice pings across the tightly packed space.

I find her sitting on a big oak coffee table, a box open at her feet. She stares in with a sort of bittersweet look on her face, like she's just found her favorite toy and it's broken. Looking down, I see what she sees.

Bundled amongst the towels and sheets sits a scrapbook—a piece of home for her and a work of art in its own right, leather-bound with an ornate glass placard. Perfectly preserved.

Mom pats the spot next to her. Crossing my legs indigenous style I sit .

"Do you know what this is, Cal?" Mom asks.

"A scrapbook?" I say.

"Is that all you see?"

"Uh, yeah?"

"It's a little more than that. You are looking at the first Kader to ever leave Iran. Well, first in our family. Your Uncle Rajan's plane landed after mine." Mom sticks her chest out and holds her head high as if she were royalty.

Her brother lives in Canada. We visited him once after my dad left. To me, the entire Canada trip is a blur. More importantly, if Mom is the first person on her side of the family to ever leave, then there's no way anyone in our family was turned into an Arc on an American military base in the forties, right?

"Before I left, my mâmân gave me this. She said we are one of the oldest families and she wants my children to know where they came from, so," Mom says, flipping the book open to pages and pages of pictures.

Old book musk escapes and finds its way to our noses. I've always enjoyed that scent.

The first few pics are ancient black and white things, yellow around the edges. They look brittle. It is sort of cool to see my grandparents as young people, though. Strange to think how cameras were rare and expensive back then. Now everyone has them in their pockets.

Plastic sleeves crinkle as Mom turns pages, a well-kept collage of people I've never seen and don't know: cousins of cousins, aunties and prom dates no one can remember the name of. Finally, Mom points to a picture of someone I have a chance of recognizing.

"That's me as a little girl," Mom says excitedly.

"No way." I look closer at my mom's cute little picture with her big hair and 70s chic fashion. Our resemblance is jarring, like I might be her clone.

"When was this taken?" I ask.

"The 90s. Maman had old magazines in the house. I really wanted to be Farrah Fawcett. Your uncle wanted to be Will Smith."

Mom points, this time to a picture of a little boy with a heavy widow's peak, his arms crossed in typical 90s gangsta pose. His track suit is loud and mismatchy. Very Fresh Prince vibes. Nothing like the proper man I met.

"That's Uncle Rajan?!" I ask.

"Yup, he was soooo cool back then," Mom says jokingly, then continues to guide us down memory lane, showing me a glimpse of the life she had before me. Letting herself remember it. A slightly older picture of my mom. She thinks she's snatched. You can tell by the poses and ear cuff. Even back then, she was so extra.

"Wait, hold on, is that you? When were you that radical?" I say.

"I was a shy little girl, and my maadar bozorg on my father's side—"

"Your what?" I ask.

"My grandmother. She asked a jeweler to make it for me. It was her way of giving me permission to be me. I think I still have this. I better still have it." Mom digs deeper into the box. I continue to flip through the scrapbook.

Why?

I don't know, it's not like I recognize any of these people except my mom, and even then only barely. Mom pulls a beautiful and very dusty golden loop from deep within the box. It glimmers in the buzzing fluorescent lights.

"Ooh, pretty, can I have it?" I ask.

"No, not everything that is mine is yours."

"But I'm your kid."

"You sure?" Mom says, laughing.

I point to a picture of her dressed in a remarkably similar school uniform.

"Okay, fair," she says. "But I made it look good." Mom has another laugh at my expense.

"Whatever." I turn the page. I forgot what I was supposed to be doing. We both did. This trip down memory lane is supposed to be about me telling her my big secret. Suck it up, Cal.

"Cal, I miss it."

"Miss what?"

"This, between you and me. I miss being part of a community and not having to struggle all the time. I'd take you home if I thought it were possible."

"By home, you mean...?" I ask.

"Iran."

"And why isn't it possible?" I ask, knowing full well I don't want to move to a different country.

"Kiran," Mom answers, turning the page to a picture of her, my uncle Rajan, and another boy as kids about my age.

"Who's Kiran?"

"Just this boy... he lived down the road from us. Always in our house. My mother would yell at him. 'Kiran, if I catch you in my kitchen again, I'm going to put you out with the dogs.' Rajan won't even talk about him."

"Why? Did something bad happen to him?"

"We don't know. But he was the first person I heard say Anhaaa keh ba atesh rah ma rewned were coming."

"The who?" I ask.

Mom mulls it over for a second, translating in her head.

"It sort of means ones who walk with fire. Arcs, I guess they are called."

Oh snap. Mom suddenly has my fullest attention.

"It's not necessarily a good thing to stand out back home. A lot of people were conservative and kept to themselves. Our family was only as liberal as we were because our village was so small. But Kiran, for such a tiny boy, he had such big ideas and feelings. He didn't fit anywhere. He rubbed many people the wrong way, but he was at home with us. Then right before the Arc occupation, he was just gone. So many people were just gone. We don't know what happened to him, but we knew better than to ask." Mom runs her hand over my head. It's heavy, as if there were some unfamiliar weight to it. Like she's pressing down, trying to remember the feeling for later.

"But he was my brother," she says solemnly, packing up the box. "If you ever see them, Cal, run the other way."

"Mom," I say, trying to race the next statement I know is coming from her, but I lose.

"They are trouble. Always have been. Always will be. Promise me you will stay far away from them, that you will keep yourself safe."

My window closed before I even knew it was open. I can't tell her now. I stare at Mom in stunned silence. This is what's best.

CHAPTER 11

Next day, we're up before the sun.

I hate it.

A sleepy morning filled with even sleepier people pouring out of their vehicles. Doors and big truck lift gates slamming shut echo through the parking garage. We got Brenda back, so maybe things are looking up finally?

"We're going to be here all day, aren't we?" I ask Mom as I hoist our donation box out of the trunk.

"They give us a bed to sleep in at night. The least we can give them is a day," Mom says.

It's a short walk from the garage to the industrial park. Their modern landscaping is just annoying. Slabs of concrete with grass springing up between them. They set picnic tables up along the edge, sorta like a giant backyard for all the businesses. I'm sure some exec said it would be good for morale and a place where employees could congregate and eat lunch. Sort of like the quad in Small World.

Volunteers from the shelter move back and forth, already setting up donation tents.

"Morning, Dena," someone says.

Mom waves.

"Hey, morning," someone else says.

It's happening again. Mom's the life of the party, even if the party isn't for her. People flock to her.

Usually, she entertains as if it were something she's born to do, hiding behind an effortless smile, flawless make-up and well-kept hair. Each acting as armor guarding the secret of how we get by.

Today's different.

She's more comfortable than I've seen her. In pastel-blue golf shorts, a visor, and a shirt depicting all colors of hands helping one another, she's never looked more like a mom or more vulnerable.

"Morning," a third person says.

"Morning. Do you know where we drop off our donations and get our booth assignment?" Mom asks.

The volunteer points to a slate building, the tallest in the plaza with dark windows.

"The bank is the only building open to us. They're sponsoring the event, which probably means that none of their people are going to show up," the lady says.

"Thanks." Mom leads us into the building.

As cold and soulless as a bank lobby should be, I guess.

Inside, Dick-Head Dylan and others load boxes of hats, pins, buttons, extra raffle tickets, and whatever supplies we need.

A group of women sorting donations smile at me.

"You can drop those off here. When the drive starts, we'll have a booth near the parking garage if anyone asks you."

I drop our box on their little fold-out table. It's mostly baby clothes and things we bought, I outgrew, and never wore.

"Hey, Kim," Mom says.

"Dena. Hey, just who I wanted to see. Would you mind being on drink duty? We need someone to run that booth."

"Whatever you need," Mom says.

Mom hugs her. She's being genuine with a stranger. That's… new.

Back at the courtyard, where most of our booths and bins are set up, Mom and I dump ice and drinks into a bucket.

This square jaw, fake tan, head full of surfer hair stands on a literal soap box with a megaphone. His entire vibe screams guy who's been saved.

"Cuomo here. I just want to tell everyone thank you so much for coming out today. You could've been doing anything else on your Saturday, but you chose to help. We really appreciate it. Give yourself a round of applause."

Everyone does. There's even a few woos. I didn't choose to be here, so I do neither.

Cuomo, satisfied with his reception, continues.

"It's like our founder, Dr. Cattigan, always says: life is helping each other hand in hand. We're giving away prizes every hour. Cash donations go towards the big raffle tonight. Item donations, like can goods, clothes, and suitcases go to the hourly one. Your section leader will come around with a revised prize list. Let's make it a great day, everyone, and remember to wear sunscreen."

Make it a great day? Like we have a choice if the universe decides to be an asshole. That last one, though, is important. It's early and already proving to be a hot-ass day. Everyone applauds again as he steps down. I even join in, mostly because I'm glad he stopped talking.

All this pep sinks me further into teenage despondence.

"Smile and act like you want to be here, Cal," Mom says to me.

"I'm doing that, Mom."

"Then act like someone who's happier and wants to be here." She leaves to get our signage from our section leader.

That's rude. It's not that I'm not happy. I mean, I'm not, but it's mostly worry. My school friends are about to meet my mom and get a very close look at how I really live. And if that weren't enough anxiety, there's all these building with geigers and cameras.

"And windows. Lot and lots of windows," Monet says coolly as she strolls up to me.

In skinny, dark, ripped jeans and a loose black band tee, you'd never guess the amount of power this girl has. She looks so normal—a lot more grunge than I expected from a soldier, but still normal.

"Let's hope no one opens fire," she says.

I didn't even think of that.

"Well, your job is to jump in front of the bullet, right?"

"No, my job is to report on who shot you. Bullet catching is his job," Monet says, jerking her thumb towards Chu.

"Only for you," he says, looking both overwhelmed and like he doesn't want to be here.

"No headphones today?" I ask.

"I thought it'd be best to not stand out." Monet gestures to her ear. It looks like she's wearing hearing aids.

"I guess that makes sense," I say.

"You know they're not real headphones? The world impresses on me constantly. If I don't deprive one of my senses, I'll be overwhelmed, and that's not good for anyone."

"Oh?" I say.

"It's rude to ask about special equipment, but today I'll let you," Monet says, tossing her hair over her shoulder and scanning the crowd.

Chu looks like he stole his wardrobe from a CW show with incredibly hot people playing mystery-solving teens. Tight-fitting jeans and boots, complete with a T-shirt that's tight enough to make the religious girls here have to say a Hail Mary for their thoughts.

Monet double-taps the tip of her nose with her index finger as if to say, *I'm right on the money.*

"Is it normal for nu- civilians to ask for handouts? What kind of society is this?" Chu says.

How do I tell him to shut the hell up without revealing I live with these people because my life is in ruins? Or pointing out the hypocrisy of his entire state-sponsored existence?

"He didn't mean it like that," Monet says.

"What? What did she say?" Chu looks around, confused.

"Don't worry about it. Just secure a perimeter," Monet says.

Right, she heard all of that. It's weird not having secrets from someone.

"Chu's an asshole," I say.

"Yeah, but we don't have homeless Arcs. From our perspective on the other side of the IMW, civilians have it all. To come here and see it's not what we thought, it's a culture shock. Our state barely has a budget but provides everything we need. Why doesn't yours?"

"Umm," I start, but I don't have an answer. I've never even thought about it. I've just been too busy trying to survive.

"Cal, who are these kids?" my mom says, coming back to our station.

"Friends from school. I told them about it and they wanted to help out." It's the best excuse I could come up with, since my plan of telling her everything fell apart.

My mom's jaw drops. I don't know if she's more surprised that people showed up or that I have friends. Not really friends, I guess. Bodyguards? Doesn't matter, they're here, so what is she going to do?

"Well, it's nice of ya'll to come on down. Cal and I think alike. I figured she'd be bored stuck here all day so and getting on my nerves. So—"

"Cal!" Yesenia says in her short shorts and tank top. Her smiling face is elated to see me. Mom brought her here, today of all days.

Like I said, variables.

My gangly princess of a best friend rushes over and hugs me. I do the same to her. It's a thing left over from childhood, where we would run at each other at full speed. It's like playing chicken with no intention of turning. This time, when we collide, Yesenia hits the floor.

"Jeez, what are you made of, Cal?" Yesenia says.

Half of my days are trekking around Small World with eighty pounds of useless crap, like that'd be helpful in a fight. Guess it made me solid, though.

"My girl's built like a brick house," Mom says. "As smart as one too."

Chu does that choking laugh thing. Yeah, I don't like that. Last thing I need is everyone piling on the "Cal is as bright as a box of rocks" train.

"I didn't catch ya'll's names," Mom says.

"I'm Monet."

"Chu."

"Call me Ms. Dena or Cal's mom."

Yesenia waves to Monet. She puts on a false smile and waves back. Yeah, this already difficult day just got awkward.

"Show them around," Mom says.

"Actually, I burn easily. Is it okay if I stay here, Ms. Dena?" Monet asks. Something's up. Why is she trying to stay put?

<Because I have a job to do,> she thinks to me.

"Sure thing, sweetheart. Pull up a chair," Mom says to her sweetly. "We have the drink station. Everything's free but we encouraged people to give a dollar for each one."

<Listen to me this time,> Monet thinks. < Stay in the courtyard and you should be fine. I will be stationed here with your mom, mostly. Chu is monitoring the perimeter.>

< I hope your backstory is A1. My mom is about to ask you a thousand questions,> I think to no response. Monet talking to my mom suddenly makes me very nervous, and I feel a swell of embarrassment. Why? I want to stay and snoop on their conversation, but Yesenia takes my arm and we skip off to explore.

"Okay, for real now. Who is she?" Yesenia says as soon as we're out of what she assumes is earshot. Arcs hear better than everyone. Feral's burpee sessions are the sole reason I no longer mutter.

"You worried she's your replacement?" I say jokingly.

"Kinda. I mean, we're a few weeks into high school and you're already friends with a cool new hot girl."

"She is hot, isn't she?" I say, looking back and noticing for the first time.

Yesenia gasps, and it makes me nervous.

"What happened?" I ask. My eyes dart around, looking for danger.

"You like her."

"What? No, I don't. I honestly sorta hate her."

"Sure, because you 're Cal and you don't like anyone."

"I hate when you quote me to me," I say.

"Dude, you're giddy around her. Well, as giddy as you get."

"Yesenia," I plead.

"No! This is all I've ever wanted. I'll run interference on the also stupidly hot guy she's with," Yesenia says.

"Why?" I ask.

"He's your competition."

"No, they're like best friends. They go everywhere together," I say.

"Sure they are. Really hot guy follows really hot girl around because they're best friends. Yeah. Okay."

"He's a terrible person."

"That's fine, he's hot."

Last thing I need is my best friend dating my shadow's bodyguard.

"Not a bad consolation prize, either. This is going to work," Yesenia says.

"Sure it is," I say unenthusiastically.

There's nothing really to see at a raffle, just the size of the affair. A few of the prizes are cool, but it would just be one more thing I lug to school with me every day.

Eventually we return to the drink booth coated in sweat. For a while I forget about everything and it is life as normal. Yesenia is her usual chatty self around me. I'm less than that. She only clams up when she sees Chu and not-so-subtly jabs an elbow in my side, reminding me of the role she roped me into.

"Ms. Dena, is it okay if we get these?" Yesenia asks, holding up sodas.

"Go ahead, baby," Mom says.

Mom looks at Yesenia as her unofficial daughter. With her actual mother passing away and her aunt stepping into the role, kind of, it's made my mom and Yesenia weird sometimes. We have nothing to give her but love.

Yesenia tosses me a soda. Monet catches it mid-flight and hands me water instead, with a glare reminiscent of Feral. Right, water.

Our squad leader threatened my life if she catches me drinking soda. I guess if it's in Monet's report too, that counts, and she's the type to snitch. A subtle head nod from her confirms it.

"Cal doesn't drink water. Everyone knows that," Yesenia says.

Both she and my mom are in awe when I chug the entire thing. Yes, it's tasteless and doesn't give me a sugary caffeine rush I desperately need, but I gotta say, today of all days, it's at least refreshing.

"I don't know what sort of voodoo you did to my daughter, but I approve," Mom says to Monet as she spots a teenage mom from the shelter pushing a donated stroller around the drive. Her hair is a stringy mess, her eyes bloodshot and face yellow. Grime clings to her like lotion. We've seen her around the shelter a few nights, always with her baby and her dad. Men aren't allowed in after dark, but he tries to get her a bed most nights and sleeps in a nearby alley. It's like he knows he needs to be nearby in case his daughter needs him. But because of my mom, that hasn't been as necessary. They've taken a liking to one another.

"Poppy! I'll be right back." The baby spits up on himself in excitement.

Yesenia cozies her way next to Chu. I sit next to Monet.

"Want to walk around and explore?" I ask.

"No," Monet responds coldly. "There are cameras everywhere. It was hard enough to get in here without being seen. Who would watch the booth? Those two?"

"Right."

After what seems like an endless amount of awkward silence, Monet speaks up. "So what was the plan exactly?"

"So you heard all of it," I say.

"Obviously."

Even on a hot-ass day, I feel my ears getting warm. "I...um," I stammer.

"You know, even if he wanted to, he couldn't. His family frowns on interspecies mingling," Monet says.

Her eyes bug when she realizes what she said, and my face starts to turn from dumbfounded to pissed.

"That sounds way harsher than I intended," Monet apologizes. "Seriously."

I decide not to be angry about it. I've punched Chu in the face over similar comments and nearly broke my hand, and from what I can tell, Monet really didn't mean it.

"I guess that's where he gets the racism? What is it really called?" I ask.

"People have been fighting about that for years. We don't even know if we're a different species or race. We're just people. And you can't blame the Myungs. They worked protection details for the most powerful and important non-combatants there are."

"The most powerful, so not the best," I say.

Monet nods at me again. "You get it."

"So, do you guys get many days out like this? I'm sorry it's not more exciting."

Monet barely hears me, but that's no different than normal. She always has this thing where it seems like she's half paying attention to everything.

"No. If I'm being honest, I thought I'd never get to be outside like this." Monet reads questions forming in my head before I can ask them. It's rude, but if she's not looking at me, I don't think she knows I didn't actually say anything.

We keep speaking to a minimum. She's either bitchy at me or instructing me to do something. She never really answers questions until she remembers she's under orders. This is different thought. This is about her, not the world or any basic knowledge that Arcs have drilled into them at pre-k.

"My arc used to overwhelm me a lot. So I was isolated and slowly weaned on to more and more chaos. Most people say they grew up alone, but I really did. I had to. Even the intercessors, the people that assess powerful or broken Arcs, thought I may never see outside, the real outside. But here I am."

"Yeah, so, full disclosure. The part of my reading that was about the camps I kinda skimmed. So I really don't know anything about normal life for... everyone else," I say awkwardly, trying not to use the A word.

"Neither do I," Monet says sadly.

"Okay, but, like, Chu and everyone's families live in camps, but that's a lot of people. Where would you put a place like that?"

"That's classified," Monet says, a little more wounded than intended.

"Oh, alright," I say, trying not to pry but really wanting to.

"I appreciate that," Monet says. "The not prying. I feel like that's all I do, mostly."

"It's fine. I mean, you sort of get used to it," I say.

A raffle goes off and someone wins something huge. A crowd erupts and everyone is ecstatic.

"There are a lot of small victories in life. I know it's none of my business, but I heard about your living situation," Monet says.

"From who?"

"You," Monet says.

Right... I thought about it. It's not the kind of thing I share with anyone. Hell, Yesenia doesn't even know. Usually, I make up a reason why we don't go to my house. While we've never talked about it openly, I'm sure Yesenia knows.

With Monet and Chu, though, the problem is a little more immediate, since the shelter is loaded with geigers at every entrance. They couldn't shadow me there if I wanted them to.

"As I was saying, there are a lot of little victories. And while you are sucking at the part of your life I'm involved in, out here, you see what you would be fighting for. Normal people. Safety of the city. Miles away from war zones and worries."

That's not the case. Wait, she'll hear this, anyway. I can't really hide what I think from her. I might as well say it.

"That's not the case. That's what you see, but to me and everyone here, this is closer to a war zone. Not every fight is guns and bullets or fists. Everyone here is fighting to survive. Many don't know where their next meal is coming from or where they're sleeping tonight. Most of them have to think about someone else, like my mom thinks about me," I say. "People walk by you day in and day out, not thinking about you or your situation. No kindness. No care. Just judgement. Today is just a day for people in that fight to know that someone takes pity on them and for a few hours try to forget about it all but constantly be reminded because they are here that they have to be. For them it's just another kind of mission, I guess."

Monet stares through me for a second.

"What?" I ask.

"There's more to you than I thought. One more point for the plus column."

"What are the others?" I ask.

"When you don't talk. You're easy to be around."

"Thanks?" I say, wondering if that's really a compliment or an insult.

"Think about this. I have a thousand minds screaming in my head constantly. Everyone has an agenda. I get impressions of all of it, from everyone but you. Like you don't have a thought in your head."

"Thanks?" I say, realizing that is, in fact, an insult.

"I know you're being sassy, but I'm serious. Even surrounded by all these people; their everythings invading my headspace. It can get overwhelming. But I focus on you and it's okay. So. Thanks."

"Did you just call me sassy?" I say.

"You called me hot," Monet teases.

Blood drains from my face as I look at her. My hands sweat, there's no spit in my mouth, and my stomach's break-dancing.

Shit, she heard that?!

"Yep. And that," Monet says lightly, poking my forehead.

Yesenia's hard laughter cuts in.

OH THANK GOD!

Her flirty laugh that's usually so cringey is a godsend.

"How's that going?" I ask, desperately trying to change the subject.

"Not well. He's super annoyed. Your friend is trying to be sweet, but to him it's torture," Monet answers.

"So you're saying we shouldn't rescue him."

"Definitely not."

Most of the day flies by like this.

Monet and I watch people in silence. That's now awkward AF, but also somehow not?

Chu rotates out from Yesenia, and I pick up that slack as my mom mingles.

With this many bodies at the booth, Mom really doesn't have to be here at all. After her latest foray into the crowd, she returns with cheer and purpose.

"Hey, dinner is coming soon. They got that man from the news to donate a bunch of food trucks. Cuomo just told me. So we got to replenish the drinks and get them all chilled. I need someone to grab some more sodas," Mom says.

"We'll go!" Yesenia says, volunteering herself and Chu. She probably wants to just watch him lift things.

"They're on the first floor of the atrium around back," Mom says.

Monet's face is always unexpressive. But I can read the micro-expressions, or maybe I just came to the same conclusion she did seconds slower. Chu can't go. Banks have geigers.

"I'll do it. You don't even know where it is," I say, trying to seem as annoyed and absentminded as possible.

Yesenia instantly pouts at me. Yeah, I know I ruined her master plan, but that's maybe a good thing.

Chu uses this opportunity to escape. Yesenia camps out as if to say "you're all on your own, Cal."

"Monet, could you help me get some ice?" Mom asks.

"Yes, ma'am," Monet responds.

Someone had the bright idea to put the all the festivities away from the bank.

That someone needs to be fired.

The atrium sits well outside our little campsite of pop-up donation tents and booths. I can hardly hear music from this far out. The enormous sign above the bank makes sure their name will end up in every photo of the day. A small little pull wagon in tow, I make my way up the ramp. It's eerier because there's no one else around. The wheels squeak with every step. My lone footsteps echo through the dark lobby. I find the supply closet Dylan and friends loaded and unpack it. Cases and cases of soda.

"This is going to be heavy," I say to myself out loud. As I pull the cart, it's exactly what I expect. A case tips over the side. As I pick it up, I realize that I'm suddenly not alone.

A private security guard towers over me. I know he's private security because it says so on his flak jacket. He carries a long gun, but otherwise he's just dressed in jeans and a T-shirt, both strapped with pouches and knives. Sunglasses cover his eyes. There are no other identifying markers. Feral taught me how single out patches and emblems that designate someone's military affiliation. She told me to look for this specifically if I ever needed to write a report about who I met in the field. She also mentioned most bad actors won't wear them, because they don't want to be identified.

"Let me help you, young lady," he says, picking up the case.

The man sets the twenty pack of knock-off Sprite in my cart and ensures it can roll.

Something doesn't feel right.

"Thanks," I say, burying every "Black girl in a horror movie" instinct I have to run. I don't think I would get very far.

As he hands the cart to me, he holds on, making sure that I know I'm not going anywhere if he doesn't allow it.

"Your name is Callisto, right? Callisto Kader?" he says with menace. Staring me down. I'm in trouble and I saw it coming.

CHAPTER 12

S hit shit shitty shit shit.

"Yeah, I thought that was you. My associates and I would like to have a word," the guy says.

At no point is it ever okay for a grown man to approach a teenage girl, or any female for that matter, like this. This is creepy, but I say nothing.

Noticing the shadows of what looks to be at least two dozen armed men only furthers the unnerved feeling.

My body goes numb. All I've done at stupid Arc school are the stupid classes and even dumber Room exercises.

When I see Mr. Rhys, I'm going to curse him out. He promised his school would be useful, but I have no idea what to do at this very instant.

The man extends a gloved hand to me. I know I'm not going with him. All I can think is five. Five. Five. The number Monet left in my phone. Shit.

"Callisto?" the man says again. "I'm not asking."

Feral's voice rings in my head. "Speed, surprise, and violence of action."

In other words, be Callisto.

I take his hand. He relaxes a bit, and I punch him dead in the throat. He drops to his knees, choking. His face turns bright red. His associates swing out with their weapons drawn. I run as fast as I can to cover. Retrieving my phone, I jam and hold five. It calls a number, picks up, and hangs up.

FWEET! A high-pitched whistle is just enough to pull my attention from the screen to the end of a rifle. An overweight dude holds a gun on me. Smiling.

I focus on the rifle and the powder burns on the end, the swirls inside his gun, and the wicked sort of smile that twists his face, having gotten to checkmate so fast. I barely recognize the man as human. There's a sinister, perverse grin on his face. He's hoping he gets to kill me. He's hoping I move so he can pull that trigger, but I'm frozen.

Fear clouds my minds and actions as I prepare for the inevitability of what's next.

My world grows darker until literal sunlight cuts through the clouds. The walls behind this goon split like the Red Sea to Moses, and Monet walks in with Chu. Before the guy can say or do anything, Monet slams his head into the counter hard enough to shatter the faux marble.

"Did you call the number?" she asks.

"Yeah," I stammer.

"We shouldn't have come here," Chu says coldly.

"We're operators. We fight and we do the mission in front of us," Monet responds.

"I'm not an operator. I'm your bodyguard," he says.

"You're in Special. Now, you're both."

Chu looks at me with disregard, then says, "I'm advising you. We need to get off the X, now!"

"I heard you," Monet says. "She's my mission and I'm yours. Do your job. I'll do mine."

Chu chews his jaw like he wants to scream and is holding back. More of the boy in the cage. Ultimately, that's what it takes to get through to him. Chu takes the guy's gun and flak jacket.

"Put this on," he says to Monet. She rolls her eyes and puts the stiff little thing on me instead. It's scratchy and stinks of chewing tabaco. I sort of zone out. Focusing on how close to death I was. I knew it. I could feel it inside of me that Callisto was gone. Even now I feel myself slipping.

THAP! A hot sting across my face wakes me up. Monet just slapped me! Looking into her purple eyes, I concentrate on her.

"Focus!" she says. "You're not dead, and if you want it to stay that way, we need you here now. Can you do that?"

I'm unresponsive, so she repeats.

"Cadet, can you do that?"

"Yeah," I drawl. "Yeah, I think I can."

"Good," Monet responds.

"What do we do now?" I ask.

"We go up," Monet says, checking the app on her phone. The wall closes up behind her, and we make our way to the elevator.

"Is that the best course of action?" Chu asks.

"We have at least a full tact team. There are civilians outside. The closest way to a secure location is in this building." Monet's never really been this forceful. She's usually quiet and laid back. Part of me wonders if all this is now because he's questioning everything she says.

"Right," Chu says. This is a different guy I'm looking at. He seems ready, like he's been waiting for this.

I see how far apart he and I actually are, because in the back of my mind, I've been dreading this.

Boots racing towards us, put a hitch in our giddy-up as we make a break for the elevator banks.

"When the shots come, get behind Chu," Monet says. "He's traditionally bullet resistant."

"What's the different between bullet resistant and bulletproof?" I ask.

"It means it hurts," Chu says.

Monet hands me the goon's sunglasses. "Put them on now."

After I slip them on, my reflection in the elevator door makes me look like The Terminator.

"Here they come." Monet grabs me, crowds me into a huddle near the base of the elevator door, and closes her eyes tight. The enemy comes from both sides of the lobby with us in the middle.

Seconds before they squeeze their trigger, I gag on the smell of burning meat. Embers fall around me. Light and pressure fill the room.

Chu's screams mix with what sounds like a thousand angry cicadas.

The louder his screams, the brighter the light until it's the brightest one I've ever seen. It attempts to crawl under my glasses and into my mind. I, being a dumbass, still try to look. I want to know why the boy screams.

Monet's grip tightens. Even looking away, these sunglasses are not enough. Through the reflection of the elevator door, I glimpse a man of crystal standing in the place where Chu was a second ago.

No wait. That is Chu!

His cry and the cicadas mingle with the screams of soldiers into a song of scorched corneas and pain.

Ding! The elevator door opens, and Monet and I fall in. Chu steps in behind us.

Instantly, the little box gets hotter. His pained tears sizzle and evaporate off his cheek.

Monet hits the button for the fifteenth floor.

"You good?" Chu asks through gritted teeth.

In the reflection from the doors, I can see his back. Where there was flesh, there's now a crystal skin, with regular skin growing steadily and a pulsing light where his heart should be. His T-shirt hangs loosely in burnt tatters.

"She's fine," Monet answers for me.

Oh, he was talking to me?!

The two of them seem at odds now.

"Yeah, I'm good. I have a lot of questions. Like what was the wall and the light and..."

"Yeah, she's fine," Chu says. "You should be used to it by now. These are our arcs."

"No, things talk to her..." I say.

"Yes, and I can talk back. Impressing my will on things is exhausting, though, especially if you're asking something to go against its nature."

I sorta think I get it. It's how she talks back telepathically and probably why her voice is quieter in my head than Mr. Rhys'. I should've seen that coming.

The doors open. Both of them are already exhausted at this point.

Chu clears our exit, and I hit a bunch of buttons on the elevator going up and down. Monet looks at me as if I'm just a kid pressing buttons.

"So they don't know where we ended up," I say.

She shrugs.

"There's a window up ahead. We get there and wait for the all-clear. Then you'll be debriefed."

Monet navigates us through the floors of hastily left desks. Seems like everyone who works here was ready for the weekend. Passing cubicle after cubicle, we finally arrive at a door that should lead to the break room.

"This is it. Window opens in thirty," Monet says.

"We don't have that," Chu responds, peering down the hallway. Shadows dance on the walls as men take positions. Our back-up should be here. They can pop out of any door. If I'm so important, why the hell aren't they?

"They should be," Monet agrees.

Then, with horror in her eyes, she turns to me and snatches my phone.

"Damn it. Call didn't go through. We've been faraday'd."

"I knew we should've gotten out," Chu says.

Monet glares at him.

"What's faraday'd?" I ask.

"The reason we don't have back-up. Your call never went through. It's like they set a pocket dimension around the building so our pocket dimension can't get us in or out of here. Not even a signal. These guys know what they're doing," Monet says.

"Then we get to the roof. This is a trap, standing here like this," I say.

Both of them look at me, surprised and stumped.

"What? I listen, occasionally. We've done like a thousand drills," I say.

"They're expecting us to go to the roof," Chu says.

"Will it matter if we can get back up?" I ask.

"First, we get out of here," Monet says.

Here is a hall sandwiched between two bullpens. This little conversation of ours has taken up too much time. Which is something we need and could desperately save if we could all talk in our heads like I do with Mr. Rhys.

<Fair point,> Monet says. <Chu, wall directly in front of us.>

<Copy,> he thinks, handing the weapon to Monet. She aims it down a hallway. Chu charges and splits the plaster and drywall in front of us, creating a small cloud of dust. Smoke grenade and flashbangs land at our feet. I kick one, sending it back where it came from. The other is a dud.

<No, I told it to wait,> Monet says as we follow Chu's path of destruction.

<Wait for what?> I think as it goes off with a large pop behind me. Soldiers hit the ground, coughing and gagging.

<Them,> she answers

<Stairs up ahead,> Chu thinks.

Bullets start flying. I watch as they bounce off of him. We slide to a stop so as not to get caught in the crossfire.

Chu winces. <Son of a bitch!>

<Watch for ricochets.> Monet's words are crisper in my head than before. Maybe it's the adrenaline, or maybe she really doesn't want us to die. Monet blindly fires down the hall.

We only stop for cover. All I can think about is my mom freaking out about all the gunfire. She knows this is the last place I was at. She's going to have a panic attack. Worse, she'll come looking for me.

<No, they have a vested interest in invisible battles like we do,> Chu thinks. <I doubt anyone outside has any idea what's even going on.>

Each sprint to cover spikes the adrenaline. Monet seems a little light-headed, teetering a bit. My hand lands on her hip to steady her and comes back bloody. She's been hit. On her side. So much blood... I.... Oh my, I'm...

<I'll be alright. Say nothing about this to Chu. We get out of here. We'll be alright. Outside, I can vaguely hear people. No one is coming close to this building.>

<You don't look so good. What can I do?> I think.

<I'll be fine.>

I wish she could tell their guns to stop firing. That would put us on some even ground. I'd take these two versus anyone on their side.

Monet smiles at me. <Sometimes, I like the way you think.> Suddenly her eyes go white, rolling back in her head. She collapses, but I catch her before her head smacks the ground.

Chu stares at me, confused. It takes a second before both he and I realize that the gunfire has stopped and we can't hear each other's thoughts.

"What happened?" he says.

"I think she impressed on their guns to make them stop firing," I say.

"No, what happened?" Chu says again. I follow his gaze to her gunshot wound.

"I'm not supposed to tell you."

Chu has a look on his face—shell-shocked, like he's reliving memories or a nightmare. Monet's so still she almost looks dead. Oh, wait.

"She's alive," I say.

"You can't be sure," Chu says.

"I can. I am." I lie. It works only on him, and it's nice. Between Yesenia, Feral, my mom, Monet, and Mr. Rhys, I'm basically forced to be truthful all the time now.

Chu isn't convinced. He stares at the girl who's gotten us this far. I guess it's his turn to freeze. I watch as everything he knows sort of ebbs away.

"Hey!" I yell. His blanking eyes focus on me. "We all have roles to play. You're stepping on mine."

Chu's prior assuredness slowly reboots.

"Get us off the X," I say.

"Okay. Okay. I'll clear a path," Chu says. "Get her to the roof. Call for back-up."

I hoist Monet onto my shoulders. I take back what I said about the eighty-pound pack hikes. Monet's a little heavier than that, but I don't keel over immediately.

"After you," I grunt.

We move from hidey hole to hidey hole. We avoid as many of their patrols as we can. This is taking too long. Each minute that passes, we grow more fatigued and they grow more desperate. Chu shares my impatience as we dip into a side hall.

Between us and where we need to be are three guys in attack formation.

"Think they know their guns don't work?" I whisper.

"Guess we'll find out."

Chu jogs down a hallway. Three guys hold their hands out, telling him to stop.

He doesn't. They squeeze the trigger, and nothing. Chu takes the first guy and launches him down the hall. He fights the next two grown-ass men at once.

While it's not the kung-fu magic of Feral, I can tell this guy is very well trained. The punches aren't my wild flailings, so that has to count for something. Between this, the light show, and the bulletproof skin, I see why they made him Monet's bodyguard.

"Stairs," he says.

I kick open the door. On the other side are two men waiting.

Shit!

Monet rolls off my shoulders and shoves the man as hard as she can. He tumbles backwards, taking everyone behind with him.

"I'm tired, I have a headache, I've been shot, and I want this to be over already," Monet says.

"More coming," Chu huffs, bursting through the door behind us. "You're alive."

"Yeah. She told you that," she says.

"Any idea how many of them there are?" I ask.

"A lot for just you," Monet remarks. "No offense."

"No, no. I agree," I say.

"They definitely knew we'd be here," Chu says, snapping a rifle in half and prying it between the door's lock.

"Why'd you break the gun?!" I ask, exasperated.

"It was out of bullets."

"There are bullets everywhere! Usually flying at us," I say.

"She has a point," Monet says, but Chu's stopped talking to focus on Monet's wound. If it weren't a white shirt, it might not look as bad.

"This can wait. It's a flesh wound," she says as we hit the stairs. She's totally lying, by the way.

<He doesn't need to know that,> she thinks to me. <It hurts like a bitch.>

Racing up each flight, we can hear people beneath us coming.

"How many do you think are on the roof?" Monet asks.

"All of them," Chu answers.

"Then maybe we don't go to the roof," I say.

"This was your idea!" Chu says, winded.

Hell, stairs even make Arcs winded. Better not tell Feral.

"Focus, Cal. Where do we go if not the roof? If you don't have a better idea, then—" Monet says.

"What if I do?" I say.

Both of them look at me.

To be fair, I'm not sure it's a better idea, just a different, more batshit one that my mom is probably going to beat me for, but it's the best idea I have.

"Cal!" Monet snaps.

"Ya see, they are expecting us to go to the roof. So we should go. That's the trap they've laid, that's where they'll be. We just need to get a call out to back-up and tell them where to meet us."

"I hate to say it again, but sometimes, I like the way you think," Monet says.

A couple floors before the roof, we realize the footsteps have stopped giving chase. It means we're walking into their trap. So we should probably lay our own. We pop into a floor off the stairwell.

"Are you sure this is going to work?" Chu asks.

"No. But I know my phone. And you said it just has to be outside the building to send a signal," I say, typing a text and hitting send to the number Monet put in my phone. "Until it connects, my phone keeps trying to send the signal out. My mom used to work in a building like this. Each floor has a trash chute that leads to the loading dock area. My hope is that it goes under whatever building insulation thing they did. If we're lucky, my phone'll connect and send the text." I hope that makes sense.

"It does," Monet says.

It's nice that she's in here with me again. I go ahead and drop the most expensive thing I own into the trash.

"Now I guess we give them what they want," Chu says.

"No, we need one more thing," Monet says.

Minutes later, we are again racing toward our ambush. All of us take a deep breath on the landing.

We had Chu take a safe out of someone's office and lug it up here. It was easy enough to find with Monet's arc. She just had to listen for something that didn't want to be found and didn't want to be opened.

From what I'm told, any other Arc could probably rip a safe out of the wall, but Chu's uniquely strong.

He kicks open the door to the roof and tosses the four-foot tall, like four-hundred-pound safe into the crowd of waiting soldiers and guns.

It hits no one.

The soldiers look away from it and train their weapons on us. They push past it in formation. The other good thing about Chu being in front. Bullet resistance.

<Not going to work. Bigger calibers now.> His thoughts betray the cool head he tries to portray. His voice in my head cracks with hints of fear. I don't even want to know how that's possible.

<Do you think my plan worked?> I ask, my own thoughts shaky.

The crowd in attack formation gets closer. We put our hands up.

The guy I punched in the throat steps forth and seems really pissed.

"Are ya'll done, or are ya'll done?"

Looking past him, I see the door of the safe Chu threw creak open slightly. Inside is only darkness. Until I see the eyes of a jungle cat. Monet sees it too.

<Everyone remain perfectly still,> she thinks as she grabs my hand.

Before anyone can register that anything special is happening, the safe erupts open!

Feral takes out the back row of their formation. They never even had a chance to react. Quick, ruthless, and bloody. So much blood.

I'd never seen her full transformation. Even now I can't. She's too fast to keep up with and too skilled to need to stay in one place. No opponent lasts more than a second against her. To think this girl is only a couple of years older than me.

Snapping limbs and wounded prayers combine in what sounds like a tornado of pain as she moves from one victim to the next, underlined by the ever-present sound of her low growl as she feasts on these soldiers. Fear takes over, and they give up their initiative of a quiet battle and train their guns on her, but no one fires.

They feel it more than we do, a ringing pressure in our heads.

They can't move. They want to, but all they can are muster are tears. Stepping out of the safe in a way that seems impossible, six-foot-five Mr. Rhys, seemingly taller and longer than usual.

"Well. Dressed. Man," Throat-Punch Guy utters in a choked, pained voice.

Feral continues to mindlessly attack anything that moves. She lurches towards Mr. Rhys. Her eyes focus ferociously like they did in class that time Mr. Dibiase took our quiz, only like a thousand times over. There's no recognition in her eyes. She truly is feral.

Mr. Rhys doesn't flinch. Slowly, he shows her both sides of his hands like he's about to do a magic trick. It takes a second, but Feral's fury and the growl subside.

Mr. Rhys' on-edge look slowly fades as he nods to Feral, and she nods back.

"We need one of them alive," Mr. Rhys says. "The others will forget." The men are all paused as our teacher and his TA make their way over to us.

We don't move. Not sure if we're going to be scolded or what.

Mr. Rhys watches us for a moment.

"You guys handled yourselves well. Good work," he says.

It's at this moment, I realize our experiences were just downloaded by the big guy.

Feral watches me. This time it's less like prey and more like a cub. It's only for a second before she switches gears.

"You two with me," Feral calls to Chu and Monet.

Chu looks at me with a conflicted emotion, like he's not sure what to say. Monet says nothing, just winces as she heads toward our squad leader. Feral knocks Throat-Punch Guy unconscious and drags him through the safe.

Chu and Monet follow.

Monet stops and looks back at me for a second before disappearing inside. I didn't need to hear her thoughts to know what she was trying to say. *Don't worry, I'll be okay.*

"What is that? Like, how is that possible?" I ask, pointing to the safe.

Mr. Rhys looks back at it and then to me again.

"Emergency window. They require a special circumstance, but they are useful. You've seen a lot of death and been shot at a lot recently. How are you holding up?" Mr. Rhys retrieves a packet of wet wipes from his inside jacket pocket.

He takes one and starts to wipe Monet's blood off my hand. I don't even realize what's happening as shock replaces adrenaline. The cool dampness slowly cleans the dry, tacky life oil clinging to the creases of my fingers. What does stick with me more than anything is the first guy's barrel trained on me. The quivering weakness I felt being so powerless, the lack of thought I had. The lack of anything, really, except resignation to my fate. The very intrusive thought squeezes tears of fear as I'm back in that moment again.

"That's to be expected. But you kept moving. You kept your squad mates alive. You out-thought a heavily armed opponent. This will stick with you. It's not something you will get over quickly." Mr. Rhys finishes wiping down one hand and moves to the other. "And if you ever need to talk about it, I will give you my ear."

I appreciate it, but I've seen tons of awful shit in my life. This is just more trauma waiting to be unprocessed. It be like that.

"It shouldn't be, though, Callisto."

When Mr. Rhys is done cleaning my hands, he removes the flak jacket, steps back, and examines what I'm wearing. The clothes are stained, but nothing that can't be explained away.

"I guess. I'll talk when I'm ready? It all just happened. I don't really know where to go from here," I say.

"Home. Your mother is waiting. Looking, really."

The sun is setting. It's gotten late. I reach for my phone to check the time but realize that I threw it down a trash chute.

Sigh.

Mr. Rhys pulls out a pocket watch dangling from his side. Of course, he has a pocket watch.

"6:43 pm," he says.

Big raffle was an hour ago. Crews are cleaning up. Mom is going to kill me. I'm about to run when I stop and look at Mr. Rhys again.

"Is that your call sign? The Well-Dressed Man?" I ask.

"When our enemies whisper stories of their worst day, it comes after the black spot: time is gone, words escape them, details are a puzzle made in sand slipping between their fingers. At some point, he comes back to them, me. But that is not my call sign. It's just a warning. One day, Cadet, I'll tell you…"

Mr. Rhys fades off as the red and blue light up the plaza from downstairs, spilling into the shadows.

"My mom called the cops?" I ask.

"No," Mr. Rhys answers warily.

"Then why are they here? I thought no one heard anything?"

"They are here because someone is choosing to be very loud."

Everything I've experienced this far into the program has been very hush-hush. The way they approached me, the way they recruited me, and half of my school days. He doesn't seem like a person who likes to make a big show of things. In fact, the only thing that's been loud was the first day at the mall with all the sirens and giegers and… oh. I get what he means by loud.

"Real Gs move in silence," I mutter, mostly to myself.

"Like lasagna," Mr. Rhys responds.

My head snaps to him in surprise.

"You may be my favorite administrator ever," I say.

The roof door opens minutes later.

I've never seen an FBI agent in my life, but I feel like I'm looking at one. His clothes are much more government than Mr. Rhys. It's not a suit that makes a statement other than one of his authority. His beady eyes, clean-shaven face, and white hair tell me everything I need to know about this guy. Definitely some kind of cop. He looks much more like CPS than Mr. Rhys ever did.

< I appreciate that,> Mr. Rhys thinks.

"Deputy Director Badge, this is a little low on your radar, isn't it?" Mr. Rhys says.

The man looks around at the bodies lying on the rooftop, the clear sign that someone was dragged through puddles of blood.

"Well, this is the homeland. We are Domestic. If there's a situation, we look into it." The man stares up at Mr. Rhys as his guys come out of the door and pause in a line behind him, all of them wearing similar suits.

"Right. And how exactly did you know there was a situation?" Mr. Rhys asks.

"How did you?" the man answers. "You're a little outside your jurisdiction, aren't you?"

Mr. Rhys chooses not to answer.

"I'll take your silence as an agreement that this is my scene now. Any of your people involved in the incident will need to be made available to me."

Mr. Rhys remains stoic.

This isn't a situation that he was prepared for; as fast as his mind is, he's not thinking of a way out and this guy is kicking his ass with the questions, like he's a kid very much caught where he's not supposed to be. But all I do is lie.

"It was just me," I say to the guy.

The guy refuses to take his eyes off Mr. Rhys until he has to and looks almost through me.

"Just you?" he says.

There's a weight on my soul as he leans in.

Oh god! What is this? It's like trying to squat lift a truck. My knees are about to buckle, and when I do, my shattering bones will weep the truth.

"You heard her," Mr. Rhys says. "I'll make her available to you at the appropriate time. We must go."

"Fine," Deputy Director Badge turns to his guys. "Collect everything. Clean the rooftop. I want no sign that this building was ever disturbed. Anyone still here and unconscious will need to be questioned... not that it will do much good."

The agents move towards the rooftop.

Mr. Rhys leads me through their line and opens the door. On the other side waits a cold and dimly lit parking garage. Swirling siren lights add an air of unease.

A few cars remain. Behind us, the stairwell door closes.

"Cadet..." Mr. Rhys starts and then pauses to gather himself. "That was reckless. Badge will do everything in his power to tear your life apart. You stepped out of line and spoke above your superior officer. Never do that again."

Getting scolded in the dark parking garage, where his booming voice echoes, makes me feel more like I'm in extra trouble. Without meaning to, my posture slumps like a wounded puppy.

"Thank you," he says suddenly. "You've bought us some time, and for that, I must thank you."

"Is he a big shot?" I ask, almost trembling.

"Domestic Branch's number two. His specialty is witness interrogation."

"By specialty you mean—"

"His arc. You felt it. The pressure."

It was as if my words had weight, and holding in things I know to be true hurt and crumpled me into a ball. In that brief instance, if Mr. Rhys hadn't stepped in, this would be over already.

Mr. Rhys resigns himself to the situation we find ourselves in because of my mouth. He stuffs his hands in his pockets and turns on a dime. Strolling into the shadows, his shoes clicking, he calls to me.

"I don't think this needs to be said, especially to you. But over the coming weeks, be especially sure not to talk to strangers. I'll see you in class."

He and the clicking of his shoes fade until both are gone.

<h1 style="text-align:center">CHAPTER 13</h1>

W ater circles the drain at my feet. How long have I been standing here? I feel planted like The Faction emblem that follows me around, and even in the locker room shower, it hovers overhead, its roots spreading to the faucet. In the dim light, it looks like a clawed hand slowly trapping me in its grasp. Feral's advice was solid—there's never anyone in this locker room—but somehow the gleaming white tiles are always clean. I'm alone, but there's no peace.

There's no silence.

Water pouring over my head fails to drown out the echoes of gunfire. Mom had a full-on fit after I disappeared and the cops showed up. It got worse when I told her about my phone. Everything is louder now. Brighter. More brilliant. Chaotic. All the sounds at the shelter that annoy me are unbearable. And there's still blood on my hands. Not really, but it feels like it.

I don't feel safe. I never feel safe.

There's good pressure, plenty of hot water, and solitude, but this shower sucks. It's not enough of an escape. Even if I stand here longer. Crumbling into a heap.

I don't cry. I'm not a crier. Not really.

I breathe. Slowly and deeply, inhaling Irish-Spring-scented steam deep into my lungs and exhaling quivering breathes full of emotion on the verge of tears over and over until I don't hurt. Until the flashes of rendered flesh no longer invade my thoughts. And the fat man's barrel pointed at my face is just an active blur, like nudity censored on TV. Until I know I buried them.

The shower faucet squeaks as I turn off the water, sitting under the trickle until it stops, and then I sit a while longer.

My shower is done, but my nerves are still raw.

132

Droplets shake free of my hair making a trail as i head back into the locker room. i lose time in front my locker, slowly rebuilding myself.

KNOCK! KNOCK!

Feral stands in the entry as if nothing happened two days ago. Like I hadn't watched her turn men into barbacoa. How much it doesn't seem to bother her, bothers me.

"It's time," she says.

Getting dressed takes seconds. My all-black fatigues make me look like a scarecrow now. My hair is still wet when I put it up in a puff. Feral waits for me just outside. Feral and I always match, unless she's covered in blood.

Moments later, we're in Mr. Rhys' office. It's cold and still.

Chu, Feral, and I watch in silence as the man thinks quietly, and for a telepath, that's saying something.

"I don't answer to them," Mr. Rhys says finally. "But my options are to comply with interdepartmental Faction regulations or don't."

Right, The Faction branches. This was in my reading. Three Branches. Foreign, Domestic, and us, Special. Each responsible for a different theatre of war. Answering to no one and each other.

"That is correct. And it seems like Domestic has their eyes on you," he says.

Cool, now we know for sure who's after me. Even with everything I read, though, it doesn't really explain why I'm in danger if they are all the same organization. Or why they are after me.

"It's... complicated. And we don't know," Mr. Rhys answers. "Any more questions?"

"Yeah, those guys that attacked us were from my side of the window, right? How are they Domestic?" I ask.

"You don't understand rhetorical questions," Chu says.

"Domestic farms out some of their actions to human contractors. Usually for operations they want plausible deniability for. None of those guys were wearing patches or emblems, right?" Feral says.

I shake my head, and small drops of water spring free of my hair.

"Now you know why."

"If we can get back to the problem at hand?" Mr. Rhys cuts in.

"Oh, sorry, sir," I say.

"I don't enjoy being put in a corner, so in the spirit of insubordination, I've listed Cadet Kader in an active operation and have informed Domestic that I will make her available when it concludes. It gives us a couple weeks, a month at most, before that deception is rebuffed. But if I'm creative enough, she'll never see the inside of an interrogation room."

"And if you're not Picasso?" I ask.

"That comes down to you," Feral says.

"What do you mean?" I say, looking around.

Everyone seems to know what's going on. I don't like this feeling. From the time I was really small, I've been aware that people have people that are much closer to them than me. It's always been that way. Everyone else has siblings or preschool friends. I don't. I have Yesenia. Even she has cousins. I'm an outsider to almost everyone, I get that, but I hate being reminded of it. As I sit there watching what's unsaid bounce between the three of them, I remember this place is no different. That even here I'm an outsider, and it bugs me that I started to forget that.

"You can be out," Mr. Rhys says. "If you want to be. Right here. Right now. But we'd have to take special precautions."

"Is this the untell me part?" I ask.

Mr. Rhys shifts his weight as if talking about erasing people's minds bothers him. Why wouldn't it? A lifetime of experiences just gone in a flash. It's just like killing someone. And the way he avoids looking at me, it seems like he's killed a few people this way.

"We'd have to change your life," he says. "Your mother's life, too, since on their side you're still a minor. Even then, there's no way to guarantee you'd be safe. They'd be coming for you and you wouldn't even know why," Mr. Rhys says. "It's a big decision. I don't expect you to make it today. Though sooner would be better. The furthest this could possibly go is winter break."

"No," Feral says. "That's not the timeframe, sir. Three weeks to a month, you said it yourself."

Mr. Rhys looks lost for a second as his eyes land on me again after looking at Feral. He seems sad, and his posture slumps. It's like he tried to do me a kindness. " Right now, all we have to do is ensure that we have eyes on you. So—"

Mr. Rhys' door opens.

Monet walks in, and my worries leave the door she entered. I've never been so happy to see someone. Crap, she can hear this. Monet turns to me and, in her sort of edgy girl way, makes a face that's almost mocking me for being glad she's not dead.

Bitch.

How the hell is she walking around like two days after being shot?

<Arcs heal faster than non-combatants.> Both she and Mr. Rhys answer at the same time. Well, that made my head hurt.

"Workout ballon versus regular ballon, got it," I say.

Feral almost smirks.

Monet stands upright and salutes. My body feels like it's straining for the both of us. She wobbles slightly. I'm not imagining it. As soon as she walked in, I picked up her burden. How is she pushing through?

Monet only ever salutes Mr. Rhys. I know that's at least partially because it annoys him. He waves her off, and she relaxes. And I guess, so do I.

"As I was saying. Cadet Kader, we are extending your protection shift. This is an operational adjustment. We know who's after you now. So, while we gather info on why, we play keep-away."

"You're hiding me."

"Pretty much," Monet says.

"This will mean less time on the other side of the IMW. We are providing you with a cover legend to explain the extra hours." Mr. Rhys nods to Feral. She places a small black and silver duffle bag in front of me. Unzipping it, I find a letterman jacket—black felted chest part with gray sleeves and a badly sewn compass on the back that has almost pulled itself free.

"Wait, I'm on varsity?" I say.

"Yes."

"No one is going to believe I'm on a varsity sports team."

"It's not a sports team. It's Orienteering," Monet says.

"What the hell is that?"

"It's a year-round club with plenty of field trips, weird practices, and something no one wants to speculate," Monet says.

"Cool. Cool. Cool, but I meant, what does it like actually mean? Like what do you do?"

"Find your way," Feral answers.

"That's whack AF."

"You get to keep the jacket only if you keep the cover," Mr. Rhys says.

It's a bribe? They should've just said that.

"I trust you can sell this to anyone who asks," Mr. Rhys says.

I nod. "Oh, umm. Yes, sir."

"The rest of you, dismissed," Mr. Rhys says.

Everyone marches out. Mr. Rhys gets up from his chair, reminding me how tall he really is. He walks over to me and sits on the wood and glass table. Even sitting, I still have to look up at him.

"I know you've been hesitant to let them...us into your life. No one wants to be on display, but people are coming for you, and we haven't a clue why. Are you still adamant about not telling your mother?"

After hearing about the occupation and the sort of fear she has about Arcs... And nearly being killed by the exact circumstance she's scared of... Yeah, I'm more sure than ever .

"We operate differently than Foreign, but I understand," Mr. Rhys says.

"So you know who's after me, but what about my geiger problem?"

"Still working on it."

"My mom is the only person on her side of the family to ever step foot in America. So it'd be impossible for me to be an Arc from her side, right? Arcs originated here."

"You've been doing your own investigation?"

"Not really. She and I just talked."

"I see."

"So it has to be my dad. I've never looked for him, but I'm—"

"Cadet, trust me, we have people on it. We have bigger issues."

Mr. Rhys is a teacher through and through. He often says leading phrases to get you to think critically about what he's trying to communicate. Which I guess makes sense if this whole organization is about forward thinking.

After a few seconds, it comes to me.

"You can't shake your own people, can you? Our agreement was that you find out who's after me, why, and take care of them, but it's your own people, so that's not going to be easy, is it?"

"No. It's not." I appreciate that he doesn't lie to me, but it makes me worry that the day he does, I won't see it coming. Funny how that works.

"Do you think it's my geiger problem? Is that why they're after me?"

"If I had to guess, I'd say yes, but if they truly thought you were an Arc, they wouldn't have sent human tact teams."

"I mean, they sent a lot of dudes."

"They did."

For a second, it all plays again in my head. I remember the rooftop and blood and guys screaming as Feral tore them to pieces. Coming after me put them in jeopardy.

"The longer I take to make this decision, the more people are going to get hurt, aren't they?"

"People are going to get hurt regardless, but yes," Mr. Rhys says.

"I don't get why this is on me. Like, I'm fourteen and I have to make this big decision about going into the mind-wipe protection program or not."

For the second time now, Mr. Rhys looks as if he remembered something crucial. He has a thousand-yard stare that settles on me with hints of shock in his eyes.

"I'm so sorry I didn't fully explain the bind you're in. Statute 0104. Anyone who is able to set off a gieger and able to serve is legally responsible for their own actions unless under orders from a commanding officer."

"This is what you meant when you said I'm a minor on their side. You're saying that here I'm an adult, but in Blackburn, to the rest of the world, I'm still a kid, outwardly."

"Yes. This is why the decisions fall on you, Callisto. It's your life."

A light feeling wells in my chest, like a void growing. It forces tears out of my eyes. All this time I've been living my dream and didn't know it. But the high fades when I think about what I'm being asked: zap my mom's memories or bring her into the fold. Either way, her life is going to change, and it's going to be on me to do so.

Stuck between being a kid and an adult, so basically just a teenager.

"I never thought of it like that. For now, you just need to figure out balance. Like, are you going to be here? We're committed to you and will do whatever we can to help. Are you willing to do the same?"

"You're talking about the shelter?" I say.

"Yes, our extended protection detail is to keep you safe. So it's up to you: keep leaving early and putting yourself and your team and maybe your mother at risk..."

"Or end up probably sleeping in my car."

"Sucks," Mr. Rhys says.

He's right about that. I have a big decision to make. Do I stay or do I go? Mom and I. Her background with The Faction. She'd never accept that I was one of them. And I'm not, but I'm here and it's keeping her safe, but for how long?

"I'm not waiting for an answer. You can go as long as you understand," he says.

"I do."

"Also, Monet insisted I remind you to not slip your protection detail. Where you go, they go, understood?"

"Yes, sir."

The meeting with Mr. Rhys took all morning. Well, not really. I think there was some protocol being put in place so that I can come back to Blackburn for lunch, not that I really want to. After what Feral said about the mess hall, who the hell would? Not to mention that's the only place I sort of feel safe, ya know? Everywhere else I find myself constantly looking over my shoulder or replaying the bank situation in my head over and over again.

"Where'd you go?" Yesenia asks, touching my arm. I jump initially, but eventually my eyes focus on Yesenia across the lunch table, staring at me with worry and unflappable determination on her face. She has questions I don't feel like answering. I've been doing my best to ignore her, but without a phone, it's sorta hopeless.

"I'm here," I say.

It's not a good enough answer, and her eyes continue to bore into me.

"Are you still mad?" I ask, trying to break the tension.

"Cal, you still haven't said why you flaked and why the cops were there. Your mom was worried."

"Now, she's just pissed."

"She's probably both. They aren't mutually exclusive. Talk to me."

There's not much to say. On a fairly average day, I was nearly murdered, fought for my life, got one of my friends shot, partially because I was wearing her flak jacket. Oh, and then just minutes later, I had to act like everything was okay.

What do I say about that?

How do I explain to Yesenia that every time I close my eyes, I can see the barrel and the fat man? How do I convey to her I knew I was going to die and was even more sure of it when I saw Monet's blood on my hands? How do I tell her all of that and not tell her my secret? The secret that's keeping her and everyone else I love safe from a threat I now know is very real. How do I tell her that I have the chance to opt out now, but that would mean leaving her behind?

"Cal!" Yesenia chirps, prompting my eyes to shoot open.

I didn't realize I'd closed them. A tear squeezed itself out of the place where all my emotions are buried. It dribbles down my cheek, and I wipe it away as low-key as I can, but she's still staring right at me, caterpillars furrowed and focused, growing worried.

"I'm fine. I get enough of this from my mom," I whine.

"You're not." She takes my hand.

I realize too late it's an ambush... another one.

Between her cold slender fingers sits an old troll pencil topper. Its groovy tie-dye hair tickles my palm as I roll it over and look at its scuffed little nakedness. As unimpressive as it looks, this is the holy grail of our friendship. Her mom passed it to her, and somehow it became our thing. It's the thing we swear on. No lies, just truth.

Fuck.

Yesenia clicks on her phone for just a few seconds and shows me the time she sets. For forty-five seconds, I have to tell the absolute truth. Before I'm ready, she hits go and the countdown starts.

"What happened last weekend?" she asks again.

Problem with best friends, they know when you lie. They know how you lie. I won't get time to think.

"I got in trouble."

"No shit. Don't be vague. Tell me the truth. Where did you go?"

From the corner of my eye, I can feel Chu watching me. Great, more pressure. If I let anything slip, it gets reported immediately.

"I went to the bank to get the sodas," I say.

Not offering any more details only makes Yesenia angry and tells her I'm definitely hiding something, trying to run the time out.

"You're really going to make me ask everything?"

I do my playing stupid look. She gets angrier.

"Were you in the bank the entire time?" she asks.

Technically, I was in an insulated pocket dimension for most of it.

"No. I left and came back," I say.

"Why'd you leave?"

"Monet asked me to go somewhere with her."

"Was she with you the whole time?"

I nod.

"Chu?"

I shake my head.

If I said yes, she'd turn her ire on him, and I'm not sure he could withstand this.

"Were you there when the cops showed up?"

"Only for a minute. I came back just as they got there and I left."

Yesenia thinks.

"Where is Monet now? The three of you are a clique."

She should be here, but she's still getting treatment. Her show this morning in Mr. Rhys' office was just that, a show. She ripped her stitches and is now on bed rest.

"At home, sick," I say.

Yesenia's rapid-fire round is over. I know there's a question coming so perfectly crafted I can't maneuver out of it with vague sentences.

"Do you have my paper, Ms. Kader?" Mrs. Stephens asks, suddenly looming over us.

The time beeps. Oh, thank god.

"Your paper?" I say, unsure of how to answer.

"About your future," she says.

"Oh, you were serious about that?"

Mrs. Stephens sort of huffs, looking down her nose at me before turning to Chu.

"Young man, what is your name?" Mrs. Stephens asks.

"Chu," he says.

"We are not colleagues. You're a student. What's your last name?"

Chu looks at me, then back to her.

"Myung," he answers.

"Mr. Myung, you're aware we have a dress code. Correct?"

He nods.

"I can't hear your head."

"Yes, ma'am," he grumbles.

"Uniforms are more than just the clothes you wear, it's how you wear them. Go to the bathroom and make yourself presentable."

Again, Chu looks to me. This time it's more of a "follow me." I'm not to be left alone. Impending death and all.

"Your girlfriend isn't the authority here."

"Ew," I blurt. "Not my boyfriend."

Chu looks wounded. Saying with his body, "Was the 'ew' needed?"

Yes. Yes, it was.

"Go. She'll be here when you get back," Mrs. Stephens orders.

At least she hopes so. Chu must be thinking the same thing. He hesitates to leave. I know I've said it a lot in the past, but this time it's literal. I think this teacher is trying to kill me. She watches Chu go, then turns back to us.

"Is everything alright, ladies?" Mrs. Stephens asks.

"Yeah?" I answer before I realize Yesenia is staring at me again. Her face is red. She's mad, big mad. She snatches the pencil topper from me and marches out.

"Ms. Kader, it seems you have a knack for trouble," Mrs. Stephens says, leaving.

Chu enters seconds later. Yesenia must've just passed him.

"The principal sucks," Chu says.

"For once, we actually agree on something," I say.

"Eventually, your friend's going to come to her own conclusions," Chu says.

"As long as that conclusion isn't that I'm a teenage super-soldier, I think I'm good. In the scheme of things, it probably won't matter for much longer anyway."

Seriously, the world must be getting ready to end, because I swear for a second, Chu almost seems to take pity on me.

"Our window opens in ten. No block A classes until we've got this whole thing sorted."

"I know."

We gather our things and wander down the halls. A crowd of chatty assholes are practically posted up in front of our window. What's the point of vacant wings if they aren't going to be vacant? The last thing we need are rumors about him and me disappearing into a classroom together. So we loiter, like they do.

"Four minutes," he says.

"I'm aware. We should talk. It looks less suspicious," I say quietly.

Chu leans against the locker across from me. "You make my job harder."

"I'm getting that."

"You don't. I cannot mess this up. This is what I do. What my family has done for generations."

"I'm sorry I got Monet shot... I should be apologizing to her, not you."

"You should be apologizing to everyone. We were only in that situation because of you."

"Okay, hold up, I'd like to think the armed gunmen had something to do with it."

"You know what I mean. And you didn't get her shot. I did."

"How you figure that?"

"I read the ballistics report," he says. "It was a ricochet."

As the bell rings and the halls flood, we check opposite ends of the hall in sync. We open our classroom door and enter. The storage cabinet in the back leads to safety.

"How is a ricochet your fault?" I say.

"It was off me. We would've never been in that spot if it hadn't been for you. I wouldn't be making a horrible impression in a new Branch of people who already treat me like an outsider if it wasn't for you. So believe me when I say if you can't keep up, I'll do everything I can to make sure we drop you."

Chu marches off as the window closes behind us. "You know where to find her if you want to unburden yourself to someone who might care."

\#

On one of the upper floors in the main hall, there's a room where you can look down on the entire campus. We jokingly call it Monet's office, because whenever she gets a chance, she's here. A floor inhabited only by Monet. I always thought it was because you get the best glimpse of how expansive and eerily beautiful this world between worlds is—trapped between day and night. You can watch the black uniforms go to and fro, watch students and staff disappear into buildings and sometimes just flat-out disappear, but after our talk at the donation drive, I know it's more likely she comes here because it's quiet.

"A little column A. A little column B," she says as I enter the room that reeks of moth balls.

It looks like an abandoned room in a mansion, like there should be dust-covered sheets draped over furniture. Except there's no furniture, just Monet tucked in a corner, huddled over a notebook.

"This used to be Mr. Rhys' office. One day he just said he felt like he was getting out of touch with everyone and moved downstairs. But if was quiet enough for him, it's quiet enough for me," Monet says.

"I never really thought about that. What's your guys's, like, range?"

Monet puts down her pen and looks at me for a second, thinking.

"Telepaths lie," she says. "Arcs lie. No one wants you to know the upper limits of what they can do."

"Because an enemy can use it against them."

"You're learning. But..." Monet points to the barracks just outside the edge of campus. It's a dark gray brick building that vaguely looks like a home for bad British kids. The training room technically sits underneath it somehow. "Mr. Rhys has heard me from there. So that's what a couple miles? I'm not sure if that's just because of our abilities or what."

She's softer today. Exhausted. Her hair's mostly up in a messy bun, but strands of it are matted to her face. She's sweaty. It is hot in here. Really hot.

"Cadet, you're staring," she says.

"Sorry."

"I don't need you to apologize. For staring or the gunshot."

"You heard me?"

Monet glances up, as if to say, "didn't we just have this conversation?" I take a step towards the literal window where I can look to Fallen Hall, where my IMW usually lets out. I'd guess that's about three or four city blocks away. Is she implying she can hear that far?

"It's not really an implication."

"You make it hard to like you."

"Do you like me?" Monet asks suddenly, catching me off-guard. My face turns bright red, or it would if it weren't for all this melanin. She looks up, intently waiting on my answer.

"I... I..." I stammer. "As, like, a person?"

Monet laughs and winces immediately. I hate her. She does things just to make me flustered. *Ask me again and I'll say no, you suck as person.* I'm glad her bullet wound hurts. Right, the bullet wound. THE BULLET WOUND! Why isn't she on bed rest?

"No," she says fiercely from her cramped little position. "I'm not going to bed."

"Why is everything an argument with you?" I ask.

Monet doesn't answer, just keeps writing in her notebook. Great, she's ignoring me, but something about this feels wrong. One, she enjoys our power dynamic. Snapping me in half would be easy for her and she never passes up a chance to remind me of this. That includes never letting me stand over her like I'm doing right now. Two, Monet's always the first out of whatever uniform we're wearing. She prefers her own clothes whenever she can, which is a shame, because she looks damn good in a uniform.

"You know I can hear you," she says.

"Are you stuck?" I ask.

Exasperated, Monet puts her pen down and looks up at me. "Yes."

I almost laugh, because she totally doesn't want me to know.

"Here." I reach down and pull her to her feet. Not as gentle as I should, because she doubles over in pain, dropping her notebook. "Sorry. Sorry."

"It's fine, just, if you can help it, don't get shot."

"That's already high on my list. You've seen where I grew up. But thanks. If it were me instead of you—"

"Everything we're doing would be done. So shut up and forget about it."

"But I feel like I should make it up to you somehow."

Monet almost pouts like a little kid and looks away from me.

"There's one thing you could do."

"What is it?"

"So, I'm going to ask you to do something. The favor isn't you doing it. The favor is you never mentioning it happened ever again. Okay?"

"Um. Alright."

"Behind that door is a shower." Monet points. "It's why I came up here originally, but I can't get my freaking flak jacket off."

"Oh, I can—"

"If you mention that I asked you for help to anyone, I will literally kill you."

"Between you and Feral, I'm starting to think threatening a person's well-being is an Arc love language," I say.

"Yup, we're just one big traumatized family."

Monet, determined to make this as awkward as it can be, goes t-pose with her arms straight out. I can't help but laugh a little bit.

"Forget it."

"No, no. I'm doing it," I say.

I unzip the fatigue top, my face just inches away from hers. I've unzipped hundreds of dresses and tops; why does this feel so different? Why am I quivering? I'm light-headed around her. All I can smell is the sweetness of her breath, like cream and fruit. *Cal, get ahold of yourself, damn it.*

Her combat jacket falls to the floor, and I steady myself as I peel the flak jacket's Velcro apart.

"You don't like things to change. You like to hunker down and wait things out," Monet says. "This isn't the time to do that. Everything is about to get harder. So far, you've been doing this as school, but this is my life, and you're about to get a real glimpse of what it's like to truly be on this side."

"I'm here, ain't I? I think I made my decision."

RIPPPP! I pull the vest, and Monet rocks forward, bracing herself on my shoulders.

She's very strong, and very um close. I realize why I'm bracing her. She holds the gnarly blood-soaked bandage on her side. No doubt she ripped her stitches again.

Monet pulls my face back to hers and looks me directly in the eyes. "You should consider Mr. Rhys' offer more seriously. Don't look back. You don't have a reason to stay here other than you're stubborn."

"I can think of more than a few reasons to stay."

I look Monet in the eye. My heart hasn't beat this hard since I set off the first geiger. For seconds we stand there, frozen. It feels like a good long while. What is happening?

Finally, I say, "Do you want me to go?"

"That's your decision." Monet pulls away from me, ripping the rest of her flak jacket off and tossing it to the floor. Her bare back faces me as she pushes open the door hidden in the paneled wall. "If anyone asks, we never had this conversation." She vanishes on the other side.

For a moment I stand there, unsure of myself. How unnatural and weird I feel. *You hate her, right?* I say it but I don't believe it. I've yelled that with more conviction at bus drivers. As I head towards the door, I catch a stray thought.

<She doesn't see how much she matters. To everyone. To me.>

Chapter 14

Less time in Blackburn means more time in the Small World. If the other branch of The Faction is next door, it would seem like I'm closer to them, but as with everything in this cooky world, it's not that simple. Small Worlds are a series of gate-locked pocket dimensions stacked on one another. Also, it means more passive-aggressive texts from my mom like "Can you answer me? I have a lot to do today and I need to know where you are. I can't get my stuff done until I know when you are."

And: "How much does your little club cost?"

But my favorite one?

"You only joined this thing because I asked you to do something for me. It's selfish, Cal. I hope they have beds tonight."

Because the shitty situation we find myself in is entirely my fault, right? Like I made all the decisions.

"Follow me," Feral says, walking past me in the quad.

"It's my free period," I say, but Feral never stops to make sure you hear her. Her word is law and it's up to you to hear it or else. When she finally stops, we're in the locker rooms again.

"These are for you." Feral hands me workout clothes: all-black leggings and a sports bra with silver trim.

"Get changed. Meet me on the training floor," Feral says.

The training floor during free period is kind of a catch-all. People are in here doing any number of things from tumbling passes, assault and tactical moves, cover to cover or making out.

It's still a high school.

Today, there are a couple operators I've never seen doing what looks like rehab on injuries. They don't matter as much as Feral, who's standing there waiting for me. We don't match; her legging-sports-bra combo is an olive green. Against her tan skin it looks like jungle camouflage. I'm about to get my ass handed to me by a lethal influencer.

"I'm here," I say.

"It's your life. Today I'm going to teach you to defend it," she says.

"What's the point? There's like an eighty-percent chance that I don't make it out of this program with my memories intact, and most of that remaining twenty percent is the chance of me dying. Even that feels conservative."

"For one, we can't just have you sitting around moping, and two, my job is to keep you alive and ready. So if that day comes and you decide to flip that switch, so be it. Until then, put your hands up or I'm going to smack the hell out of you."

Immediately, my hands go up.

"Footwork. Balance. Technique. Proper technique keeps you from hurting yourself while you hurt others. Let's get started."

Little did I know that this was the beginning of how I would spend all my foreseeable free periods and sometimes after school: getting beaten up, almost exactly like middle school. We don't talk, but I don't mind. We spar, I lose, she instructs, we repeat. It's very hands-on learning. Dare I say I like it. I mean, being tossed on the ground over and over again, not so much. But I'm allowed to hit her if I ever make contact. A few days in and her combat drills are proving to be the source of all my bruising.

"Move your feet, Cadet," Feral barks on the training floor.

We've covered close quarter hand-to-hand a bit. Now we're on to grappling.

In a wrestling clinch, my head next to Feral's, my arm draped around her shoulder and back, I try to shove her, but she doesn't budge.

When fighting, there's this sort of carefree thing I really freaking appreciate, but I find freedom whenever it's socially acceptable for me to be a hot mess.

Our hair dangles in a stringy, matted mess, and we're both slick with sweat. Her muscles ripple as she stops me from gaining leverage. Our feet dance in circles as she tries to trip me. Feral pushes, but I dig in and stop her. As soon as her forward momentum stops, I'm looking at the ceiling as she tosses me over her hip, violently slamming me into the training floor with a loud THUD. All of her weight lands on me, pushing the air out of me quicker and bruising my tailbone. I yelp in pain.

"You good?" Feral asks.

"I'm good," I choke out in a pained voice.

"You swing like you aren't afraid to break your hand. That's good, but fighting is more than about your fists. Your center of gravity is also important. Feel your opponent out. It's not enough to react or anticipate what they are doing. Inform it," Feral says.

"Not sure how to do that," I say.

Feral sits next to me. "Why did you push against me?"

"To stop you from pushing me over."

"Was I really going to push you over, or did I just want you to push back so that..."

"...You could throw me on my ass," I say, after thinking about it for a second.

Feral nods.

"We're training so your body knows what to do, but that won't counter informed actions. It's the difference between being trained to fight and knowing how to fight. It's easier to make those choices before you get into a conflict. You have to make a decision or one will be made for you, both in life and in a fight."

"I get that, but—"

"Don't do that," Feral says.

"What?"

"Lie to yourself."

"I don't lie to myself. Really, I lie to others. But that's not what I was doing," I say.

"What you say matters," Feral says. "So if you're scared, it's okay to say that."

"I'm not scared of anything."

Feral sits indigenous style in front of me. She pats the ground, telling me to sit. I do. Her delicate eighteen-year-old girl hands start to carefully unwrap my own future killing instruments. Her Arc pushes claws out of the tips of her fingers like she's a giant house cat. Little slits on the tips of her finger tell the story of their change and the effects of it happening time and time again. It leaves a small scar that doesn't heal, which is saying something, because they heal from almost anything.

Without her Arc, her hands are incredibly normal: plain fingernails with knuckles covered in bruises that heal before my eyes. No callouses, no nicks, no other scars. These are hands that should get manicures or play sports or do dumb dances on social media. They should do anything, really, anything other than the thing I know they've done.

"You know why you keep seeing him?" Feral asks suddenly.

"Who?" I ask, playing dumb.

"We're going to act like you know my boss is a telepath who downloaded a mission report from your brain. We're going to act like you remember my nose can smell fear. And Cadet, you stink."

I'm just going to say it. Our relationship is weird. Anyone else telling me I stink would be in for an ass whipping, but she's earned my respect, fear, and endearment. I know she doesn't mean it meanly, just says it harsh enough to get me to focus on what she's saying. She only doles out affection, if you can call it that, at her liking.

Instead of giving her the Callisto special of lies and lashing out, I just ask, "Why do I keep seeing him?"

"It was your first conflict, and you almost died," Feral says gently.

"That's it?"

"Yup, it's as simple as that. Almost dying puts a point on things. Bringing other things into perspective."

"Like?"

"For you? If I had to guess... It's all the lies you tell people about why you don't try. You're starting to think they are true and that it's too late for you to make anything of yourself."

People telling me about myself bugs, especially when it may be true. Irrationally, I lash out. "No, you're scared."

I feel like a child. But Feral looks at me calmly.

"Very much so," she says with all-too-honest eyes. They border on lost, the way they did when she went, well, feral. I remember the rooftop and the classroom. Something snapped in her to make her perceive everything as a threat. Is that what she fears? Not being able to come back? Feral holds up her hands. All five fingers splayed out before me. She does the same card-dealer motion I saw Mr. Rhys do to her on the rooftop.

"What's this?" I ask.

"Blackjack hands," Feral answers. "You're getting better at fight training, and if I lose myself, this is your only chance at stopping me. It reminds me that you're not a threat."

"Ouch," I say.

"Don't take it personal. No one is really a threat to me." It sounds arrogant, but I know her well enough to know she doesn't mean it that way. It's just the truth. In a fight, there's very few people she can't take.

"Any other wisdom you want to pass along?" I ask.

"Everyone's waiting on you to make a decision, but no one's taught you how. No one ever teaches us."

"Oh, I, um—"

Feral spots Chu and Monet walking towards us on the training floor. "But that's for another day. Club Time." Feral takes the ball of tape that was just wrapped about my hands.

"I thought Orienteering was just a cover?" I say, flexing my hand and coaxing the blood back to my knuckles.

"It is, but it still needs to stand up to scrutiny," Monet answers. She's already stripped out of her uniform. We don't wear them much on this side. Her silky black hair flows freely like she couldn't be bothered to pull it back. In her all-black combat fatigues, she seemed more at home, but not necessarily more comfortable. She looks a little odd dressed for war with a lime green backpack strapped to her. It's the same one she used on the other side of the windows. No doubt it's used for all her Blackburn bullshit.

"Okay, so what do we do?" I ask.

Monet throws me a book. *Orienteering: The Sport of Navigating with Map & Compass.* There's some girl on the cover running through trees with a magnifying glass and a compass. If the inside is as dull as the outside, I'm going to take a nap.

"No, you're not. You're going to read that so you at least kind of know what you're talking about. I'll work on falsifying club activities."

"You said it wasn't a sport."

"Yeah, well, I also told you Arcs lie."

"What's he going to do?" I ask, pointing to Chu, who sometimes fades into the background if you're not looking directly at him. His fatigues fit like an itchy Easter suit. Just a general uncomfortable vibe from him.

"I don't care, but I also don't want to look for you if something comes up." Monet says

.

"Kahn's homework, tracing my bloodline," Chu answers.

"Ooh, can I do that instead? I need to do that." I'm not keen on spending time with Chu. Especially after his threats, but anything would be better than reading this damn book.

"I don't want the company," Chu says.

Monet doesn't say anything for a second.

"Monet?" I say, shaking her out of her own thousand-yard stare.

"Oh, you guys don't listen. I said I don't care. Just leave me out of it."

"Cool. Where do we start with that kind of research?" I ask.

Chu begins to answer, but his face falls flat when realizes he doesn't know. Both of us turn to Monet. She doesn't look up from the records she's already started falsifying.

"Fallen Hall. It houses the most detailed reports of all the branches," Monet says.

"Why is it called Special exactly? Like, I get the Domestic are like FBI cop people. And Foreign are soldiers, but Special?" I ask.

Monet wants to throw this question to Feral, but our squad leader, like most seniors, didn't want to sit around and listen to a bunch of freshmen squabble. She's incredibly quiet when she wants to sneak away.

"Special investigations. We track threats in the gray area. Ones that may start on homeland and go abroad or vice versa. We do a lot, actually. We have all the Arcs that don't fit neatly in the other boxes," Monet says.

"Because Arcs were divided by ability for the branch they best fit," I say.

"At first, Special was a recon unit, because we had all the fliers. Then a couple people who could teleport, so we became transport. Slowly, we evolved into support and intelligence. And intelligence keeps detailed records. The most detailed records." Monet points toward Fallen Hall with her pen.

"You sure you don't want to show us?" Chu asks.

"I'm not allowed," Monet answers.

I hate being in sync with Chu, but we share a dumbfounded look.

"It's how they keep their secrets, secret. Can't have a person like me in a room full of classified documents screaming their contents in my head. Now can I do this in peace, please?" Monet says.

I don't get what I mean to her. That's what she said, or, um, thought. What did she mean by that? She was very serious about never talking about that day either. She's been colder since too, or maybe just preoccupied?

A short walk later, Chu and I find ourselves in the mouth of the place that birthed all my current problems. The hall is where I talked to Chu's mom and we remarked about how the medals mark the sacrifice of soldiers. I wonder if she hated me then, given how I'm firmly on the other side of this Arc/Human thing.

"So I know why I'm here," I say. "But why are you? Don't you know your great-great-great-grandfather?"

"You heard Monet. Special's records are the most meticulous. In Domestic, all records are buried under miles of red tape. Here, it's a classroom assignment," Chu says.

I can tell when people are hiding something. This dude is saying a lot when he thinks he's saying nothing, and whatever it is, it's painful.

"You underestimate how difficult this is going to be. You have to account for an army base of people and then extrapolate their bloodlines and cross reference their abilities for seventy years."

Yet another reason why he's unlikeable. He's that "I know more than you" guy. Which sucks because we're in the Faction, the thing that's been his very life for all fourteen years. So on this side of the window, unfortunately, he does know more than me.

Behind the door waits a sanctuary to secrets. There's a reverence to this place that simply doesn't exist anywhere else. You can tell by how all the documents and books are perfectly tucked away in dark wooden cabinets with glass doors. Deep red carpet beneath our feet invokes this idea of blood in the soil, as if standing on hallowed ground built by my forefathers. Which is exactly what I'm here trying to figure out.

I look around, but there's no one to be seen. It's eerie how all it takes is a person to not be where they're supposed to be in a place like this and you suddenly feel like you're in a horror film.

"I'll check the stacks," Chu says.

I snap and finger-gun towards the viewing room. Thick, enveloping book musk makes this place my kind of vibe. Low-hanging chandeliers mimic the idea of candlelight. Each step barely makes a sound on the lush carpet. If there wasn't this inherent sense of taboo, this place would almost be cozy.

"Hello?" I call into the viewing room.

My words fade into the shadows. As I'm about to call out again, an old-timey radio voice booms from some unseen speaker.

"The Exodus Engine was a product of American ingenuity."

That... That was weird.

I push forward, guided only by touch as I trace the rows of bookshelves towards the only sound in here: frustrated groans as someone works.

"Hello?" I call again.

This time there's an answer. Sudden churning makes my heart jump a beat. The projector powers up, sounding like a small generator. It whirrs to life and casts an image over me. Pale silverly light bleeds into the stacks, illuminating the hints of titles.

On screen, Arc Walt Disney sits on the corner of his desk, puffing a skinny cigarette in his three-piece suit. Even though the images have faded and colors dulled, his eyes glisten a sharp blue. It's like he sees me and only me.

Why can't I look away?

Why would I want to?

His thin mustache curls around his lip as he sips his drink and smiles.

"The Exodus Engine is a product of American ingenuity. It was to be the first of its kind."

He puts out his cigarette and maneuvers around the office with a view of some sunny coasts.

"A research group found a way to power the future using a completely new discovery in thermodynamics. Scientists uncovered what they believe to be a previously undocumented form of energy known as Eileithyia. Named for the Greek goddess of birth, it was hoped that this would pave a path of unprecedented human progress and ingenuity. However, during their test, an exposure event occurred. The base, as well as a nearby town, were engulfed in Eileithyia. Not unlike the Chernobyl incident that would occur a little over fifty years later. Those who survived the exposure gained fantastical abilities and would come to be known as Archetypes, or Arcs for short. An ability is comprised of two things. The first: Eileithyia, atomic building blocks for energy, imbuing each cell with fantastic power. Second, and arguably, the more important, is known as a Life Echo. The founder developed the term to describe how one carries themselves or learns to carry themselves through life. It determines the technique during The Bloom and, in the early days, if you even survive ignition."

The film suddenly ends.

No! Where did he go?

Deep set panic sets in. My chest heaves, but I can't move. I stare at the blank screen until it finally goes dark.

"Can I help you, dear?" someone says.

Panic subsides. Slowly, I turn and focus on the tight-faced woman with dull eyes, slender with thin hair and blotchy skin. As she clicks the projector off, I can move again. It's weird. I check my hands and make sure I'm all there.

"It's the arc, dear. Try not to think about how it still works despite him being dead for fifty years."

"I wasn't going to, but now that you mention it..."

"You have a little something," she says, gesturing to her own lip.

I realize I'm drooling. Why am I drooling? How long have I been standing here?

"A hypnotism arc is better used for educational films than his other hobby," the lady says.

"His other hobby?" I ask.

She gives me a knowing look, one that sort of says all it needs to.

Oh, that's disturbing.

I check my hands again as blood seems to warm in them. It feels like I drank hot soup and it's flowing through my veins. I didn't even notice I was getting cold.

I look back, and the woman and her little book cart have disappeared. I follow the squeak of wheels that need to be greased.

"You're searching for bloodline records," the woman says.

"Yeah, Cadet Myung and I came here to track our family tree. He went to the—"

"I'm right here, Kader," he says, appearing from the other side of the stacks. "You found someone."

"Yeah, the librarian."

The woman puts the book down and stares at me with eyes glazed over with cataracts.

"I'm not a librarian. I am the Book Keeper," she says with wounded pride.

"Sorry. We're just trying to track our family tree," I say.

"Myung? Old family," she says.

The woman's hand glows a sickly green. The things that look like liver spots on her hand swell in the light's presence. The glow charges the gold-plated railing on the shelf but stops as she takes her hand off of it; it's as if she just remembered something.

"Myung's not a Special family," she says quietly to herself.

I know what she meant, but the way she said it was kneecapping. Chu's hopes deflate a little bit.

"And you're exempt," the woman says, turning her glassy gaze to me.

"From?"

"Kahn's assignment."

"Oh, no one told me," I say.

"I need an explanation," Chu cuts in. "Why can't I see my records?!"

His tone doesn't offend her. I know the look on her face; it's disgust and terror. She looks at him, then past him, in the distance. Following her gaze, though, there's nothing there but stacks. She cocks her head back to him.

"You know why."

"That shouldn't matter. I'm here. I'm in Special."

"That remains to be seen, but what you're asking about is a war matter, and there's only one person to talk to about a war matter," she says with a solemn gulp, again glancing in the distance.

Chu fumes.

I don't like Chu, but watching his hopes crash and burn isn't satisfying. Weirdly, I feel bad for the dude, like there was a lot more than just answers to a class assignment riding on what he would find.

"Look, lady," I start, but Chu stops me.

"I don't need you to fight my battles," he says and storms off.

Glancing at the old woman, I somehow missed that the sickly energy she charged in her hand was still there. She's holding it. Her muscles ever so tense. As calm as she looks, she's prepared for a fight. A fight with us. From everything I've seen, they really care about their history. I can only imagine what kind of monster they have guarding the records.

"I think you have somewhere to be, young lady." Her tone invites me to leave.

Does she know something I don't? Dumb question. What does she know that I don't? Back on the training floor, Monet's already done.

"I was hoping I'd have more time to myself." She sighs, upset.

"Where's Chu?" I ask.

"He was with you."

"Yeah, but the lady wouldn't give us our records, and he got upset and stormed out."

"That's annoying," Monet says.

"Tell me about it. I mean, I was made exempt, which I don't mind, but I don't understand why I wasn't told. Or why Chu wasn't given his. He's been in The Faction all his life. She said it was a war time matter."

"Our history is long. There's still a lot about us you don't understand," Monet says gravely.

She has answers that she's not sharing. That bugs. Feral was right about me not knowing how to make a decision. In order to do that, I need all the facts, and clearly Monet is right. I still don't know a lot.

CHAPTER 15

Staring straight ahead, we wait on line for Feral. Operators run drills all over the training floor. Half the time it's full of grunts, thuds, and muffled gunfire. It smells wet, like dusty pavement and hay, strangely enough.

Feral marches in quickly, not slowing down at all.

"Follow me," she says.

We do as we're told.

Are we doing the Room again? That would suck. I'm too tired to do any critical thinking today.

Feral whips open a door just off the main room. Inside sits a partition and, on the far side of it, targets. It's obvious enough what this place is, but the gun locker next to us might as well be a billboard. This is the shooting range.

Feral stops and salutes a heavy-set, jolly-looking son of a gun. In any other school, he'd be the shop teacher for sure. He greets her with a warm smile that shakes free bits of metal shavings from his graying beard. "This is Gunnery Chief Black Box. You will call him Mr. Davies," Feral says.

"These are your pups?" Mr. Davies says with a chuckle, his voice gruff and manly. "I expected more. Anyway, like she said, I'm Gunnery Chief. This makes me responsible for all equipment you take in the field, including your load-outs and special equipment. Today we're only worried about the basics."

Mr. Davies walks over to the gun safe and draws out two weapons. The pistol looks like a bee in mid-sting. The rifle vaguely resembles a bird in mid-dive.

"Your standard Hawk and Hornet," Mr. Davies says. "Faction caliber, standard twenty-eight and eleven count mags, respectively." He unloads the weapons, then reloads them.

"Our mission system is based on the primary munition used for a mission qualification. First, we have blue clips," Mr. Davies continues. He gestures to the blue light emanating from where the bullets go in. "These missions will make up a majority of your freshman and sophomore field ops. Things like evacuations, crowd control, babysitting non-mission-critical sites, goodwill missions, maybe some light escort duty. Stasis rounds. The non-lethal option. Hurts like hell. Can simulate complete biological shutdown. On to red."

Biological shutdown? He means death.

A high-pitched whine interrupts that terrifying thought. With a click, the blue light turns red.

"Red clips are Arc standard issue AP rounds. The light itself is a deterrent to anyone who may have negative aspirations, known colloquially in some areas of the world as the pistola de sangre. Blood gun. Missions where deadly force is authorized. Even if it is authorized, it should not be your go-to first option. Don't kill unless you have to. These are missions where if it comes down to your life, the life of your principal versus a combatant or mission failure, you should walk out of there alive. In order to pass this period each of you must complete the marksmanship certification. Only then will you be issued your own personal firearm. That requires a thousand hours of range time. It's noon now. At the end of today, you will have exactly 996 hours left. Any questions?"

Great, more homework.

"Fantastic," Mr. Davies says, barely waiting for a response. "Now, let's cover weapon safety and etiquette."

Nearly four boring-ass hours later, we finally are placed behind a weapon. It's all bolted down. We couldn't even move it if we wanted to.

Cadet Myung is first and, as expected, he's an excellent shot. Each round sounds like thunder and makes me jump. Even with earplugs in, my ears ring. Being this close to gunfire makes me. Occasionally at night, I hear them going off in the distance. Every shot makes the room smell more and more like burnt steak. So with every shot, I breathe a little heavier.

"Looks like Domestic did something right when they taught you to shoot, kid," Mr. Davies says.

Chu smirks proudly, looking at his target read-out on the monitor.

Am I tripping or was that kind of dickish thing to say?

It's Monet's turn, and surprise surprise, she's good at this too. Though most of the time I get the sense that she's easily distracted, today her only focus is on the crosshairs.

"Cadet Kader, you're up," Mr. Davies says.

Before I can even look at Feral, she speaks. "You're here. You shoot."

I gulp down fear in exchange for courage. Fixing myself behind the Hawk, I press my glasses into the scope. The target is nothing impressive, just zones marked out on a slab of what looks like concrete.

"Remember to squeeze, not pull," Mr. Davies says.

BLAM! The rifle recoil jams into my shoulder and hurts like a bitch. Worse, I barely wing my target. I feel a jolt of adrenaline through my body. I both love and hate it. Violent mania courses through me. The muffled gunshot through earmuffs is still a near-deafening pop.

"Your stance is too narrow. We're defensive shooting, not hunting," Mr. Davies says, his voice barely above the tinny ringing in my ear. I fire again, still missing.

Cadet Myung snickers.

Mr. Davies walks over to me and holds out his hand. I look at him, confused, before he gestures to the glasses on my face. I hand them to him.

"Put your eye on the scope and tell me when," he says.

At first, everything looks like a kaleidoscope of soft lines and tones of gray, but slowly everything becomes sharp and crisp. That's not a slab of concrete but some kind of bullet-monitoring motion computer. Sleek and silver.

"That's good," I say.

"Fire at will," he says.

The first shot misses left. I take a deep breath and focus solely on the target and breathing.

"Whenever you're ready," Mr. Davies says.

I get it!

Staring through the scope, preparing myself for the pop, and focusing on the target. It goes blurry again. I adjust the scope, and it comes back into focus. For a second, I see myself instead of the target.

I pull away. Still huffing.

"Weapon free, Cadet," Mr. Davies says.

Screw it! I place my eye on the scope and fire.

BLAM!

Again and again and again. I keep doing the same thing, losing track of the munition. The weapon clicks when emptied.

"Release." Mr. Davies' command to back away from the weapon. I do. "Learn to count your shots."

"Oh, okay," I say.

"So what happened? You adjusted the scope again," Mr. Davies asks.

"It was in focus and then it wasn't. I don't know," I say.

Cadet Myung seems upset as Feral looks over to a monitor. It reminds me of bowling and how you can see scores. All three of ours sit there, but I have no clue what to make of it.

Mr. Davies looks over the target with Feral, and these two must talk regularly. There's a non-verbal communication between them.

"You do much shooting anywhere?" Mr. Davies asks.

"No, sir. That. That was my first time," I say.

"Maybe you're good for something after all," Feral says, showing me the target. There's one hole in it.

"I only hit once," I say.

"You were almost impressive," Monet remarks.

"No, Cadet," Feral corrects. "Every shot after your correction hit dead center. It didn't waiver. Even Kahn can't do that."

"Yeah, if we had you, maybe we wouldn't have had to recruit him," Mr. Davies says with a little disdain.

Oh, wow. I did a good thing? It feels conflicting since, ya know, the deadly machine there gives me the power to take away someone's life. I don't know if I'm ready for that, or if I'll ever be.

Mr. Davies studies the scope and my prescription. Something isn't making sense to him. I get that look a lot here.

"I've never seen an Arc who needs glasses, but since you have 'em, you might as well get this prescription updated," Mr. Davies says.

I can't afford that. Those frames and lenses are like eighteen months old. I have another six months before I can even think to talk to my mom about glasses.

As he holds the gun with his burly frame, I can't help but think of the bank again. My chest feels tight like I'm being squeezed. The sounds from a nearby range don't help. Each volley strangles me a little more. I do my best to hide the heaving.

I barely hear Mr. Davies say, "That's it for today. Remember, 996 hours left."

"Dismissed," Feral says.

I'm first out of the range. I can barely breathe. As I walk past the other ranges, I realize they are empty. The sound of gunfire echoes solely to me. We're done for today.

My bus stops with a hiss.

"Broadway and Clayton," an automated voice chimes. Stepping off the bus, I'm greeted by the crunch of leaves. Apparently, it was too much to ask for IMW access closer to my house to save bus fare.

Days are shorter during fall. It's almost dark already. A bitey breeze sweeps through the streets, carrying the pretty great smell of recent rain, stirring trash and leaves. It would cut through me if it weren't for a hoody and the letterman jacket.

Pulling my bribe closed, I march through the battleground of city budgets—a neighborhood torn between new construction and houses as old as the city. I can't tell which side is winning.

Someone somewhere is using a leaf blower, and there always seems to be a trash truck backing up, but despite the noise of people, there aren't many to be seen. They hide away in their homes, out of sight as if they know something I don't, but at this point, who doesn't?

The shelter sits on this side of the line that separates the good community from the bad, making it just like every other part of my life: unpredictable.

Staring at the geiger as if it may bless me with answers, I walk through the sliding doors, and Mom barely notices. She's already doing "career development." Which is code for visiting with Mrs. Cooper until they open beds.

Shelter serves as a soup kitchen for dinner. It shuts down about an hour or so before beds open. Usually, there are a few people here, but tonight, it's already almost full. It'll be nearly impossible to get a bed.

Feral's training sessions have transformed my body into ninety-percent bruises. Hiding the marks up and down my legs takes priority over moving without a Charlie Horse. One's definitely easier to explain than the other. Perched on a chair, I rest my head on my knees, a big hoody draped over me like a portable blanket.

"Start your homework," Mom says, still pissed at me.

It's been a couple of weeks and she's still mad, barely speaking to me. It's my own fault, though. In a very short amount of time, I got into a fight and went missing twice. Not to mention losing a very expensive phone she had to replace. In a perfect world, I'd spread out how much trouble I cause.

My mom watches me like she's trying to solve a puzzle. After being a bit of creeper, she finally asks, "Girl, whose jacket are you wearing?"

"Mine," I answer sheepishly.

I've had the jacket for a little while, but only recently has it been cold enough to wear it. I told Mom, but apparently not listening is hereditary.

"You really on a team?"

"Yes, Mom. I'm a varsity alternate for the Orienteering team."

Mom looks down her nose at me as if she knows I'm lying. I mean, I am, but she doesn't, like, really know that. No wonder she's mad at me. She thinks I'm just being a shitty kid who doesn't want to hang out at the shelter. Which is all true, but I have a reason.

"So what's going on between you and Yesenia?"

"Nothing. We're fine?"

"You sure? Her dad says ya'll ain't talking."

"No, it's school and—"

Now that Mom mentions it, she and I haven't talked in a while. Not since that day in the cafeteria. Was it really that big a deal?

Mom must've seen the "oh snap" look on my face, because she says, "Don't forget who your people are. And do your homework."

"Ma, I'm hungry."

"There's soup."

Soup isn't food. So, I guess I'll starve.

My hunger drives me towards irrational rage. As my stomach gurgles, my face twists into a frown. In my chair, I angrily type and delete half a dozen messages to Yesenia, unsure of what to say. It feels forced, and that's new for us. I'm trying not to direct my anger for my mom or from hunger towards her. Mostly, I'm frustrated. Yes, part of that is Yesenia, but I guess most of it is Monet. We've been weird since that day in her office. We barely speak, and I can't get over the thought I heard from her. I mean something to her. Which is great, I think, but all the secrets bug me. Still, when I close my eyes, all I see are hers.

UGH! Why am I like this? Why is this coming up now? Why are all my thoughts invasive? If it's not nearly dying... It's her.

Everything's so weird now. Is this a crush? Why do people make it seem like this is great. This sucks. Usually, when something as big as this happens, Yesenia'd be the first person I'd text, but I guess things are a little different now. I have so much to worry about that crushes and friends and everything that my life used to revolve around just seems small. I'm supposed to be making the decision and that timeframe is almost up. If I have to say goodbye to Yesenia, it should be on the best terms possible. We won't remember it, but it matters to me. If these are the last days of Callisto Kader, I should be the best friend I can to Yesenia Barros.

"You were right, and I hate you for it," I text, waiting for her response while taking in the depressing cast of characters at the shelter. A few of the more well-to-do homeless, if that's even a thing, wait here in the open mingling section. We've become regulars here, sad to say, so there's some I recognize, a lot I don't.

"Thigh contusion. Wrap with a wet bandage. Frequently ice the injury for ten to thirty minutes," a man mutters, staring at my leg. His hands grip the wheelchair as if not by choice.

I pull down my hoody enough to cover the bruise peeking out from underneath, but he continues to mutter to himself. Gray, thinned hair, drool hanging thick off his crusted lips. His eyes glazed over.

"Sorry," one attendant says. "Doc is still diagnosing people."

"Wait, he's really a doctor?" I ask.

"He was, but he lost everything when the market crashed. One diabetic coma later, he's here."

As she rolls him away in a wheelchair, he continues to mutter diagnoses to himself.

Some people refuse to come off the streets unless it's the direst situations. No one trusts this place, but with tonight allegedly being the coldest on record, I can't blame them either way they decide. A bunch of people who no longer fit anywhere but here. A few guys off their meds, the drug addled, the abandoned, the convicts, and the fleeing abused all huddle here hoping not to freeze. We're all just broken people in a broken place. It makes sense I call this home.

More attendants and more security help for peace of mind, I guess.

"Turn it up," the soul-patch goatee security guard says as everyone fixates on the television, even my mom.

Peeking over the heads of kids who are somehow shorter than me, I watch a camera focus on drones hovering over foreign skies. There's enough of them to be alarming. From a distance, they could be mistaken for a flock of birds. A really menacing flock of birds.

The anchor on the news speaks, doing their "this is serious and be scared" voice. "Mysterious drones have continued popping up all over the world, surveilling top priority targets in Nagpur, India; Dar es Salaam, Tanzania; Taichung, Taiwan; Lima, Peru; and Bucharest, Romania. They hover for exactly seventeen minutes before dispersing and reappearing days later. Authorities will not confirm if this is an attack or a prank, but they have roped Arc leadership in to aid with the investigation."

"Easy to rope you in when you're part of the problem," one regular says. He lives in his corps jacket. It's soiled from nights on the street and sizes too big, telling the story of the man he used to be. His body withered and hardened, his eyes wide and manic.

"Dad," Dick-Head Dylan whispers, nudging soul-patch security guard towards the guy.

"They ruined my life. Out here!" the regular continues.

His yelling woke up Poppy, but as just as the whining starts, Grand-dad is on top of it, grimy face and all.

Soul-patch kneels next to the veteran guy. "You and I both know that's true, but I'ma need you to keep your cool, soldier. We can't have these civies getting up in arms. Understood?"

The regular mutters to himself and begrudgingly salutes.

Wait, did Dylan say "Dad?"

...

...

DICK-HEAD DAD!

It shouldn't have taken me that long to think of. He seems like the type to blame everything on Arcs, but in this case, at least, he's not wrong. Mr. Rhys did say he was going to get creative. It's a daunting sign for me, because it means I'm almost at the end of my rope.

"We will monitor the situation and have updates on the hour," the anchor says.

"If it's not them, why don't we as people get to know what they look like?" the regular says.

Funny enough, I had to study exactly this for Arc government exam earlier.

After World War II, Arcs wanted their independence and realized that it would come with reprisals and no true equality, so they arranged for anonymity as well.

"I usually am, but about what?" Yesenia texts back finally.

For a little while, even texting is like I'm firmly back in my old life. She's bitter about the radio silence—I can feel it, but she never says anything. Partially I think me admitting to liking someone distracted her from that. It's nice just to talk about something that doesn't have a real possibility of death or a decision. Her advice is all bad though. Send her a text or let Yesenia be my wingman again. Put moves on her. For one, I don't have moves to put on anyone. I kinda want this to not be a thing.

Mom knocks my feet to the floor. I nearly drop my replacement phone.

"Get your feet off the people chair," Mom says.

I roll my eyes. If it had been anyone else...

"Come with me. I want to show you something. Bring your stuff," Mom says.

"But beds are about to open."

"Hush and follow me," Mom says.

Snatching all my worldly possessions up, I stomp after her.

Mom leads me away from the crowds of people to a hallway. I've never been over here, because in this building I only go where I need to and this hallway, last time I walked by, wasn't built.

This wing of the building is all new and attached to the former club. You can feel how the sound changes as you move seamlessly from one building to the other. The shelter's coming together quickly, but not quick enough to have the elevators working yet.

Mom jogs up the stairs, oblivious to the amount of stadium stairs Feral had us run this morning and how close my legs are to seizing into a tight web of deadlock muscle tissue. I'm about to flip Mom off when she peers back at me to make sure I'm following.

"Use them young legs," she says.

Ugh.

Up the stairs and around a maze of narrow halls decorated with dollar-store art and off-white wall paint. The hardwood laminate floors creak under our feet.

Mom allows herself to smile as she unlocks one of the many pastel-green doors.

I peek inside at the very cozy bedroom with kitchenette. It's about the size of Mr. Rhys' office. I don't know if that means this is a small room or he has an enormous office. A door leads to what I assume is a bathroom. It's cheaply furnished, but everything looks nice. There's a bed and chair. Fixtures on the wall tell me the TV has yet to be mounted.

"What you think?" Mom asks.

If I'm being real, it's better than the last several places she and I have lived. For one, it has proper floors, insulation, and isn't on four wheels. I can only think about how cold the last place would've been tonight. It's enough to make me shiver. A giant south-facing window on a normal day would let in plenty of light. On a day like today, it's great for watching the gray clouds fade into a dark sky.

Paint and wood lingering in the air tell me they only recently finished this place. It beats the stench of dry rot any day.

"It's nice," I say, turning around, catching keys tossed at my face.

Mom gives me a look that she's slightly impressed.

"Keys?" I ask.

"While you been messing around, I've been handling business. This is our room. Perk of now working here," Mom says.

Having our own room with a locked door certainly feels like a step in the right direction. I'd be lying if I didn't say this feels a bit more permanent than I'd like, but we're here. Might as well make the most of it.

"Hold on, you work here now?"

"When this wing opens up, they are going to need resident advisors. I start training on Monday. Ms. Kim said it was speaking four languages that really put me over the top."

Okay, face, don't betray me. Be genuinely happy, or at least look it. My eyes go huge and I smile, then my voice jumps an octave or two as I say, "Oh, cool!" and go to hug her, but Mom stiff-arms me right on the tender spot on my forehead.

"You and I need to talk," Mom says sternly.

Right, having our own place also means the privacy for her to yell at me again.

"I know I work a lot, so you have freedom to get in trouble. I know I ask you to put up with more than a kid should, Cal, and I leave you to fend for yourself a lot. But that's all changing right here, right now. Do you understand me, Callisto Alexis Kader?"

"Why you out here sayin' my whole government name? Jeez."

"Little girl!" Mom yells.

"Yes, ma'am."

"So whenever you're done with your little club at school, you better come right here. If you're not, I'm busting ya behind."

Mom's threat isn't an idle one, but less scary after you've seen your squad leader turn half a dozen dudes into flank steak.

We don't carry much with us, so unpacking and making the room feel like home takes no time. Mom even decides to feed me. I watch as she sleeps. It's one more thing to feel bad about. She's trying to carve this whole new life for us, and I'm about to take it away. She's made so many decisions for the both of us and I can't even make one.

Being an adult sucks.

Chapter 16

—·—

New semester. Same shit. My deadline has long come and gone. Over the long break, it didn't seem like anyone was interested in hearing from me. No one pressed, so I didn't offer my input. Now that I'm back, everything around here feels busier. Frantic.

Dressed to the nines in a properly fitted uniform, I wait uncomfortably in front of the launch doors: giant bullet-dinged metal ones. Long benches, like you might find in lock-up, stretch across the entire wall. We're still in the dam, just another location, deeper. We're underground. You can sort of feel the world around you somehow. My foot jitters nonstop.

"I got you something," Monet says, nervously fishing around in a pocket of her flak jacket. Seconds later, she retrieves a delicate water lily pendant. It's silver and is immediately the nicest thing I own.

"For your birthday... and I guess Christmas," Monet says.

Downside of being born ten days before Christmas, that's not the first time I've heard that exact sentence. Winter break in the shelter was cold and lonely; most days I didn't leave the room. I was instructed not to. It wasn't the greatest birthday or Christmas. This makes up for it.

"Monet, thank you. I—"

"T-Minus sixty seconds!" Feral calls out.

"Not the best timing, I know. But this is a mission. Even if it is just a security sweep."

Sixty seconds till my first mission. Is this the decision that I didn't make?

"Don't overthink it," Monet says.

"Is seven of us going to be enough?" I stare down the line at Chu, Monet, Lockheed, who now has hair, Cabbage—that's officially his call sign—and a girl I've never seen before. She looks like a Slavic princess from a sad poem, huge blue eyes and hair of unsifted gold. I know her name is Avenoir, just the same way I knew Lockheed's call sign.

"We have two units and Feral. It's overkill for a security sweep. But it's baby's first official mission," Chu says.

"You guys have already seen action," Lockheed says with a hint of envy.

This isn't the same as some training exercise. We've done tons of those, and the last time I went into the field, well, it was more like the field came to me.

Mr. Davies enters, and everyone jumps to their feet and salutes.

"At ease. You're all fitted with Hawks and Hornets. We're undermanned, so you're going into the field prematurely. That being said, only one of you has put in the recommended hours to use them in the field."

Cabbage pats Lockheed on the back. Chu sours.

"Unless it's absolutely crucial," Mr. Davies continues, "do not take them out of their goddamn holsters."

"All three of them have call signs and he's already put in his range hours," Chu grumbles.

"They had more time than us. They started at the beginning of the semester. They're all from here. No one's migrating or been recruited," Monet says.

"Yeah." Chu walks away and stands at the door.

"I think that's his point. We don't belong here," I say.

"Let's freaking go!" Feral yells.

BRRRNNK! The rusty doors open just enough for a gust carrying the funk of mildew to sweep in and for us of all to pile through. Damp carpets beneath our boots squelch. We fan out, taking defensive positions in the office suite of a long-abandoned mall. Some of the grime-coated displays tell the story of what this place used to be: for lazy afternoons and last-minute gifts. It's outlived its purpose. I hope I'm not about to do the same.

Arc field trips are the best.

Feral's the last in. The IMW slams shut behind her. Her first glance is at Monet.

<Can everyone hear me?> Feral's voice comes through.

Lockheed and his group seem a little disoriented by a voice in their head. I guess we have a leg up there.

<This is one of our forward operating bases. Domestic's increased scrutiny puts places like this at risk. Any team we have to relocate that might use this place would be at risk. So

we're going to clear it. We are splitting into three teams. Lockheed, your unit will take the north wing and lower levels. Monet and I will coordinate and take east and half of south. Cadet Myung and Cadet Kader, west and the other half of south.>

The increased scrutiny is because of me. No one's said it, but it doesn't take a rocket scientist. Mr. Rhys listed me in an active operation and suddenly they go radio silent and all the bases like this one are being targeted.

"Neither of them have call signs. Are we sure they're up for this?" Lockheed says.

Chu and I both stop ourselves from punching him in the face. Not sure how I know that, but we both felt it.

"Don't ever question my order," Feral says.

"Yes, sir." Lockheed shrinks.

"And she'll be fine, Chu. There's no place safer than with me," Feral continues. <I hope the same goes for Kader.>

"Yes, sir."

We all split up.

Why am I stuck with Chu of all people? Why not Monet or even the Cabbage kid? Chu pushes past me, probably thinking the same thing. And I thought we were awkward at school.

Where TVs and monitors once hung, now only holes and jutting wires. Cables run the length of the hall, leading from nowhere to nowhere. And if you listen, you can hear water dripping off in some forgotten corner of the complex. I'm amazed that Special uses this place at all. What I saw the day I was recruited was nice and elegant. This forgotten dump is a shit hole. I'm surprised Mom isn't paying rent so we can squat on one of these office futons.

"So what exactly are we looking for?" I ask while we walk through the corridors.

<Sectors one through five clear,> Lockheed says our heads.

"It's just like our room clearing drills. Check for signs of people. Check for traps."

Yeah, we've done them a lot, and almost every time I've set off the trap.

"And try not to set off a trap if you find one," Chu chimes in.

Chu and I do our best to open tiny offices and check for lights and around corners. So far nothing, and it doesn't feel like we're going to find anything.

<Sector 6 and 7 Clear.> Lockheed again.

"He's trying really hard," I say.

"It's protocol," Chu says.

"Okay."

"Why are you still here?" Chu asks.

"We were ordered to go off together? I can't exactly leave."

"No. I meant about your choice. It seems obvious to me. You don't belong here."

He's totally a douche, but at least right now it's comforting that someone wants to talk about it.

"Look, I know you don't want me here."

"I don't, but that's not what I'm referring to. It takes hours to find out if you're an Arc, days if it's obscure. You've been here for a semester. You should've been out well before the ambush if you're not one of us. Even before Domestic had a good read on you," Chu says.

"I haven't heard anything other than your old Branch is after me," I say.

"Funny they want you but they didn't want me."

"What?" I ask.

"Nothing. Just, everything isn't what it seems here."

"Really? Like what?"

"I'm enough of an outsider as it is."

"You want to tell me what's up? Like, why you're a dick to me or why your old Faction didn't want you?"

"No," Chu says flatly.

"Do you want to maybe tell me why everyone around here treats you like an other, then?"

Chu's head snaps to me. It's like he had been invisible against his will and someone just acknowledged they can see him. He hangs his head and speaks low.

"That day in Fallen Hall made something really clear to me. It should've made something clear to you too."

"What's that?"

"Something's being kept from you. They know what you are. They don't want to tell you."

"I wasn't asking about me, I was asking about you. They wouldn't let you see yours either."

"It's not about me. It's about the organizations and who they are to each other. The thing no one is allowed to talk about. And about me? Everyone thinks I'm something I'm not, like I have some agenda more than just being a kid who didn't want to—" Chu stops himself suddenly as if what he was going to say next would break his heart. He murmurs, "Never mind."

<Nore's got something,> Lockheed says.

"Nore?" I ask.

"The girl," Chu says.

<Ow, shit,> Monet chimes in. <Brace for it, people. I've never done this.>

Suddenly, my head pounds like there's a railroad spike being driven through my eye socket. It takes everything I have not to scream. When I look up, there's two different images, one in each eye. Very clearly. I'm staring through someone elses pov—not Lockheed's, because I can see him holding the flashlight in this dark room. This must be Nore. In front of her, a sleek air-filter-looking thing, cylindrical and stout. Cabbage traces the power cord to the wall and points out how it branches to other parts of the complex.

<It looks like an improvised explosive. It was rigged not too long ago,> Nore says.

<How can you tell?> Feral asks.

<I don't know. It's something Cadet Kader is about to say.>

Something I'm about to say? What the hell is this girl's arc? Something behind Chu moves. No, someone.

<Kader?> Feral asks.

<Guys, we aren't alone.>

Corridors push into uniform darkness. We move in a straight line, guided by Chu's beacon. He holds up his fist, signaling a stop. Its glow ebbs softly like a firefly at night. A few seconds later, I stop next to him, laboring under fifteen pounds of gear. Extra mags, body armor, and an oversized helmet make me feel more like a pack mule than a soldier.

Chu peers around the corner, his eye fixed through the scope of his Hawk, pressing the butt of it against his shoulder, his finger hovering over the trigger. For moments we wait as he stares into the darkness.

<Monet, focus,> Feral says.

<Sorry. I've got it.>

<Repeat transmission.>

<I don't know who they are. But he jumped me. They're strong too. I hit him and he didn't go down. I think they're Arcs,> Chu says.

<Lockheed, get your team to the door. Secure it. This is still a blue clip mission, but if anyone who's not us comes near it, make them extinct.>

<Yes, sir,> Lockheed says.

Maybe it's imagined, but I swear I hear hesitancy in his thoughts. Why wouldn't there be? He's looked forward to this his entire life. There's probably some military superstition about your first mission going off without a hitch and what that means for your whole career. Then on his first outing a girl not much older than me just ordered him to be a very violent Hodor.

<Cadet Myung, Cadet Kader. Get to extraction,> Feral says.

<Yes, sir.>

<We're clear,> Chu says.

Then we're off again, racing through abandoned office suites—a place that's outlived its purpose. Wet musk lingers in the air with the echoes of our footsteps.

<Monet, get to the window. I'm going after them.>

<I'm not leaving her.>

<I'm ordering you.>

<And I'm superseding it,> Monet says.

"What do you think is going on there?" I ask.

"Huh? What are you talking about?" Chu says.

Did he not hear that? Did I imagine it? All this weight and momentum sends me flying forwards when my boots catch on torn carpet. My chin stops my fall, scraping along the subfloor. It hurts, but I don't have time for pain or embarrassment. I leap to my feet and fall in line. We exit one wing and enter another.

Bringing up the rear is easy when you're by far the slowest. Paranoia creeps up my spine, quickening my breath as I stare behind me into the inkiest of shadows at our six.

Not a problem for the assault leader. Chu clears rooms like a boss. His arc is like a tactical spotlight emitting from his hand as he swings his weapon. He's gotten proficient at using his ability.

Mr. Kahn thinks his talent comes from his eagerness alone. I don't think he's wrong. Dude is desperate to prove himself. Every waking moment that he's not with me or Monet, he's in the range, desperate to earn respect and a call sign. I, on the other hand, can barely hold a Hawk or Hornet without imagining being on the other side of one.

We duck down in the conference room, a place that's seen a firefight or two judging from the rounds lodged in the overturned conference table.

Good, a chance to get my second wind. Sweat drips down my forehead, irritating my already irritated eyes. Taking off my glasses, I wipe away sweat with my sleeve.

Chu barricades the rear entrance. One way out now. His beacon burrows through the darkness ahead, showing a path with treacherous edges.

"What's at the end of this hall?" Chu asks.

Next to me, a fire evacuation map is covered in soot and dirt. Not much information other than a layout.

"Any time now," Chu persists.

"It looks like a couple of stairways, the elevator bank, then an overpass and the east part of the complex," I say.

<You mean west,> Monet says.

"Uh," I stammer.

Chu looks at the map. "We've been going the wrong way."

"I've been following—"

Chu, annoyed, hushes me. He listens for a moment.

"Shit, thanks, Kader. We have to move."

He hears them before I do: enemy combatants.

We sprint, ill-fitting boots be damned. The conference room barricade does next to nothing as it explodes when the door opens. I open fire. The Hawk only looks like its namesake but sounds like thunder. I tell myself it's like paintball, but I've never played paintball. Each time I have to fire, that day I buried uncovers itself and becomes fresh again. Each time I'm forced to tuck it back into the place where I tuck all my worries to remain undealt with.

<Contact,> Lockheed says.

Suddenly, more pops in the night erupt from deeper in the complex. We're not the only ones in a fight for our lives. Who are these guys and why are they here?

<Be aware, the bridge is out ahead,> Monet calls.

I see it as she says it, a courtyard of glass and broken lights. Across the man-made canyon, another tunnel into darkness.

Chu runs to the edge of the bridge and leans over the side. <Over the side. I'll launch you. >

This maneuver sounds like a bad idea, but as I sprint towards him—my chest heaving and my muscles about to fail—and the broken bridge, I realize it's actually a horrible idea.

Leaping over the railing, I catch his waiting hand. Of everyone in our unit, he's by far the strongest and most physically gifted. Chu swings me with ease.

Between my heartbeat and the air rushing past my ears, I hear nothing. I focus on his grip and try to imagine that I'm just on a roller coaster. Yeah, that's it.

Suddenly, his body jerks. His grip lessens until his fingertips are a recent memory. For moments I'm suspended in mid-air and disbelief. Three stories high and floating. Nothing moves, but the world gets taller and the sinking feeling gets more profound. Past my stomach, creeping into my throat, then I stop abruptly with a thunk and the crunching of glass and metal as my body caves in the top of a car.

Impact forces me to exhale.

Everything goes numb, and there's a blanket ringing in my ears. My head feels like someone read the assembly instructions wrong. It needs more screws. Lying there for a moment, I take in all I can see with blurry vision. My glasses didn't make the trip down on my face.

I should be dead. Why am I not dead?

I watch Chu's blurry form repel off the side, haphazardly crashing and rolling.

"Get up!" he yells as more rounds pepper the ground around him. I roll off the car, and he slides into place next to me. Bullets tatter the car like violent hail.

"How are you not dead?" Chu asks.

<It's the compression suit she's wearing. Made special by Davies,> Monet answers.

<We're pinned down. And I'm hurt,> Chu thinks.

I look at his arm and realize he didn't drop me. He was shot. His arm slowly turns gray before my eyes. The color and life flowing out of it.

"What's happening to you?"

"Blue clip stasis round. We're definitely dealing with some of our own."

< Good,> Feral thinks.

On the other side of the car, we hear boots hit the ground.

"Reloading," one says.

From the tunnel in front of us, a full-on lion roar. Bassy and deep, rattling everything in me to the bone. I'm not going to lie, a little pee comes out. A blur parkours over us. I don't need to see it to know who it is.

Seconds later, Monet follows and trains her weapon on the fight, but she doesn't fire. It's already over.

Feral yanks me to my feet. I start blackjack handing immediately.

"I'm good," she says.

It's weird—this time she's not covered in blood. I don't know what's odder, the fact I was expecting it or the fact that it's not there. Feral looks over Chu, and the gray on his arm is spreading faster.

"Shit." Feral trains her eyes on me. "Listen, I need you to be here with me right now."

This is what I was afraid of. I was afraid of conflict. I was afraid of the orders. I was afraid of being indoctrinated into their club and what they may ask of me. But when I look in her face, I don't see anything but a friend, and everything else melts away.

"What do you need?" I ask.

Feral smiles. "Mission parameters have changed. Chu will be out of commission shortly. If that happens, leave him. His mission becomes your mission. Get Monet to safety."

"Wait, what?" Monet says.

"It's not Domestic. It's Foreign," Feral says. "It's Foreign."

The second time is said with more weight and understanding. Something invisible happens between them.

"Okay," Monet concedes.

I don't like Chu, even a little bit, but even I'm not okay leaving him behind.

"Get on your feet. Everyone is trying to leave you," I say.

Chu groans picking himself up. Monet hands me her Hawk. I am not a soldier, but I am a girl who will fight for her friends. I take the Hawk. I know better than to ask what Feral is going to do.

"The three of you take care of each other," Feral says.

We watch her change, incisors growing larger, what sounds like eggs slowly breaking. Her claws poke out the tips over her fingers, each one long and razor sharp. There's fur, but it's raised like a dog's hackles when they're about to attack. It's so light you can hardly tell. Both guys on the ground have been wrecked. Feral takes their weapons and heads into the tunnels on the opposite side.

For the first time, I notice it's night now. We haven't been here long, but wherever we are must be far enough north for the sun to have already set.

<Four minutes till window opens. Is anyone coming?> Lockheed calls.

<We're on our way,> Monet thinks.

I can't see really well, never found those glasses, but if it moves, I'm going to shoot it. This might make it easier for me.

Monet helps Chu along, listening for the signs of people coming or going. It's harder than you think. Most of the complex sounds like a safari gone wrong—roars, yelling, and gunfire.

"We're almost there," Monet says.

Chu leans on her for support. Most of his left side has gone numb already, but he keeps the eye that's still alert trained on the darkness in front of him.

The rear again is my duty, and I'm not playing; if it moves, I'm shooting.

<We're almost there,> Monet thinks.

As we near the window, it gets hotter. Much hotter and smellier. We duck behind a set of filing cabinets. Lockheed and his team are guarding the door from behind the desk. A majority of the room is clear, except for pillars and, behind those, enemies peeking out, taking pot shots. Getting across no man's land is going to suck.

The opposition just keeps firing as Lockheed shows impressive stamina by lighting as much as he can on fire. His legs are basically a flamethrower. This doesn't add up; we're fighting Arcs. So why aren't they using their arcs?

<Hiding their identity. They're not supposed to be here. If we ID them by their gifts, they'll be in serious trouble,> Monet thinks.

< So why is Lockheed being a flamethrower? We're not supposed to be here either.>

< He's dumb,> Chu thinks.

< Mission parameters state I have to use whatever means I have to secure this door, nameless,> Lockheed chimes in.

Nameless? Ooh, the karma of the guy who nearly outed me as Arc-less being similarly insulted is sweet, or it should be, but right now all I can think is *that's my teammate, asshole.*

<Where's Feral?> I ask.

<Don't worry about me. Get through that window...or I'm going to kick your ass.>

"Where's back-up? They're at the window," one of the guys call into his radio.

It blares to life a second later. "We need all available hands on our location now. It's Feral."

Spying around the corner, I watch the assault team look at each other with nothing but fear and indecision. Finally, something gives.

"Permission to go red, sir?" the guy asks.

Red? Shit.

Chu heard it too.

<Windows. Open,> Cabbage thinks.

"Get on her back," Chu demands to me.

"I'm not using her as a body shield," Monet says.

"I'm good with it. Can't have you taking two bullets for me."

It seems like a weird time to play horsey, but we do it.

<Fall back,> Monet thinks to Lockheed. <Cabbage, can we get a wall?>

Suddenly, there's a cabbage hedge. Something that will make you feel useless? Have the girl you like carry you like a backpack across a battlefield. She's faster and stronger than me, so I get it, but at the same time, it's very embarrassing.

We hear "go red" just as Cabbage's wall gets torn to tatters. Standing between us and them: Chu. Half of his body gray. He steps back as each bullet ricochets. I slam my eyes shut. Then I feel it again, this time brighter and more desperate. It's taking everything he has. Chu's light covers us. He lets the bullets push him back until they stop firing and all we can hear is their screams.

We stand on our side of the window. A dozen operators I've never seen have their weapons trained on our launch doors. Some of them have yanked and secured Lockheed's team already. Now they are separating and sequestering Monet, throwing me to the ground in the process. Chu collapses, finally giving in to the gray. One of the operators catches him; they aren't even worried about their hand burning. Just before Chu's eyes shut and the window closes, the most dreaded sound echoes from the complex.

A cat's swan song.

"She's down. She's down," their radios scream. Just as the window closes.

A short time later, Monet, Chu, and I are in the med-bay, a very sterile, all-white room lined with hidden cabinets. A place that smells like tongue depressors and antiseptics. My body tingles and reeks of Icy Hot. My chin scrape stings as the junior nursing assistant applies ointment. Her hair is pulled back in a dreaded ponytail and she has a nose ring.

"There you go," she says, placing a Band-aid on my chin. My reflection in the mirror is wild. Frizzy cornrows, soot-stained skin.

"I look like scamp."

"Yeah, you kinda do. But it's cute."

"Thanks, uhh..." I say, trying to drum up her name.

"Call signs only work when mission system is active. I'm Khadijah, a basic but all-around badass."

"Thanks, Khadijah."

She fist-bumps me and spins in her little stool to Chu, who lies nervously in a hospital bed.

"Now the real work begins," she says.

Graying skin on Chu's arm slowly eats its way towards the rest of him. His fingertips twitch as if the last bits of life are sputtering out.

"Turn away for me and tell me what you feel," Khadijah says.

Chu turns his head as the girl pokes his arm with her pen. Chu doesn't respond.

"Okay."

"Are you done?" he asks.

"Yeah." Her voice is flat as she goes to one of the hidden cabinets. She sets up an IV.

"What's in that exactly?" Chu asks.

"Epinephrine and stimulants. It'll shock your system and start reversing the stasis effects."

"I'm bullet resistant," Chu says, stumbling over his words.

"I know. I have your file," Khadijah answers. "Give me a second."

She searches through other bins and cabinets.

"What's your name?" he asks.

"Was you not listening?" she asks.

"Ears are gray."

Khadijah leans in close and says her name again, but in a whisper. Chu smirks.

"K-uh-D-EE-j-uh," Chu says.

"You got it."

That's some grade-A flirting. Who knew he had it in him? She attaches a booster, a sleek metal cylinder that reminds me of a fuel injector. I watch the girl load bullets in its chamber and sweetly look at Chu. She takes his hand. Monet covers her ears, so I do too.

Right as Khadijah is sure he's relaxed, she jabs him in the arm and fires. *BLAM!* Like a firecracker going off in the room. It smells like it too. When the smoke clears, a series of needles are wedged in his arm.

Chu's mouth falls open. He's in shock and trying not to admit it hurts so bad. You can see the tears in his eyes. Finally, he gasps for air like a bad kid who's been whipped and cried all the air out of their lungs.

"Sorry, but it had to be done," Dijah says. "When the IV is clear, you will be good to go. I'll leave you to it." She exits leaving the boy from a different branch, the special girl, and me, the girl who's not from this world— three little outcasts stew in silence.

"She's good at her job," Monet says. "For a minute you weren't even thinking about Feral."

"That's not true," I say.

Denial is what I do. It's not that I wasn't thinking about hearing her cries. I was trying not to think of them.

"I know," Monet says.

"No offense to anyone in this room. Or all offense to everyone in this room, I don't really give a damn. I just lost maybe the only friend I have here. I want to know what's going on."

"It's complicated," Monet says.

"That's not good enough," I respond.

"Soldiers lose people. It happens," Chu says.

"She's not an operator like you and me. As much as other people may have a problem with you being here, we were sworn into this. She is not. Our burdens aren't hers." Monet finally comes closer. She'd been moping on the other side of the room. Everyone here had a complicated relationship with our squad leader. Her and Monet seemed to argue more than talk and if she wasn't correcting Chu, she was ignoring him.

"Then what am I doing here?" I ask.

Monet looks at me as if I wasn't supposed to speak.

"This was supposed to be a couple weeks tops, and now I'm just here, and how do we fix this?" I ask again.

Neither of them have an answer; both just look at me, unsure of what to say.

"Why is Domestic after me and Foreign after you?!" I scream.

Monet again says nothing.

"This is bullshit. How can you expect me to make 'the decision' if I don't have all the facts?" I mutter.

Chu's eyes flutter as he has an epiphany. "She can't say anything. She's under orders."

"So you know, you just won't say." I'm getting angrier. At this point I can see them both clearly without my glasses, and I'm not sure how. Even through the tears, both of them might as well be in 4k.

"Can't say," Monet says.

"There's a cold war between branches," Chu blurts, but Monet covers his mouth.

"Never talk about it," Monet warns. "You don't know the rules here. Talking about it would be bad for all of us."

Monet turns to me with huge, sad overtaxed eyes. Slyly she takes my hand, and with it comes a jolt: a message.

<I swear to you. I will explain, but not here. Not now.>

Chu catches it. He tries to relax, but his arm is returning to color slower than it turned gray. Right now, it's just dead weight.

"What are we now? Without Feral?" Chu asks. "What are the two of you?"

Both Monet and I turn to look at him. I'm not that obvious, am I? Well, if I am, then why hasn't she said anything? She gave me a gift, but that doesn't help much. Why am just languishing in hell over where we stand? Before her I didn't even know I liked girls. I've had so much other shit to worry about in my life, including right now.

"We're all assignments to one another," I mutter angrily, plopping myself in a chair.

"She's right. And I think it may get us killed. We don't work well together at all." Monet sits on Chu's bed.

Chu's vitals ticking on a machine underline the dread and silence we all feel. Mr. Rhys is nowhere to be seen. No doubt losing Feral hurts him too.

"I'm the reason we went the wrong way. I should've chosen a route that didn't require throwing you across a chasm. That probably would've been a sounder plan."

I'm surprised Chu ever admits being at fault. He's usually Mister Perfect, or at least tries to be. His brief moment of humility, if you can call it that, is followed by him gesturing to us.

The floor is ours.

Monet never steps up first. This is pretty much saying it's my turn to go.

"I can't pull my weight, and that's before the gear and crap. No one taught me to read a map."

"You didn't read the orienteering book," Monet says.

"We all knew I wasn't going to read the damn book. Can you just let me finish?! Firing a Hawk is... difficult. When we're out there, it's obvious to me I'm out of my depth."

"Bingo," Chu says.

"Ya know there are other options than just always being a dick?"

"I should've known they were there," Monet confesses.

"What?" I ask.

"Everything is constantly pounding in my head. It's so much information. So many impressions. I should've been able to sift through it all and know from the minute we stepped in the building that we weren't safe. I'm the reason Feral is gone."

"You're not. Have you tried having a conversation in a high school cafeteria? You can hardly hear the person next to you. If your head is anything like that, I don't blame you."

"That's not good enough. We're not good enough," Monet says.

"So how do we get better?" I ask.

"All I'm hearing is that you're the problem." Chu points to Monet. She glares at him.

"What's he talking about?" I ask.

"You've already done the math. You've put two and two together. So just say it," Chu says.

"He's saying someone needs to take charge in the field and suggesting that it's me," Monet answers.

"I guess that makes sense," I say, trying to remember how we actually choose what we're doing when we're out there. Typically, it's one or both of them just yelling at me.

"I was sworn into service last semester," Chu says. "Kader hasn't been sworn in at all. And you took your vows when you were three. So would it make sense for Ms. Arc-less to lead us, me the bodyguard who takes all his cues from you, or—"

"Got it, now shut up," I say. "I nominate Monet to lead us in the field."

"Of course you do. It doesn't work like that, but hey, why not. I second the nomination," Chu says.

"Fine," Monet says.

"Wait, now that she's the leader, are you still going to undermine everything she says out there still?" I ask.

"Ooh, good question," Monet says, finally thawing a bit.

"You two are cute, but this is over now. I'm going to be on my way." He stands up and rips the IV out of his arm. "Don't forget what we talked about, Kader."

What we talked about? Right, on our assignment he claimed they know what I am and they're not telling me. Finding out there's a cold war and knowing there's something bigger out there potentially. In his own way, I feel like he's trying to say, *I know you like her, but don't trust her.*

"Had no idea that he was such an asshole," Monet says as she follows him.

"Truly an asshole, but he brings up some great points," I say to myself.

We're still not friends, but at least now we're a squad. We have to be.

CHAPTER 17

Flowers don't bloom in Small World. Still somehow you can still tell it's spring. Months have passed since Feral... um, yeah. No one seems to care that I haven't made my decision or that I don't belong here. And as dumb as it sounds, even if Feral's not here, I don't want to forget her, though it seems like everyone else already has. No more free periods. The quad is always empty now.

We're nearing the end of the school year. We hardly see the inside of a classroom these days. Readiness drills, patrols, and guard duty take precedence. All windows must be guarded, and every student must have a shift, no exception. Except Monet, who's rarely on guard duty with us. But since Monet and I are both targets, we are given less crucial infrastructural objectives. I know it's killing Chu that Lockheed is guarding Fallen Hall and he's stuck with me guarding the steeples of the Claremont Building.

What do these gods amongst men worship? Anything that any one of these people can do would be viewed as a miracle in most cultures. Maybe there is no Arc religion and the only reason for this place is the reason I'm guarding it. Maybe it's just a fallback shelter to be used as a field hospital and bunker for conscientious objectors in case of an attack. Though no one will acknowledge that there may be an attack. Because no one will talk about this cold war, which really sucks, because that's all I want to talk about.

"You good?" I ask.

"We still can't talk about it," Chu says standing next to me on the adjacent side of the door. We've been better since the n the med-bay. He's been nicer to me. We still don't talk much, but that works for us. There's less tension in it now.

"You've changed," I say.

"So have you. You kinda walk like her, ya know." Chu marches back and forth, mimicking the way Feral would walk onto the training floor. She did stomp a lot for someone who was supposed to be cat-like. I laugh, and it's good to laugh for once.

"Thanks for that. I appreciate it," I say.

"You two were close, and I know what it's like to lose a sister."

What? That's new. Suddenly, flashes of his mom and dad's pained, resolute salutes come to mind. I thought they were heartless the way the sent their child off to possibly die. Now I know they didn't have a choice; they'd just lost a child and had to send the other one to the same fate. It's really freaking sad.

"Blackburn has spring formal coming up soon," Chu says, wanting to change the subject, before I offer him a thousand condolences I'm sure he's already heard.

"Yeah. Wait, you're not asking me, are you?" I say.

"Hell no! But I was thinking about maybe asking Khadijah."

"She's too cool for you. And is that even allowed? Her going to that side?"

"I wasn't thinking about that. I just thought…"

"You want to go on a date with a pretty girl." I laugh.

"Yeah, I was hoping you could help me."

"Me?"

"Yeah, you're good at lying. You could say we need extra bodies on your security detail or something."

"Bold of you to assume I'm going."

Yesenia would kill me if Chu showed up with someone else—not that she and I have had a chance to talk much recently. We text, but it's not the same.

"If you ask Monet, she'll probably say yes. Hell, you don't even have to ask her. Just tell her you're going and she has to come," Chu says.

"Forcing someone on a date with you feels sorta wrong? And if I'm being honest, I think you were right. I think she's keeping something from us."

"Something like?"

"What does it mean to supersede an order?"

"Someone gives an order, but you outrank them. It almost never happens."

"Huh, weird."

"Why?"

"Something I either imagined or overhead," I say.

<Facing an oppositional force starts long before any blood is shed on a battlefield.>

"Ahh!" I yelp, surprised by the voice suddenly playing in my head.

Mr. Rhys' telepathic lectures can reach us anywhere in Small World. Why go to class when the class can come to us?

<Planning for a conflict and the means to which you reach your desired outcome is a strategy. The individual steps, the decisions on how you go about executing all of this, those are your tactics. Good decisions are the basis of everything that follows. Who you choose to bring into your infantry to the dignitaries you have lunch with. This class is about deciding,> Mr. Rhys' voice says, prompting me to enter the class. His thoughts stop and his voice takes over as the door opens.

That's a little passive aggressive, but okay. Mr. Rhys is easy enough to tune out. The rest of the lecture plays in the recesses of my mind, like an annoying pop song with a catchy hook.

"Relief is here," Chu says, pointing to the unit walking down the path.

I don't know them. The mission system isn't up, so their names don't feel the gaps in our minds, but they look like jocks. Which is saying something in a school full of super-soldiers.

"Let's go," Chu says.

We wave, but they don't wave back; they just keep talking to one another, not acknowledging we even exist. Whatever. One of the guys shoulder-checks me, hard. If the ground weren't so soft, I'd have a bruise on my ass. I'm about to break my hand on his face when Chu beats me to it. He clears the first guy with ease. But we're outnumbered because they actually have a third. Oh, never mind, first guy is stirring, but he's not getting up. I jump to my feet, and Chu and I prepare to take on the two remaining ass clowns.

"Nameless and an Arc-less. Light work," the kid says.

What did he just say? My eyes bug out. Chu's do too. Shit.

"What did you just say?" Monet comes up behind us.

There's fear in their eyes. Real fear. The "they know something about her we don't" kind of fear.

"Nothing. Just..."

No point in trying to lie. Monet sees something in them. She looks at the two of them, then the one on the ground. She turns to campus with the end of the world movie look. You know the one, where the hero sees a giant tidal wave bearing down.

"Shit," Monet says. <Mr. Rhys, her cover is blown. Everyone knows. How do we proceed?>

<So by extension, it's a class about life,> Mr. Rhys says, still droning on in his lecture. There's a moment of silence.

<Get her off campus. We'll trace the leak and see if it's linked to our other problem later. She's not safe, especially where you are right now.>

Monet looks back at the Claremont Building ominously. I don't know if I was supposed to hear any of that, so I keep my trap shut.

"You have peer mediation. We need to change. Chu, grab our go-bags," Monet orders.

We sprint to the women's locker room and change quick. Monet is nearly panicked. I've never seen her so shaken. Something is up.

"Are we going to get in trouble for the fight?" I ask.

"What? No."

Chu meets us at Fallen Hall with a pair of duffle bags. His uniform is sloppy as usual.

A drab classroom waits for us. It's like walking out of Oz back into Kansas. Everything is sorta painfully dull.

"Let us handle this. You need to go be a student. Do peer mediation. It'll wait till you're done," Monet says.

My normal life is calling.

Once a week I get to sit across from cornrows and an attitude. No, I'm not looking in a mirror, unless it's a funhouse one that made me much taller, much lighter, and chapped my lips. Maybe I'm being the asshole. I mean, Chu and I didn't get along, but we found common ground.

Alani and I are the same, grew up in the same area, go to the same schools. Surely there's something redeemable about her. Right?

On cue, she gives me a hood girl scoff.

Never mind. Dirty-faced girl.

A room in this forgotten wing of Blackburn that smells of chalk and Doritos, pockets of others troubled kids also sit around tables. Each of us no doubt looking like delinquents. All we need is that strict teacher from a different walk of life to set us on the straight and narrow. That isn't by any stretch of the imagination Mrs. Stephens, who oversees everything. With this many kids beefing, it's hard to believe that Alani and I are the only ones who've come to blows.

Zero tolerance, my ass.

We sit in a circle around the table like it's a campfire. Yesenia sits on one side, the mediator on the other, and across the table sits Alani. Excellent choice. With all the things currently going on in my life, this is the last place I want to be.

Monet and The Faction are definitely keeping something from me. My secret's out on that side, and I'm not even sure what that means, really. Feral's gone, and Chu's the closest thing I have to an ally.

Monet's conversation with Feral in the mall forwarding base plays over and over in my head. She superseded the order. There's also Mr. Rhys telling her to get me out. And in Fallen Hall that day, the Book Keeper's look of fear. Is it Mr. Rhys she fears? How much more don't I know?

The mediator's stuttering interrupts my slow swirl down the drain. "A...a...as a reminder, we have all agreed to the rules of engagement here. That means no cursing and no threats."

What? When did we agree to that? That's like ninety percent of my personality.

"Yesenia is here today since she's a trigger for the conflict and we can get her take on what happened."

"How's that fair?" Alani bleats. "They lovers."

"We really aren't," Yesenia says.

"Mm-hmm. Does she know that?" Alani says, gesturing to me with her big-ass head.

"So, Callisto," the mediator starts, fumbling over her notes. She's flop-sweat nervous.

Alani chews on her lip. The usual sign that she's about to say something off the cuff. Her stink eye eggs the mediator to hurry, which only makes her stumble more.

And yes, it sucks, and I feel bad for the girl, but on the other hand, this is what Alani does. If I just stay composed, everyone can see she's the worst human ever and maybe, just maybe, people will realize I'm not the bad guy here.

Yesenia reaches over to our mediator. "Desirae, it's okay."

The girl takes another breath and starts again.

"Callisto, you started the fight. What problems do you have with Alani?"

My first instinct is to call her a bitch, but the no-cursing rule. So I think again with clarity. We keep rehashing this day and our conflict without ever gettign to the heart of it.

"For the record," I start, "I think this is dumb. Alani spent all of middle school talking smack about me. Cool. I ignore it. Be the bigger person. Even when she threw things at me. Called me names constantly. Cyber bullied me with her Insta-Stories. Tried to get me jumped. Did get me jumped by lying on me in middle school. Not fun, but it happened. Whatever. This whole time I took it, being the bigger person. But she crosses the line and I hit her in her face a couple times and now I'm in peer mediation. Where was peer mediation when all that other shit was happening?"

"Ms. Kader. We told you the rules. Don't step out of line again," Mrs. Stephens cuts in but still doesn't answer my goddamn question. It wasn't rhetorical.

"Um," the girl stutters. "Alani—"

"No," I say. "I'll answer your question, Desirae. I don't have a problem with Alani. She has a problem with me. But if she stayed in her lane, we'd be fine. All she does is talks shii—crap about everyone, and picks at them and thinks people will let her get away with it. And for the most part, everyone does. So she just gets to be a bully unchecked. Until one day I checked her."

"I understand. Alani, how do you feel about what Callisto said?" Desirae asks.

Alani's lips smack as she starts, "I think she lying. I think she don't care 'bout nobody but herself and she mad she broke so she take it out on people at school."

What does that even have to do with anything? I frown so hard, my own cornrows tighten. I'd reach across this table and choke her, but last time I did that, my world sort of imploded.

Alani continues after a huge, overly dramatic eye roll.

"She only act like she's that girl's best friend so she can have an excuse to fight people. If she was really her best friend, Yesenia wouldn't be crying in the restroom by herself over her dead mom!"

The whole room stops and turns to us.

"That's not true!" I say.

Yesenia's face blushes with all kinds of embarrassment.

Wait, that is true?

"Okay, I think that's enough for today," Mrs. Stephens cuts in. "Alani, I think you should leave. You two wait ten minutes."

"So she doesn't even have to apologize?" I ask.

"That's enough, Ms. Kader," Mrs. Stephens snaps.

Errr, these people are infuriating. Let the bully out there in the hall so she can plan her ambush. Ya know what? I want that. Please let her say something stupid to me outside of this room. It'll be worth getting expelled.

Alani slinks out of the room, and I turn all my fury towards Yesenia, doing my best to soften my outrage.

"What the hell?" I say under my breath. "You've been crying in the bathroom?"

"Oh, don't even, Cal. It's not like you tell me everything. I'm not stupid. I know what's going on."

Uh-oh.

"What are you... um, talking about?"

"Cal, I know you better than anyone. I've known you the longest. You didn't think I'd notice how everything has changed with you?"

Where is this going? Please don't tell me another one of my secrets has gotten out.

"How long has it been?" Yesenia says, dropping my heart into my stomach. Oh, crap. She knows about me being kinda an Arc and she's calling me out here, of all places. Through the door partition, I see Monet's face for a second. She can hear me. What do I do? Do I answer her?

Monet is silent.

Yesenia's big brown eyes stare through me. Waiting relentlessly.

Oh, this is going to suck.

Sighing, I lower my voice just enough.

"You can't tell my mom. She'd freak out, but it's been since the beginning of the school year."

"Cal, you've been homeless since the beginning of the school year?" she says in disbelief.

Wait, is that what she knows? Wait, wait. Did she seriously not know?

"Oh, um, yeah, that," I stutter.

Yesenia reels back in realization. "What did you think I was talking about that you didn't want your mom to know?"

"No, I just don't say it out loud, and, well, you know my mom. She's a private person. She doesn't even talk about it to me. So it's kind of taboo to talk about it to anyone else."

"You're lying again, Cal," Yesenia says.

"I'm not," I say. "The donation drive, that's why we went. We're staying there right now, but we're not a part of it or anything."

"No, I believe that. There's something else going on with you and you don't want me or anyone to know and it sucks."

Yesenia hates confrontation. Right now, though, she stares at me with anger like she could fight me.

She knows how I lie. The one downside of having a best friend. I wish she could just go along with it blissfully. I have so much other shit to deal with right now. But this is the problem in front of me.

"School's been stupid hard. Home has been harder and you're not around. I told you. I told you I didn't know how I was going to get through this year without you. And I'm the only one of the two of us who isn't a liar!" Yesenia yells.

"I've never lied to you," I say.

"Really? Then what happened that day at the bank? Who are Chu and Monet and why are they hanging out with you all the time? Who's your small school department head? When did you join Orienteering?" she says, flicking my jacket.

I knew I shouldn't have worn this, but I was cold. Damn. Damn. Damn. Damn. Damn. "Uhh."

Wrong answer. Before I can even finish stammering, Yesenia snatches her bag and storms out.

I immediately follow. I grab Yesenia and she physically can't get away from me, even if she tried. I'm so much stronger than her. It reminds me of when Feral first grabbed my wrist. No, I don't have time for that now. Chu was right; she'll come to her own conclusions if I don't set the record straight. I'll tell her everything. Monet glances at me like she wants to stop me, but she's busy on the phone.

"Give me the troll doll. I'll answer you," I say.

"Why? So you can lie on our friendship again? Cal, people grow apart in high school all the time. I never thought it would happen to us." Yesenia stares me down with tears in her eyes. "Keep it." She shoves the thing into my chest. I let go just as she pulls away.

It's weird to watch her go, but I can't help but feel like she's right, like the last fragments of my early days are walking out the door with her. It's emptying. For moments I stand there alone, waiting for what's next. I don't want her to not be around. I should run after her and fix this, but I know that's selfish. Part of me knows I stayed for her, but I haven't even been around, not like she needed. So why am I here? She should know. Especially since everyone knows, even if she's going to forget or I'm going to disappear.

"Thanks so much, Ms. Kader," Monet says, snapping me out of my trance.

"Were you just on the phone with my mom?" I ask.

"Orienteering has a field trip you forgot about," Monet says. It's scary how good she's gotten at lying.

"I've been learning. Sorry about your friend," Monet says. She realizes there are too many ears around. < Your secret is out on our side. We can't trust the night team to keep you safe. You have to stay with us. We've set up a hotel. We'll convene and try to figure this thing out.>

"Lead the way."

CHAPTER 18

The sun has barely gone down, but Monet is already sleep. Sometimes I forget the toll their arcs put on them. Maybe she's not bitchy, maybe she's just tired all the time. She was spent by time we got to the hotel and snuck them in through the kitchen. It became obvious very quickly that she was going to take the overnight shift.

This day has absolutely sucked. Yesenia isn't talking to me. I think our friendship is officially is done The Faction has me out in the cold for a reason I'm still not clear on. And I was forced to lie to a concierge to get us in this very chic Best Western... actually that last part I don't mind.

Every fiber of my being feels like it's been tapped, but unlike Monet, I can't sleep. I'm worried about my mom. If the night shift can't be trusted to look after me, how do I know they'll look after my mom? And I can't text her; she's asleep so she can continue her own overnight shift.

No word on what we're supposed to actually do, just camp here and wait.

This place isn't anything to write home about as far as hotel rooms go—itchy sheets and things you shouldn't lie on without first disinfecting the entire place. It smells of stale laundry detergent and old potpourri. We moved the bed away from the window, it's effectively in the closet. Anything tall enough to block the windows is doing exactly that. From the outside, it probably looks sketchy, but we sprung for the suite. I can think of other sketchier things people do in hotel rooms. Okay, that's gross even for me, it makes me itch. I sit up in bed.

"Can't sleep?" Chu asks, propped up in a chair that sits in the bathroom, just off the front door, hornet in hand. It was in the go-bag. So were fresh clothes. To anyone who asks, we have to look like kids on a field trip, so the varsity jackets are a must. There are other high school teams around here, too. Apparently there's a meet or something. I have no clue how Monet pulled this off so quick.

"Nights suck," I say.

"Well, my heart is a small sun. It mingles with sunshine and replenishes itself. But on days where I use my arc a lot, or just on some days. The nights are sad and long. So yeah, nights suck."

"Sounds like a night in the shelter. Any tips?" I say.

"I just try to make it to daylight." He holds his hand up to hush me as he listens intently in the hallway. Chatty people walk by.

"I like that, but it would be easier if I knew what was going on."

If you don't make a decision, one will be made for you... I know how to make it to daylight! I know how to make this go away. I know how to keep them safe. I know how to reset everything, but first I need answers.

"Chu, can you step out? For a second?" I ask.

Chu turns to me like I'm dumb, but he looks past me.

"It's alright," Monet says, sitting up.

"I'll secure the perimeter. You get five minutes, that's it." Chu hands our one Hornet to Monet and leaves. For a few seconds, I sit there trying to figure out how to start. I know she can hear me, but it's like that damn troll doll. She won't answer anything I don't ask. We sit on the bed across from one another. The neon sign shines through the window. Its red glow make her eyes look purple.

"I need answers," I say forcefully. The lights flicker a bit, but Monet only focuses on me. Her head tilts sideways like a puppy.

"Ask them," Monet says.

"You heard them already. You're not wearing headphones because you're nervous and out here you need to hear everything. Only if I'm grounding you. If I'm your silence, I've been noisy as hell. So talk."

It's Monet's turn to compose herself. "Remember when Mr. Kahn asked us about our call-signs and how only precious people give them to you?"

"No, not really."

"Yeah, of course you don't. Call signs mean something because they founded The Faction on an Army base. Soldiers give soldiers nicknames, because—"

"You can't give yourself a nickname," I say.

"Right, and after the ignition, individuals were taking down symptoms of one another to report to the medical teams. All the people closest to you, like friends and family, would notice the symptoms enough to diagnose. Nicknames and diagnosing became what we know as call signs."

"What does that have to do with us?" I ask.

Monet hesitates to get to her point. She listens to the world around her, trying to make a show of the possible lurking dangers out there, but my attention stays on her. She wrings her hands, pulling at her fingertips. Eventually, after a deep breath, she starts, "There was this boy I used to play with back in my camp. He was a couple of years older than me and shrouded in this silvery haze, but so was everything back then. We'd play hide-and-seek. God, he loved hide-and-seek, even though I could always find him. He told really bad jokes too. His favorite one? 'What do you call a factory that makes okay products?'...A satis-factory." Monet smirks to herself recalling it, like it's still funny to her. "I remember laughing. I couldn't stop laughing, marching around butchering the word 'satisfactory' the way toddlers do. My dad asked what I was saying and where I learned that word. So, I told him the joke the boy told me, and for the first time, my dad's hue changed. It went from the pretty silver to this acrid yellow. I learned later that's the color of panic. My parents tried to act as if everything was the same, but the yellow infected everything. They would ask me questions about the boy, and each time I answered, the yellow grew more intense. It wasn't long after that Mr. Rhys showed up, showered in these blues and greens and so much of that silver. So many colors I'd never seen before. It looked like a painting. The boy must've thought so too, because he just said, 'Monet.' I remember looking at him as if I already knew it was my name."

Monet loses herself just a minute, taking a break on her trip down memory lane.

"Who was the boy?" I ask, my voice trembling as if I already knew.

"No one. Just impressions left by my brother who passed long before I was born. He echoed around the house, making him as real to me as you are. He had my mother's eyes," she says in bittersweet reflection.

Monet wipes away tears and continues, "Mr. Rhys understood instantly what he was looking at, of course, and recruited me. The sort of dusty silver haze always surrounded my dad and mom and lived in my house that I never thought twice about was their secrets. I can see secrets, Callisto. They had been keeping the truth about my brother away from me, and when Mr. Rhys told me the truth, the silver went away and eventually the yellow faded. I miss the silver. It's my favorite color. As I started to work in The Faction, my first job was to figure out if people were lying. So this stupid trick I mastered as a child, seeing lies, became useful. Ya see, I didn't need to know if they were telling the truth. I just needed to know if they were hiding something. So, all I would do is look for my favorite color."

A heavy silence sits between us as Monet stares through me.

"Okaaay," I say.

"After that, Mr. Rhys trained me and gave me my second assignment. Finding what they're hiding."

Monet reaches across the bed. Her cold fingertips caress my face and press against my temple.

"Nothing," she says.

"I'm lost. What just happened?" I say.

"The lights flickered. I'm surprised the geigers didn't go off. But you didn't even realize it. You still look confused. Cadet, think about it. We're an organization who guards secrets. How are we able to do that?"

"The head guy is a telepath and you're a telepath."

"I get impressions. I'm much more than that. I'm a spy hunter. Special has to take precautions. I'm it," Monet says.

When she says it aloud, the revelation hits me like a bag of bricks.

"Wait, you think I'm a spy?!"

"Your timing wasn't necessarily convenient. Neither was Chu's. No one defects Branches, really, and on the day this mysterious girl is being recruited our forwarding base is targeted. That wasn't a coincidence. Someone told them about it."

"I was told they were there for me."

"That's kinda what we thought originally. The guy we brought back from the bank, the one you punched in the throat? We sorta learned they were there for us, not you. Wrong place wrong time."

"If you've known for that long, why didn't anyone tell me?"

"Above my clearance," Monet says with a shrug.

"It doesn't seem like there's much above your clearance."

"There's not, but that's a rabbit hole. I don't know what I don't know. Other than your sketchy entrance, there've been other questionable things about you. Like why you haven't set off a geiger since that day? And how well you case people and rooms. You seem to pick up crucial things but you're never paying attention. But the biggest red flag was that day at the range. Like, you can shoot really freaking well. The only people who shoot like that are Arcs or soldiers."

"Oh. I didn't know that. Sorry?"

"Yeah."

"Who else has Arcs, if it's not Domestic?"

"There are governments with Arc contractors, but who shoot like that? Only Foreign. And after that day at the mall… we know you aren't Foreign."

"Why are they after you?"

Monet traces her fingers along the edge of the Hornet's grip. "They are better equipped to infiltrate us than Domestic. I'm the sole thing stopping that from happening. I've been doing this all my life, and if we have a spy, it's not you."

"Then who? Chu?!"

"Doubtful, but like I said, I don't know what I don't know. Just like you don't know what you don't know."

"You're being cryptic."

"What if you were a plant being used unknowingly? What if the bank and the mall were really extraction attempts? Maybe that's why they want you so bad? It makes more sense than Chu; given everything that happened with his sister, I doubt he'd tow the company line."

"I don't know all the details about his sister, but I can tell you, it's not Chu."

"I said it's doubtful. Look, we don't know what this is. Something's changed. This thing between the Branches has been going on longer than either of us has been alive, but suddenly when you show up everything kicks into high gear."

"Is that why I had to leave Small World?"

"No, that was more for Mr. Rhys' sake than yours. There is a power structure in place, and arc-less aren't a part of it."

"So they know I'm arc-less. Like for sure."

"Unofficially? We've known since before Mr. Rhys recruited you in the laundromat. It took Mr. Rhys twenty minutes to find your dad and mom's entire history."

She says it so cavalierly, like it's insignificant. The one thing that turned my life upside down and put into question everything I know about the world and myself is a footnote in her whole story.

"So why am I here! Because you think I'm a spy. I'm some pawn in your game?" I yell as best I can, being mindful that we're still technically on the run.

"I...I really don't know. I can tell you that's the reason your records are sealed. They don't exist officially in our ranks. But I simply don't know."

It's all a lot to take in. It's making me lightheaded—well, that and that we're sitting inches from one another. We haven't been this close since that day in her office. Sadly, that may be the most intimate exchange of my life, but I try not to let it distract me. I believe her, but I can tell from the way her body language shrinks there's more. There's something she knows and has to say that she doesn't want to. Nothing she's under orders not to say, but something she's embarrassed to say.

"How are you so good at that?" she says, still reading my thoughts. "I don't get it. If The Faction had you, maybe they wouldn't need me." Monet shrinks a little more under her unburdened sadness.

"Dude, it's me. I'm sure you just broke a dozen orders telling me what you told me. And we're close, right? You gave me this." I gesture to the necklace I haven't taken off since it was given to me.

"You can talk to me," I say.

Monet takes a deep breath, preparing herself. "We're not close."

"Huh?" I ask.

"I'm a spy hunter," Monet says. "I... I need a way in. With Chu, that's easy. I'm his principal. His Domestic programming makes it an ideal relationship for me to observe his behavior, but you? We had no idea, but we needed you to trust me, to like me, even."

"What are you saying?" I ask, reeling back. All the warm and fuzzy feelings I've had about her, all the confused feelings about what I am now that I apparently like girls, all of that shit gets drained away by rage.

"I gave you a nudge. Not intentionally. When I received my assignment, it was the first time I really got to go into the field. I just told you how I grew up. Alone. Going from one assignment to the next. I never got to experience even the little bit of a childhood like most Arc children do. I've never been outside, especially on your side. So, I was excited, and my emotions sometimes get passed on to others and change, and—"

"I picked up your emotions just like I did your thoughts," I say, realizing what she's saying.

"Wait, what?!" Monet asks.

I know what she meant now when she said I don't know how much I mean to her. I'm her mission. I'm the key to her pipe dream of a normal life.

This hurts. My gut burns, swelling with anger from deep inside. Confused tears of heartache and betrayal make her a blur. I've been played. Me. This entire time, I thought I had feelings for this girl. Even right now, it feels like I do. She smells sweet, like flowers mixed with gun oil. Her violet eyes, the things I dream about.

It's all a lie. Why am I here?!

"None of this makes sense. Why won't they tell me what I am? Why would they ever bring me in? I'm just a normal-ass girl who gets in fights and can't afford lunch."

"Clearly, you're not." Monet reaches over to comfort me, but I swat her hand away immediately.

"But I am! I'm letting down people I care about and putting them in danger!"

"The Faction is keeping your family and friends safe," Monet says.

"I'm not talking about them. I'm talking about you, asshole! You got shot!" My voice peaks, shrill and rough, dancing into all the corners of our suite. It makes silence ripple between us. By time the air is placid again, I've calmed down and Monet's orders and rank have fallen to the wayside.

"And now I don't even know if that's real," I say.

Man, this hurts. Only one time in my life have I felt like this. Back when Mom and I lived in a house and we lost everything. Having stuff taken away from you isn't fun. So I stopped caring. And I recognized the world doesn't want me to have things, so I stopped wanting things and liking things till I came here to this stupid school where it was okay to be brash and violent. Where I was encouraged to be paranoid about my surroundings and challenged in school for once. I found a sister who wanted nothing from me but for me to be better than I was and really meant it. An asshole who was treated like an outsider by everyone just because of where he came from and a girl who grew up by herself, with too much damn responsibility. I never wanted to relate to her. I never wanted to like her. But I do and I do.

Damn it, I should've known better!

This isn't the streets that I'm used to. When people lie to kids there, complete with all the promises of the life they can have, the lie is obvious. It stares you in the face. The people we see every day, our parents, our teachers, bus drivers, they're all a bigger clue to the lie that the younger generation is told. There is no great hope for the future. The world chugs on, and it needs you to do the same.

Here, I don't have those same clues. There are hardly any adults around, and anything they don't want you to know is classified. I don't know if the lie is the same, and I didn't know if they kept their promises. But I see them now.

I unconsciously focused on the girl's violet eyes.

I guess it's my turn to be stared at with burrowing intent. Every thought that pings through my head, pings through Monet's.

My inner monologue is hers.

As quiet as a whisper reaching the far back corners of my mind, so quiet it's barely more than a suggestion in my head's narration...

Monet's voice, distant. <Servitium Sacrificium. It's our lie. It's our promise. We've been in an age-old war for survival. We need bodies.>

"That's all I am to you?" I ask.

"For what it's worth, I'm sorry."

"I've made my decision and I want out," I whisper.

"You don't get it," Monet says. "Domestic knows about you now. If they think you have information, they won't stop. And since you've been exposed on our side, Mr. Rhys won't have the resources to relocate you. This is going to cost us everything! Domestic will use you to tear apart Special."

"So what? Someone else using me to get what they want. It'd probably hurt less."

Monet is speechless. I grab my book bag.

"I could order you," Monet says. It's more pleading than everything else. I can see it in her eyes. She's scared for me. All that does is make me angrier. Knowing how much I've been through because I've been here. People I've lost or nearly lost. Without saying another word, I leave.

CHAPTER 19

It's late when I get to the shelter. My fight with Monet took everything out of me. Dragging myself up the stairs, I can barely unlock the door to our apartment.

"I thought you had a field trip," Mom says, her attention still on fixing her makeup. She's already dressed for her shift, jeans and a baby blue polo with the helping hands logo.

"We do. I feel sick."

"Cal, the reason you have a phone is so you can call me for stuff like this."

Mom's right, and I thought about it, but part of me just wanted to ride the bus and reflect. Another part of me sort of hoped that Domestic would make their move. Decisions are hard.

I collapse face-first into bed.

"What's really going on with you? You're not acting like the kid I raised."

"Nothing. I'm fine."

"Lie to me one more time. I dare you. Do it and don't even think about going to your little after-school club."

"That's fine. I quit."

"When did you do that?"

"Today."

"Mmm," Mom says knowingly.

"What?"

"What did she do?" Mom says.

"What did who do?"

"Monet."

"What makes you think this has anything to do with her?" I now have to talk about that lying, backstabbing bit—

"Since school started, you've been secretive. Lying, not saying everything, keeping something from me. Trying so hard to not talk about her, right?"

"I mean, I guess."

"You joined the club because of her too, right?"

"Yes." It's more accurate than Mom knows.

"So imagine you're me. Your daughter has exactly one friend and then this other little girl pops up. All they do is hang around one another. I'm not stupid. So what did she do?"

"She lied."

"You do that all the time. You did it just now when you came in."

"Not like this. I can't trust her. I can't trust myself around her."

"Cal, I mean this with all the affection a mother can: You're an asshole."

"Mom!"

"It's true. It's why I can never get you to behave. You're wild. Around this little girl you were as tame as I've ever seen you. Which makes my life easier, trust me, but it isn't you."

She doesn't know. She doesn't know how I hemmed and hawed trying to protect her and her life. I'm such an idiot. Of course Monet played me. I thought I was being so clever.

"You can be with someone and lose yourself, Cal."

"YOU DON'T KNOW!" I yell suddenly.

Why am I yelling? Why are there tears in my eyes?

My mom stares at me in stunned silence. My entire life, I've never screamed at my mom before. Just here and now, I can't take having everything I've been through excused as "I've been in your shoes." I know better.

Mom waits for me to finish.

Am I done? I think I'm done.

All the soft shoeing. All the lecturing. This year has been absolutely miserable and now I'm getting scolded and lectured like she knows everything, but she doesn't!

No, I'm not done.

"This isn't your life, Mom!!"

"Cal, who do you think you're talking to?"

"You! The only other person here! I've never liked anyone, and now I like someone and she lies to me and you tell me it's my fault?! You tell me I'm the asshole!"

"That's not what I meant. You didn't let me finish," Mom stammers.

"I can't lose myself, because every day I find out something new about myself I didn't even freaking know. Like I pushed away the only friend I've ever had. I didn't mean to, but it was kind of a relief, because being her only friend is sometimes exhausting! Being the child who rolls with the punches when we're evicted and living in a homeless shelter is exhausting! Having to console your friend after everything is exhausting. But I'm supposed to go to school and get good grades when we don't even know where we're sleeping at night. And I don't complain. I just do it. I let you make all the decisions because you're the parent and you're supposed to know better. But I don't think you do! And I'm not acting like your kid, because you didn't raise me to be that! You want me to be another you! And I really don't want to be. I've seen how that turns out."

Shit, I think I went too far.

Mom looks at me with more hurt in her eyes than I've ever seen anyone have—and I saw Monet get shot. Tears well at the corners of her eyes, but she delicately dabs them away. Mom doesn't say a word, just chokes down hurt and leaves, not even slamming the door as she does.

Mom was right, I am an asshole.

Our apartment shudders; a cold wind echoes through the tiny room, though it seems bigger when it's just me. Even after a couple of weeks, the smell of paint still lingers. Lying there trying to force myself into the comfort of sleep is useless. An errant streetlight peeks past the blinds and into my eyes. Something feels wrong, or I'm tired; it's funny how often those two go hand-in-hand.

Getting up, I shuffle over to the big chair facing the window. My sweats and a hoody drape around me like a moving blanket. My headscarf tied tightly around my head, that's how you know I haven't gotten a wink of sleep. Usually it's wrapped in a pillow when I wake up.

Tucking myself into a ball, I look down at the streets. Sirens dart by, spilling red and blue lights into the shadows; with darkness hiding all the unsavory parts, it almost looks nice. I lose myself in the view, drifting closer and closer to sleep, when someone shuffles in the hallway. That's all it takes for me to cling to consciousness against my will. Groaning silently to myself, I listen to hushed footfalls coming from the hall. They're quiet; fresh wood floors creak under the steps.

It's like three am; no one should be out there. The shelter still has a curfew. Is that why they're sneaking? A shadow stops at our door and waits. My heart flutters as I unintentionally hold my breath, trying not to make a sound.

Maybe it's Mom checking up on me? No, not after that fight. We probably won't speak for days.

I wait a couple minutes, but the footsteps at the door don't move. Time to do something dumb. Just hours after back-to-back screaming matches, I'm still drained.

Monet...sigh.

I crack the door open, and Poppy's grandpa creeps down the hallway.

"Um, hello?" I say through the chain, keeping the door closed. Every apartment in the shelter has them. Mom gave me a tour, a useless one, since they are all basically the same.

Poppy's granddad's head swings towards me, alert.

That's weird. Men aren't supposed to be in the shelter. Should I call my mom? She is the RA, so she should know. The small man holds his finger up to his mouth and shushes me. As if he knew what I was thinking.

No doubt, he's sneaking in to check on his grandson. He dotes. I guess that's alright? But why do I feel like it's not?

I watch as he creeps to the end of the long hall, doing everything to keep his sweatpants with newspaper patches around his waist. He opens a door and disappears on the other side.

Something is still wrong.

Taking a deep breath, it hits me: the smell of ozone and the pulsing heave of electric breath lives in my ears.

He didn't step through a door. He went through a window!

Instinctually, I pull out my phone and go to dial five, but who would even come? I back away from the door slowly, until it starts to feel like I'm walking in quicksand. What's going on? My knees buckle.

THUMP! My body crashes to floor to in front of our bedside table.

The world blurs. Did I lose my glasses? Feeling my face, they're still there, just not doing shit. Everything is out of focus. I'm aware of my heart as it slows and dances to a new beat;

the sweat on my forehead is cold, and my skin is clammy. My eyes, which refused to shut minutes ago, can't stay open. All the dizziness turns my stomach into a blender. I'm going to vomit.

My entire body locked in a Charlie Horse or something. It's hard to breathe. I can feel myself fading and starting to seize as an uncontrollable quiver like lighting rattles my body against its will. My knees knocking against the floor sound like my mom's drunk line dancing. After a long bout of this, my body lies still and somehow even more spent. From the shadows steps the grimy man. I expect him before I see him. His slight frame, which once seemed malnourished, now seems stronger than humanly possible. Somehow I missed the obvious signs that this man is without question an Arc. The dirt that sticks to his skin and, I'm guessing, his soul seems authentic enough. So do the bags under his eyes, the grease in his shaggy hair, and the smells of cheap liquor and unwashed ass. Right now, I'm glad I can't breathe. Worn clothes soiled from nights on the street and a beanie to keep his head warm. It's all been a deception.

"All this for me?" I drawl to the man hovering over me as my eyes close.

CHAPTER 20

And my eyes open. Like the blink of an eye, I'm somewhere else.

Where am? Where am I?

My breath quickens. My chest heaves. Straps pin my arms to a chair.

Straps?

Why am I...?

My head swings around, searching. It's not just my arms that are strapped, though. Leather bands fastened across my chest and around my ankles make sure I'm not going anywhere.

Why?

They are forcing me to stare ahead at a giant mirrored wall sitting on a track. Through it, I can tell I'm not in our bedroom anymore. The rest of this place looks like a garage—four solid cement walls.

I struggle against the bindings on my arms, chest, and legs until my flesh is raw and I'm spent. My grunts and screams bounce off the walls and go unheard.

What seems like forever passes as I'm left alone, forced to stare at my disheveled, highly pissed reflection. My headscarf drapes around my neck, having come undone during transport. My cornrows are fuzzy. All I can smell in this place is my sweat and grease.

CLICK!

On the other side of the mirrored wall, something turns on. People shuffle, seats are dragged out and pulled in. Sounds like class right before it starts.

Finally, there's a light. The reflection turns off. Staring at me with his government-issued haircut, Badge. This asshole drinks coffee as if this is just another day in the office. As if he isn't on some sex-offender-type crap having a teenager chained up in his garage.

On his side of the wall, though, it looks like an office. There's a row of desks behind him and a couple of Domestic Agents are typing on computers and monitoring me.

"We need to get on the same page. This here is an IMW with an emphasis on window," Badge says, gesturing to the window wall. As he steps towards me, gears whir, moving the screen along with him. "It allows me to not be physically in a room with you, but in a room with you. Sorta seeing all that's going on and communicating in real time. Why is this necessary, you ask? You're in a Hush. Zones we use to contain Arc prisoners like yourself. Faraday'd black sites completely run and operated by D.O.D. vetted contractors. Every door requires pass keys, and every door in the facility, every literal window lined with geigers. Said geigers are rigged to trigger an explosive isolating you in that part of the complex until you or your corpse can be retrieved. That's why I'm here, not there. And that's why there is where you will remain until I say otherwise."

"I'm a minor. Don't you need a parent or guardian to question me?" I ask on the offshoot chance the police guy would stick to the law.

Instead, he picks up a tablet and says, "Cute. I have to say they did a number building your legend. Callisto Alexis Kader, born December 15th…" Badge reads in silence for a second. "Mother Adena Kader. Yeah, okay. Callisto, I have a theory about you."

"Cool. Let me go and we can talk all about it," I say.

"I could, but I like a captive audience."

Great, we've moved on to puns.

Badge puts down his cup and sits on a desk just inches from my face.

"So let's start. On paper, you're this human kid, one friend, poor grades, destined for an unremarkable life as far away from The Faction as possible. It's all very detailed. But I know, as you have probably well 'forgot'," he says with air quotations, "that there is no such thing as a false positive for an Arc. And you've set off a geiger, so we know you're, in fact, one of us. So how does someone who's never set off a geiger before suddenly make one pop?" he says with a snap.

"I've been asking that exact same question."

"Well, here's a thought: maybe you were always an Arc? Maybe they had teams turning off geigers for you everywhere, or maybe it was a proximity trigger. Whatever it was, first day of high school something gave and exposed you and your assignment."

"You know that's really dumb, right? Like, I'm failing out of high school and I know that's dumb."

"I said it's a theory," Badge remarks.

"A dumb one. There's no assignment worth paying a guy to press buttons for me on and off when I go get burritos."

"But there is. It's an absurd theory; I'll admit. Until you take into consideration what you are. That you're it. *The principal.* The one person in The Faction who knows where the engine is."

"Wait, the engine has been lost, right? Please say that's right, it was on a pop quiz a—"

"Come on now. That's the ghost story we're told so that no one goes looking for it."

"So whack theories and ghost stories. Got it."

"I'll let you in on a little secret. The first part you know. There are three branches of the Faction. Domestic has an endgame playbook dedicated to the fallout of another engine burst. We've never stopped scouring for it. The same, I'm told, is happening in Foreign as well. In fact, the only Branch not looking for it is Special."

"So?"

"So? This thing gave birth to our kind. Our garden of Eden. Not looking for it means you already know where it is. So how do you hide something that everyone is looking for? How do you keep it safe? What resource do you have that you can use that no one else has access to? Something so rare, they are once in a generation, and now you have two."

"A telepath," I say aloud on accident after solving his breadcrumbs.

Badge snaps and points to me. "So you hide this impossible thing. Entrust its secrets to someone, or a family of someones. Then erase entire parts of those people. All to keep a secret."

It sounds legit insane, but he's convinced. His beady eyes watch me as he continues to spew his crazy.

"The Faction is one tree with many branches," I say, recalling The Faction's emblem and what it means.

"It's hard to be on the same team when we're dying out and they're hiding the key to our salvation."

Badge is very serious, and as batshit as all of this sounds, it explains everything. Why I was recruited. Why my records are classified. Why Domestic is after me. This could all be above Monet's classification, right? The whole damn thing fits.

Does that mean my mom isn't my mom? Or that we've had our previous lives erased and ended up in this shitty one? Does that mean I've met Mr. Rhys before?

"There it is. You're seeing it for yourself. All the pieces coming together," Badge says.

"Why are you telling me all this?" I ask.

"Because my Arc requires you to know what I'm looking for. If I ask you a baseless question... you can't lie about it, but if I ask you something you definitely know and you try to lie... well. You'll feel it.

"So, first question. Our contractors there want to know, for their safety. What is your Arc?"

Right, they don't know I'm as human as they are, but is that keeping me alive or hurting me?

"I don't think you need to know that," I say.

Oh, shit!!!

As I double over in pain, the straps hold my weight. And there feels like there's tons of it. Like they have bundled me in a blanket and put heavy weights on my chest. It's not just the weight, but the powerlessness I feel—unable to do anything to save myself. A clawing urge against the coming death overtakes me.

"Oh, you know something. I should mention, avoiding answering my questions is the worst thing you can do. Tell the truth and you'll be fine," he says, but I hang on as long as I can, full of panic and pain.

"I don't have an arc," I blurt against my will. When did I start talking?

Immediately, the pressure stops, but I ache. I can clearly feel where the elephant's foot was on my chest.

Badge examines me closer.

"Oh, of course you don't. Just like you don't have a call sign. Things I'm sure Rhys plucked from your brain. He is thorough."

"Say that's the case. Everything about previous me is gone. Here and now, I don't know what you want. Even if it is tucked away in my brain somewhere, I don't have access to it. So what are you hoping to find?"

Badge seems to have been waiting for me to ask this question. This whole interrogation stinks of the kid in school who actually did the entire presentation by himself. Overachieving ass bitch gestures to the row of agents behind him. "These folks aren't just here for their health. Domestic doesn't have a telepath, but we have data and a way to interface with surface memories. So, first, we're going to break you. Once the nut is cracked, we'll dig around and find what we're looking for. In a word, we're looking for clues. You'll give them to us one way or another."

The door behind Badge opens, and in walks Poppy's granddad. I must've been out for a while, because the shower required to get him that clean would've taken days. His shaggy hair has been trimmed into a corporate haircut, and he wears a suit from the same place Badge got his. Honestly, I preferred him in the sweatpants with newspaper patches. Gone are the bright smiles of a guy playing with his grandson. This guy never smiles; he, like, only plays sudoku or something else joyless.

"You know our man, Opium," Badge answers. "He's been watching you since that first day downtown. Hard to stay off Rhys' radar for sure. You lasted roughly four seconds after my last question. How the brain perceives time... well, that's Opium's territory. His arc simulates an overdose, but if used just right, it can make every question you don't answer, every lie you tell... feel like days. Do you love Adena Kader?"

"Yes," I say. Just then, an image pops up on the screen next to me. Weirdly, it's what I was thinking about. That time at McDonald's right after we ding-dong-ditched our last place. How are they doing that?

"Do you think she loves you?" he asks.

"Yes." Where is he going with this?

This time I see the countless times Mom kissed my forehead or hugged me.

"Do you think her life would be better without you?"

"Yeah."

The image is Mom sleeping in the car and me eating while she watches. I can't believe I yelled at her. I'm such a tool.

Badge's face frowns in a way that sorta shows that he's impressed. What is this? Why are they only asking me personal questions?

"You've lived in your car," Badge says.

The dozen or so times flash onscreen.

"Yes."

"You've stayed at friend's houses. Including a person your mom used to write bad checks with, a former drug dealer, and an armed robber. And a storage locker. Dangerous situations."

I see all of it. Why are they asking me about this?

Badge paces, and I watch him. If I could rip his throat out, I would.

"You've squatted in abandoned houses. You currently live in a women's shelter. You've had a hard life. Not enough food. No new clothes. You're on track to be a degenerate. You don't even have enough to help your best friend, who is going through something truly devastating."

Yesenia weeping as I hold her. I remember this—it was right after her mom died. All she did was cry for weeks.

Why is he making me relive this? This fucking asshole. Why is my life on display?

It hits me just ask Badge asks his question, "Is Adena Kader a good mother?"

He thinks I'm someone I'm not. He wants to break my life apart to find out what's beneath. What if there's nothing beneath? It suddenly occurs to me, I won't be there when Mom comes home. Before I can even think not to answer that in my own brain, the pressure starts, the weight of my soul burdened by a question.

The Faction ruined my life. Foreign took my friend. Special kept me in their path. Domestic kidnapped me and is putting me through this. They don't get to ask me this question. Not this one.

I will never answer them.

I strain against invisible weight as my organs feel like they've turned to lead and want to fall out of me. My veins grow flush against my skin as I no doubt pump more blood through my body than I ever have before. Catching my reflection on the corner of Badge's mirror wall, I watch veins bulge in my forehead. My heart beats double time.

I cannot answer.

I will not answer.

On the screen, I watch Mom smile at me again.

I barf and black out.

0500:

How much time has passed? How long have I been out?

"Is she good?" Badge's voice says.

Right, we've been doing this for days now. It has been days, right? Who's touching me?

A woman contractor places an IV in my arm. She doesn't look old enough to be a soldier. She should be in college studying poli-sci. Her eyes settle on me for a second. Her team of three stand nearby with their guns trained on me.

"I asked a question, contractor," Badge says.

"What don't you understand about a joint operation?" a woman says, standing on the edge of the room. She's dressed like a politician on her way to a subcommittee hearing. There's a subtle aura about her, a power that makes her small frame seem statuesque. It reminds me of Monet.

"The part where you're as invested in the outcome as I am," Badge says.

The lady takes a step toward me in awe as one of the contractors puts a hand up, warning her not to come closer. Like I'm that dangerous.

"She's just a child," the woman says in awe.

"When the men and women are gone, the children will fight their wars. And when the children go to war, what's left in their wake are monsters. We're running a tight ship here, madam. Can we get back to it?" Badge says.

He doesn't run things here; she does. That's her arc, I guess. Her power. Subcommittee lady raises her hand toward the contractor.

"She's good for another round of questioning. We're going to need to get a feeding tube in her soon," the contractor says.

"No," Badge says.

"Your job's to ask questions. Our job's to keep her alive and secure," the contractor says, emboldened by the subcommittee lady. They're all ignoring that Badge could kill them all if he chose to.

"Well said. You have an hour," the woman says.

BUZZ!

The door sits seamlessly in the wall. It pops open, revealing itself. Everyone files out, leaving me alone.

"So, Callisto. Your time in The Faction," Badge starts, but I tune him out. His last question haunts me still. Again on screen I see my mother. Knowing this may be the last time I see her. Right now, she only exists in my memories and on that screen.

Badge is surprised to see the image.

"We're moving on. Do you hear me?" Badge says firmly, but I don't answer.

The worst thing you can do is not answer.

2100:

"Don't breathe, just relax," a woman's voice says. It's the contractor again.

There are more soldiers here now.

Three to keep guns on me. Three to hold me down. One tilts my head back. The woman takes a goopy tube and shoves it up my nose. My eyes water, and my body spasms. It's like inhaling pool water, but like a million times worse. I pull against the straps of the chair. This sucks, this super sucks.

Violently, I cough. I can't stop coughing. I feel sick.

"You need to eat," the woman says.

But this ain't eating. Against my will, my belly fills. There's no taste. Just the perverted satiation. I was starving. I wanted food, but not like this. Behind her, Poppy's granddad watches through the screen. He's just a blur through my tears, but I know it's him.

1700: I look like a mess. Alone in the room for the first time, only long enough to see what I look like. Dried spittle and sweat coat my skin. That took everything I had. Why?

How long has it been?

Do they know I'm missing?

Do they care?

Am I going to die here?

Tears and snot pool out of my face. Dried bits of food I barfed stick to my sweatshirt. A *CLICK* on the other side of the window brings dread.

"Are you ready to continue?" Badge asks, having stripped his suit jacket.

…The worst thing you can do is not answer.

1400: We've been at this for so long. For weeks now. Time and time again. Feeding tube after feeding tube. His shoes entering the other room cue me that he's watching. I can hear my mother scolding me in McDonald's for fighting Alani. Badge's exasperated sigh.

KNOCK! KNOCK! KNOCK! His knuckles on glass, begging for my attention. I don't move.One of the contractors lifts my head.

"You want to kill me, don't you?" Badge says, staring at me with his beady little eyes.

That's an easy one, but I can't answer his question. None of his questions, I can't answer. And that causes problems. First the weight, like an invisible vise closing in on everything.

POP! My arm snaps.

A guttural scream erupts from me. One that would give Feral a run for her money. My muscles tense around the break, around all my bones. Flailing and screaming, my own body disfigures itself. My joints creak as the pressure slowly increases. Badge looks down at me, cold, smug, and frustrated. He's made it personal.

My head slumps. I hang there for moments.

"We're getting nowhere. We need to move on to something more drastic," Poppy's granddad says. Opium, that's what Badge called him.

Badge says nothing.

"This is all-out war. If that's what we're risking, then we should make the most of it," Opium says.

Badge lifts an eyebrow. "It's only war if they can prove we ever had her. We'll pivot to a different phase if it breaks her, make sure Special can't pin the remains on us."

????: Chiming and whirring. Chiming and whirring.

"Hey, get up, kid!" a voice says.

Hovering over me, the subcommittee lady. She was with the contractors. Her power is gone—in its place, palpable fear.

Behind her, Badge's torture wall lies shattered. The whirring I now recognize as a siren. Around me, three contractors lie dead. Yellow lights flash from silent klaxons—the only light in the powered-down halls.

"What's happening?" I ask, my throat raw. I sound like how sandpaper feels.

"Everyone in this facility is going to die if you don't get out of that chair."

"I can't. I forgot how," I say. "I've been in this thing for months."

The woman grabs my face, ignoring how rank my breath is. "It's been four days."

"No. No. It can't be… wait," I say, slurring my words.

"You sound drunk, kid. And if we get out of here, I'll make sure you're old enough to get drunk. I've turned off all the geigers in the facility I can. The exterior ones are still active but the ones inside the facility are off." The woman gestures to the swirling sirens.

"You need to go. I need to go. Do you understand?"

She's close to me. Too close to me. Looking down at my chest, I realize what the chiming is. The straps being undone. Nothing on my hands or body. Suddenly, I reach up and grab her throat. All the strength I have goes into trying to rip it out. It's not very much, but still. She hits my elbow and frees herself from my grip. I didn't expect that.

"I'm not here to hurt you," the woman says. "I'm offering you a chance to save yourself and everyone else."

The woman backs away, leaving me in the chair. Out in the hallway, she turns and flees.

Cal, what are you doing? You can't stay here!

It's not enough to get me to move. Numbness courses down my veins like blood. The pinpricks of limbs being asleep is the only thing I can feel.

Mom is going to be worried.

Nothing.

Yesenia is going to have a fit.

Still nothing.

Monet, Chu. All the thoughts I think to motivate me do absolutely nothing to stir my limbs. I lie there like a discarded doll. Until I think of one thing.

Badge needs to die.

That sends a surge through my body like nothing else. It gives me focus, the kind of focus I had the first day I set off the stupid gieger. There's a surge of stability in me. The world sharpens. It's enough to get me on my feet. I can stand, but I'm still disoriented. I throw myself against the wall and use it to brace myself as I make my way into the hallway. There, more dead bodies. Ravaged. Subcommittee lady didn't do this.

Dragging myself along while my stomach dances to a song of churning bile, I try to think of a way out of this maze. It's really just a concrete building. It reminds me of the training rooms, thick walls isolating us from the outside. This whole place seems like an office building. There are no windows. Each door on the outside looks like it leads to a submarine. I try to focus on getting out of here, and to my surprise, I know where I'm going. This must've been the route they took to get me in here, but how could I know that? I was out cold.

Rounding the corner, I run into a fleeing soldier. We hit the ground at the same time. He has the same look of fear in his eyes.

"Shit, another one!" he says.

What does he mean, another one?

He goes for his weapon, and for no discernable reason, I bite his hand, clamping down as hard as I can. He screams! As we scramble to our feet, I try to kick his nuts into his throat. They don't get that far, but it's more than enough to make him pass out.

I've got to get out of here. Up ahead, a small unit flees something. They open fire. Their muzzles flash brilliantly in the facility's darkness. Desperately they reload, emptying more ammo into the shadows ahead of them. What inspires their fear stirs me to life. Over the tatters of their gunfire, their shrieks and the sirens, I hear a *ROAR!*

Noooo.

Seconds later, the soldiers lie mauled as a hunched-over, worse-for-wear brunette covered in blood turns to me. Feral.

It can't be. It just can't.

Her eyes hone in on me, glinting in the lights the way a cat's do. She bares down, racing toward me at full speed. I'm in shock. She's alive. The relief I feel makes me almost forget what I need to do. Holding my hands up, I show her there's nothing in them. I blackjack hand and watch her come back to me. The mania subsides; so do the claws and eyes.

She's weary and even more dead on her feet than I am.

"I heard you. So I came," she says, fainting in my arms.

She heard me? I vaguely remember screaming when my arm snapped. Oh yeah, my arm. I test it out and it's fine, better than new. Weird. Wait, she was here. They had her? It's been weeks. That pisses me off, but not more than me missing her. I hold her tightly, forgetting where we are. Not caring, rather. We sit there like a puddle, the two of us.

I can hear their boots as they close in from both sides. Probably all the remaining guards in the facility descending on us. I get what the contractor meant now. She said everyone in this facility was going to die unless I got out of that chair. They didn't stand a chance against Feral as long as she was feral.

"Face down on the ground, or I will shoot. Do you understand me?" one of the soldiers barks.

We must look strange sitting here, blood that's not ours pooling around us as it drips off of her. I'm zoning out and don't answer the soldier.

The worst thing you can do is not answer.

How did I get here?

Make a decision or one will be made for you.

It feels inevitable, kind of, like all my life I knew I would be here at the end of a gun.

No, that's not it. That's not it at all.

Make a decision or one will be made for you.

Every moment before this, I fought to keep things the way they were because I didn't want them to change. I wanted to be a kid, no responsibilities, no weight of the world. None of that. I was being self-indulgent.

But eventually I knew I'd have to grow up. That's what feels inevitable. That's what, in this moment, I begin to accept and scares me more than death. I have a say.

Suddenly, the lights in the facility pop on. The klaxons stop spinning, and the sirens quit their yawling. The subcommittee lady said that was all because the giegers were off. Does that mean they're back on? What about the bombs?

"Little girl," the guy says again.

Make a decision or one will be made for you!

I've made my decision. We're not going to die.

My reluctance gives, popping like a bubble and fading into the ether. Deep inside, I scream. Imagining all my frustration, rage, and fear pouring out of me. My Feral-like bloodlust, like a river pushing deep through me. As much as I pour, it never empties, just echoes, louder and louder.

THRUM! THRUM! THRUM!

The contractors stare at small boxes on the walls. Something I hadn't noticed before until their lights cascade toward us in flashes of red, accompanied by the ominous slamming of fire doors in succession.

Geigers? No, not just geigers.

The facility rumbles along with bellows from elsewhere in the complex and the coughs of goons. Explosions. All that is secondary to me as I continue to hear the terrifying sound of my own heartbeat echoing through me.

THRUM! THRUM! THRUM!

It throws the security team into chaos. They weren't expecting to die today. I'm hoping not to die either. In slow motion, we watch as the pillars disintegrate and turn to powder in mid-air.

The creaking and crumble. The roar. The screams.

All of it.

Smoke tries to force their way into our lungs. Huge stone pieces of rubble collapse all around us. Knocking like death. Feral clenches me as the floor gives. We sink in a quick succession of stuttering stops, until we can fall no more and the light dies, leaving us in the dark.

CHAPTER 21

In clouds of shadow, there's no way to tell up from down. Moving or choking, those are your only options.

Having a building fall on me is just the latest in a long line of shitty things I've had to deal with lately. For months, I've just been losing things, our place, Yesenia, Mom's trust, Feral.

I've never seen her this bad. I pulled her leg free of debris and applied a tourniquet from one of the restraints she still had attached to her. Wherever they had her strapped down at, she didn't seem to care much for it.

Waking up to that much blood, I knew I couldn't wait. There's no way to know if the rubble I move will cause everything to collapse around me, no way to know if I'm running out of oxygen or if Feral will survive.

"I'm going to get out us out of here," I say.

Surrounded by darkness, I push things aside to make room for us both, then pull her along behind me. There's more clarity down here and with what I'm doing than dealing with Monet and Special Branch. But I'd be lying if I didn't say I miss them. I'd be lying if I didn't say they made me feel like I belong, even though I very clearly had no business in their ranks. The Faction is one tree with many branches. I may not be one of them, but Feral is. They won't leave her behind if they know she's here. Trees stick together. Great, now I'm using puns. Bad ones.

It's been hours.

How am I still going?

I haven't eaten in I don't know how long. A couple hours ago, I could barely stand, and now I'm here moving shit I have no business being able to move. Only now I realize I don't have my glasses and can see fine.

Not that it helps down here. I listen more than anything. Hoping the shifting of rubble will warn me of a collapse. Mostly it does, my surroundings telling me when and where to dig. So I listen to everything. Right now, water pouring rapidly nearby brings its own kind of anxiety and thirst.

Amongst the stink of dusty rubble lingers the scent of our sweat, the acidic smell of my sick that sticks to me faintly, and the copper metal odor of blood.

"You're too quiet. It's making me nervous,"

Feral doesn't answer. She's out and she has been this entire time. The small heave of her chest and the slight purr from her is all that lets me know that she's alive.

I'm tired and fading, I know that. I can feel my muscles slowing down and cramps edging to take center stage.

A quick breather, that's all.

I rest on the opposite side of the tunnel I'm digging, if you can call this that. Feral talked about how she never slept, but this isn't sleep. They deprived her of everything and she shut down. We'd probably still be in the facility if she hadn't gone ape-shit. Feral's curled up like a wounded cat. I wonder if her arc does that, or if it's learned behavior. A faint light from somewhere gives us an even fainter impression that we're facing one another.

My breath grows heavy, but I feel alright. Ironically, I have Feral's conditioning to thank for my quick recovery. So I get back to it. Both of us no doubt can notice how much more potent the scent of blood is, and we're in active denial about it. Cool, I can deal with active denial.

Feral's breaths grow shallow.

So do my own. We must be running out of oxygen.

She will not die here. If I get to choose anything in this life. If I get to exert my will over anything. It starts with this. My body feels different. Stronger. It's nothing for me to keep going. Every four feet I clear, I pull her along with me. It's slow but steady work. Sweat and dust coat my face. Breathing this in can't be good, but the alternative of not breathing is obviously worse.

I'm running out of time.

Tossing aside pieces of debris, I try not to think about it.

Focus on her breath and moving the next stone.

My fingers leave traces of blood as I go further and further. Like swimming though sandpaper, the coarse grit tears at my flesh, but I keep going.

Reach the exterior. Maybe I should've chosen a different wall, but I don't need to get free, I just need to get closer. I'm not a really religious or spiritual person, but the subtle moves left and right feel like an experience all on their own. I know I'm getting closer.

"Closer," Feral groans. It scares the crap out of me. I nudge her, but she's still asleep. They'll come for her. They have to. She got me this far. I'll get her out of here. It spurs me to keep going. Sweat stings my eyes along with the probably toxic amounts of dust I inhale.

I can hardly breathe.

I shouldn't be able to move.

I should stop.

I have to stop.

How long have I been digging?

My muscles scream and quiver.

The more I dig, the more I uncover my own buried panic.

How do I tell my mom about this? Do I tell her? Is she okay? Is she even my mom? How do I explain being gone? Will I die before Yesenia and I figure our crap out? Am I going to die?

"I don't have to worry about any of that. The Faction will do right by me," I say aloud. I just needed to hear a voice. Even if it's mine as a forty-year-old woman who smokes a pack a day.

Am I digging the wrong way?

Am I wasting the time she has left?

This is impossible. I don't know how far I have to go. But I don't have to get to the surface. I just have to get close enough for Monet to hear me. To hear my pleas for help.

Why can't she hear me?

I'm spent. I can't move an inch further.

"This feeling right now. Remember it. Know that every order I give is to stop you from feeling like you do at this moment." My deprived brain remembers Feral's words as if she's speaking them to right now.

"Yes, sir," I say.

"Dig," she says. Or at least the imagined voice of hers in my head says that.

So, I do. Hand after hand, scoop after scoop, fistful after fistful. Blood-soaked fingers dive into the mountain's remnants again and again, time after time. Pulling back sand

and all the kinds of rock I didn't pay attention to in class. It all gets tossed behind me, bouncing its way down the tunnel. I move rebar and stone.

We scoot. I do it again.

Each time, my thoughts scream, <Here I am!>

Keep going, Cal. You can do this. It's dumb. It's frustrating. How much dirt do I have to dig through? The more I dig, the more it seems to help. It parts around me, aiding just a bit. I'm hallucinating, aren't I? I can't think about that.

The more I dig, the more I have to dig.

It's insurmountable.

We're going to die here.

I try not to think like that, but it's the thought that's constantly buried at the back of my head. The fear of dying. The fear of being unremarkable while doing so. Failing. To save myself. To save Feral. To do anything right that Mom or any of my loved ones could be proud of. Shit, I'm getting low. Really low. This is hopeless. Utterly hopeless. We're so deep underground. No one need is going to hear me. My exuberance wains until it's just like another night in the shelter. I'm lying awake in my cot listening to the night terrors and snores, trying to keep the sadness of my reality at bay while I wait for Daylight.

As I think it, a hand breaks through from the other side, extended to me. So warm as it grabs onto my forearm and pulls it free of the ground. I glimpse him, silhouetted by the sun: Cadet Chu Myung. He pulls, and two more hands grip me around my shirt and yank me free. I land on the person pulling me. Her eyes are whited out. I watch as they slowly return to their hazy, overly bluish complexion. Like watching paint swirl in reverse until they pool in near-violet pupils that stare back at me. Monet's expression is, as always, unreadable.

I missed her stupid face, even if it's covered in dirt and soot. Even if the signs of her own firefight and battle are written all over her. I can tell she hasn't slept in days.

Looking at Chu, it's more of the same from him. I welcome his warmth. The tunnel was colder than I thought. The sunburns on his neck are the story of how exhaustingly he's been arcing.

These assholes haven't slept in days. They came and they've been fighting for I don't know how long. I knew they would come for her.

HER!

I leap to my feet and race back to the tunnel. I nearly Bugs-Bunny-dive in. Chu and Monet scramble after me, confused. They pull me out again, but by then I've wrapped my arms around Feral's waist. I won't let go. I can't let go.

"Let go," Chu says.

Never. He yanks hard enough to pull us free, and we sprawl on the ground.

Chu and Monet look to each other first. They are both shocked.

"You didn't know she was here?" I ask.

Both shake their heads slowly.

"So why... why are you here?"

"For you," Feral says softly, still unconscious.

"Oh," I say. The last word I can muster before exhaustion wrestles me down and I pass out.

There's dust in my lungs, the ground shifts around me, and the pressure of a building sits squarely on my shoulders. Death's icy grasp tugs at me slowly. Ignoring it, I continue to scoop debris out of my way, cuts on my hand stinging each time they dive into dirt. I've done this before. I made it out, but something's different this time. This time, while weaving through the Earth, there's a voice. More of a faint echo, but it tells me what to touch, where to go, what's up from down. It guides me to the surface.

My eyes shoot open, slowly adjusting to the med-bay's pristine whites. It still stinks of tongue depressors, but the gentle beep from machines plays like a lullaby.

Monet sleeps in a chair at my bedside. She's always asleep. At the door, Chu sleeps in a different chair, both still in soot-covered uniforms.

"You're awake," Monet says. She was listening to my thoughts, waiting for me to gain consciousness.

"Yeah," I say with a voice I don't recognize. Is that what I sound like now? It's a harsh, dry rasp. When will this go away?

<You don't have to talk, remember?> Monet says.

<You were down there with me telling me where to go, weren't you?> I ask.

<No. I mean. I don't know. When we got there, it was already pretty bad. The building was a heap and people were combing the wreckage for survivors. I started impressing as far down as I could go, hoping to reach you,> she says.

There's a lot between us. A lot that needs to be figured out and said, but all I think is, <It did. Thank you.>

"You're up," Chu says.

"Some bodyguard you turned out to be. Sleeping on the job, Daylight," I say.

I take a second to register it. The name came on its own like second nature, as if it's always what I called him.

"Daylight?" I say.

I swear pebbles are going to shoot out of my mouth the way my chest feels. A flash of his hand into the dirt and his silhouette come to me. The cadet formerly known as Chu Myung stands there wearing pride on his chest.

"In pulling your ass out of the fire, I found a way forward," he says.

"So this means we're best friends, right?"

"I hate you," he says earnestly. Maybe not best friends, but at least friends. I could use one of those right now.

"Where's Feral?" I ask.

Both Daylight and Monet look at me. Neither say a word. Sworn to secrecy again, I see.

<It's alright. You can tell her,> Mr. Rhys says.

We all hear it and look around as the door whooshes open like we're in Star Trek.

Mr. Rhys enters as clean-cut as they come. Both Monet and Daylight shoot to their feet to salute.

"At ease," Mr. Rhys says. "Can you walk?"

"I don't know," I answer.

"Have you shown her a mirror?" he asks, looking at my squad mates.

"We weren't sure if we're supposed to," Monet answers.

"What's that about a mirror?" I ask.

Mr. Rhys walks over to the tall, long mirror next to the closet. He flips it towards me.

Slowly, I examine a girl who looks just like me. Her face beat up and cut. Same for her body. It's taut and lean from days of hunger. She's wearing the same hospitable gown, has the same hairstyle, same skin color, same nose, except her eyes. They shift incandescently in the light, back and forth—black, blues and purples like ink on water. Lines on her skin glow ever so slightly.

"Is that me?" I ask.

"Yes. The pattern seems to follow Blaschko lines. Migrational cells every human has at birth," Mr. Rhys says.

"So I'm glowing? What does that mean?" I ask.

This is a lot to take in. I glow now. Cool.

"There was another question you asked earlier we should address first," Mr. Rhys says.

Monet scoops me into a wheelchair Daylight retrieves. The three of us follow Mr. Rhys down the hall. Armed operators stand in front of a different med-bay door.

"Step aside," Mr. Rhys says.

It takes a second before they do as ordered.

In a different med-bay suite, Feral lies unconscious.

"She's been in and out of it. Mostly out," Mr. Rhys says.

Pulling myself out of the chair, I make my way to her bedside on shaky legs. I take her hand and feel the smallest squeeze. It's far from the one that almost broke my wrist at the beginning of the year.

"I'll be alright, thanks to you," Monet says.

My head snaps to Monet as it takes me a minute to realize what's happening. She's channeling Feral. Tears creep down my cheek, and I wipe them away quickly.

"You saved me first," I say.

"You need to be debriefed, Cadet," Mr. Rhys says.

"Fine."

I follow Mr. Rhys out of the med-bay, stubbornly marching down the halls after him. I really should've stayed in that chair, but there's no way I'm letting him push me around. Monet and Daylight follow on my wings, ready to catch my wobbly ass.

"Foreign typically moves with a lot of chatter. They are brutal and efficient. The fact they kept her alive this long is surprising," Mr. Rhys says, leading me down the hallway to his office. The one with seemingly thousands of doors.

"Why do you think they did that?" I ask.

"I'm sure one day she'll tell you the story." Suddenly, Mr. Rhys stops at one of the doors and goes through it. We, of course, follow.

On the other side is a room unlike any in Small World. It's a home office. Like a 90s home, the ones you see on HGTV that have "good bones" but haven't been renovated since 92. Everything is light wood colored and floral. Also, if those shows are to be believed, all these walls are load bearing.

Mr. Rhys takes his place behind the desk. Daylight rolls one of the dated cabinets up next to him and points it at me.

"Monet, if you would," he says.

Monet squeezes my arm and smiles at me as if to say it will all be okay. She steps out, and Daylight of course follows her, with a pat on my back. Mr. Rhys opens the cabinet doors, careful not to cross the front of it. Inside sits another geiger, like the one he had on his desk that day.

"The Eisenhower?" I ask.

"The Reagan," he answers. "More portable, just as accurate."

The thing is pointed at me, but it isn't doing anything. I catch my reflection in the dusty mirror hanging in the office. My glow has faded. So weird. Mr. Rhys, with his hands firmly in his pockets, looks at the thing and then at me. When nothing happens, he sits across from me.

"I need to debrief you and be fully transparent."

"So what am I, and how did I get this way? What's in my records that you're keeping from me? Am I the principal or whatever craziness that Badge guy was saying?" I ask.

"The truth? Your mom isn't an Arc. Neither is your father. Nor anyone in their bloodlines. You're something improbable. You're a girl who developed an arc. And we have no idea how. Yes, I knew this in the beginning and I still recruited you. Nothing Badge said was anything more than a story a very desperate man tells himself in the face of what he believes will be our extinction. Ironic he almost killed you."

"So why did you recruit me if you knew?"

"I was curious. My position relies mostly on probability. I inherited an intense game of Mahjong in this cold war between branches. There was the chance that one of them or our other enemies were using you as a ploy to plant you amongst us. It's atypical of their other moves, but it had to be considered. I had to know if you were a threat to just Special or the entire Faction. I also thought you might be from one of the lesser families. The most improbable thing being that you are what you are: an Arc with no origin."

"That's not possible without the engine. They think you have it," I say.

"Clearly, it is. But they don't know that, and if it ever gets out that your bloodline isn't tied to ignition, this war will get worse."

"They'll think you have it and are making your own Arcs."

"Exactly. We know now that Monet was offered up to Foreign by Domestic as a way of distracting us from you. Our resources would be aimed at recovering her and not covering you. They used our forwarding operating bases to plan their operation. Ones we were aware Domestic knew about. Feral was being housed in the same facility as you. This all speaks to their collusion." Mr. Rhys doesn't seem happy about that in the slightest.

"There was a woman there," I say trying hard to remember. My brain fog hasn't completely lifted.

"Yes. You should forget about her for your own sake," Mr. Rhys threatens, but I have a vendetta against everyone in that facility who Feral didn't kill, including a couple assholes who were there but on the other side of the window.

"Kay. I want to know what's going to happen to Badge."

"He's Domestic's second in command, so for the time being, nothing."

That doesn't make me happy. Not in the least. Feral is in the hospital, and I probably should be too.

"If you really think I'm just going to allow them to take two of my operatives, then I really haven't introduced myself very well. There's no power on Earth that will protect them from what's coming," Mr. Rhys says with a deep, bassy menace. It reminds me why people who know of him fear him. More than anything he's ever said to me, I believe that. "I'm sorry I put you through all of this. I forgot to take in the humanity of it all. And left a young girl vulnerable against very desperate people."

That sorta pisses me off. It's minimizing everything I went through because these people brought me in and didn't trust me. That's why I'm here. So he can apologize. Debriefs are a psychic thing, so the after-school special is kind of insulting.

"You're only partially right. This was so I could apologize, but mostly I wanted your approval on the house. Once your mom gets here, we'll begin the swearing-in ceremony and—"

"Wait, time out. My mom's coming here?"

"Yes, this house is for you, or her, rather. This is a camp for Arcs. Your mother won't know most of them have gifts. And it's imperative that we hide your father's origins, but—"

"No," I say, realizing what this is.

It's a bribe. This is everything I've wanted for my mom and myself. Stability. Mr. Rhys knows that.

Athletes and musicians buy their moms houses all the time, and I may never get another chance to do that, but this isn't right. Feral almost died. Monet was shot. I had a building dropped on me. And Daylight. Daylight's parents lost a kid and sent another one off to serve and nearly die.

"We're long past making the decision, Cadet," Mr. Rhys says. "It was either leave, have your memories and everything erased, and be relocated, or have your family brought into the fold. No matter how you got here, you're without a doubt one of us. The decision has been made."

Make a decision or one will be made for you. Did Feral know I would end up here? Is that why she told me that? Mom won't sit by while I'm out there nearly dying and she worries. She won't go for this. Neither will I.

"There's another choice," I say.

"I don't think there is."

It's been at least four days since I went missing. I was down in the hole for what felt like days, and who knows how long I've been out. Mom must be worried sick. She'll think I ran away because of our big fight and she'll blame herself. She'll think that I think she's a terrible mother, and I don't. I'm a really shitty kid. She's the reason I never said a word to those assholes in Domestic. And it sucks she won't believe this is the lesser of two evils.

"She won't believe what is the less of two evils?" Mr. Rhys asks.

"Me. I join The Faction alone and my mom lives her life. This world never crosses her doorstep."

"Cadet..."

"PROMISE ME!" I say with all the might I have.

PZZTS! Mr. Rhys studies the Reagan. Smokes billows from somewhere deep inside like it short-circuited. The front part of my brain tingles like I inhaled fizzy water as almond creamer invades my taste buds. That's how I know he accepts the terms of our agreement, it's like his psychic handshake.

"Welcome to The Faction."

* * *

ACKNOWLEDGMENTS

The road to publication has been long and arduous. It's not possible without help from special individuals.

Alexandra Ott your in-depth review of the manuscript, the questions you asked, and the proofread made it possible to execute a story that lived only in my head.

Doug and Sarah, this last stretch was an uphill climb. Without your guidance, I'm unsure if we would've reached this point.

Rowan, thank you for the cover mock-up that got us headed in the right direction.

Richard Rios, the MVP. Thank you for the time and consideration and your talent that you put to use in promotional materials. You made more of that than I ever thought possible.